NO SECOND CHANCES

MARISSA FARRAR

BOOKS BY
MARISSA FARRAR

CONTEMPORARY FICTION NOVELS
Cut Too Deep
Survivor
The Sound Of Crickets

THE MONSTER TRILOGY
Defaced
Denied
Delivered

THE SERENITY SERIES
The Vengeful Vampire (free short story)
Alone (free first novel of the series)
Buried
Captured
Dominion
Endless

THE DHAMPYRE CHRONICLES
Twisted Dreams
Twisted Magic

THE SPIRIT SHIFTERS SERIES
Autumn's Blood (free first novel)
Saving Autumn
Autumn Rising
Autumn's War
Avenging Autumn
Autumn's End

Underlife
(*Go Back*, the prequel to *Underlife*, is now free to download from Amazon)
The Dark Road

NO SECOND CHANCES

ONE

GABI—SIX MONTHS EARLIER

"Last day before you go home, Captain Weston!"

I turned toward the male voice, a smile on my face as I adjusted the waistband of my ACUs—my Army Combat Uniform. "That's right, Private Jeffers. One more day and then I get two whole weeks of watching crap television and eating pizza."

He laughed. "And drinking cold beer."

"And hot showers and sleeping in my own bed."

"A real bed," he replied. "Make sure you enjoy it."

"Oh, I will." I noted his Kevlar helmet, like my own, his protective gear, and the ammo strapped to his chest. "Where are you headed?"

"Just got a call that a lookout post on the west corner is one man down. Private Moss has been taken down with the stomach flu."

"I'll go," I offered. "I'm at a loose end today anyway, just trying to get things tied up before I go on leave. I don't mind swinging around there for a couple of hours."

The young man's eyebrows lifted. "You sure, Captain?"

"No problem. Just carry on doing whatever it was you were doing."

"Thanks, Captain. And enjoy your time at home if I don't see you before you go."

"Will do."

Home to me wasn't the same small California town I'd grown up in. I'd left that place ten years ago, and while I felt bad I'd barely visited my dad during that time, I didn't have any intention of going back. I'd left only a matter of months after my eighteenth birthday, joined the Army, and the rest was history. These people were my family now. My father had more interest in finding the bottom of an empty bottle of Jack than he did spending time with his daughter, so I doubted he even noticed I was no longer around. Mom left us when I was two, claiming this wasn't the life she had signed up for and she couldn't handle being around a toddler all day. Dad had been great when I'd been little, though I thought he'd always been drinking—he just hid it better back then. But the older I got, the more I noticed the empty bottles in the bin, and the smell on his breath. He didn't like having someone around who would question him, so gradually he started to shut me out. I didn't even care by that point. I had my own shit going on, and what teenager wanted to hang around with their dad anyway?

I headed out into the hot Iraq sunshine. The wind blasted my face like the air from a dust-filled hairdryer. One thing I looked forward to heading home to was the change in light. Everything here felt burned by the sun, the ground a scorched yellow sand, the buildings—those still standing—the same faded sandstone. Even the occasional piece of vegetation—the tall palm trees—felt like the color had seeped from their leaves. The dirt didn't help with the lack of color. Thick yellow dust coated everything, filling the air and settling on anything that stayed still long enough.

Thoughts of home stayed with me as I walked. My fantastic father-daughter relationship wasn't my only reason for leaving, but I tried not to think about that. I tried not to think about the life I could have been living right now. I'd made a lucky escape, even if it hadn't felt like it at the time. At the time, it had felt like I'd left with my heart shattered into a million tiny pieces, and that I'd never be able to glue it together again. But I had. Perhaps my heart wasn't in exactly the same shape as it had been before, but maybe that wasn't such a bad thing.

I crossed the small, dusty town, my weapon at my side. The town was quieter than I had imagined before I'd been deployed out here. I'd been expecting a constant warzone, but it wasn't like that. Yes, reminders of the war could be found everywhere, from the bombed buildings, to the malnourished children, and the almost constant chatter of distant gunfire. But it was also just a town with its inhabitants trying to live their lives the best they could in the circumstances. The locals hawked their wares on the side of the street—cheap imported radios that were falling apart, and stacks of old VHS tapes no one could watch—while feral dogs and tick-infested goats dropped feces all around them. I buried my face down into the scarf around my neck, trying not to inhale both the dust and the stench of rotting trash in the heat. There were no waste disposal services here, and everyone lived in the streets. A group of children, with threadbare clothes and skinny brown limbs, kicked a half deflated ball around in the dirt. They glanced my way as I strode by, but barely reacted to the sight of an armed soldier, and a woman, at that. The local people had gotten used to seeing us here now.

I approached the lookout point which was currently undermanned. The soldier on watch, Private Thomas Moss, spotted me approaching and lifted his fingers to touch his forehead. "Captain Weston. I wasn't expecting to see you over this way today."

"Private Jeffers mentioned you were a man down, so I figured I'd make myself useful on my last day before leave."

The young man grinned. "That's good news, 'cause I've been dying for a piss for about two hours now."

I laughed. "Good thing I'm here then. Hey, how's your new baby doing?"

Tom's wife had given birth only three weeks earlier, and I knew it was killing him to be apart from his family so soon after the birth.

"She's good, and Kimberly is doing great, too. She's got her mother staying to help out with the baby, so I doubt she's even missing me."

"I'm sure that's not true," I replied.

I moved to enter the building, planning to climb the steps in order to reach the lookout spot, passing the other soldier on his way out as I did so, but the growl of an engine made us both stop and look in the direction the sound was coming from.

I frowned, instinctively reaching for my gun, and Tom did the same.

A small car hurtled around the corner, yellow dust billowing in a toxic cloud from beneath its wheels. I heard Tom swear, "What the fuck!"

I didn't have time to say anything myself, alarm and fear bursting inside me, threatening to wipe out my rational thought. But my training kicked in, and a calm voice spoke inside my head. *Take out the driver.*

He was headed right toward us, his foot down hard on the accelerator. I caught a glimpse of a set of dark eyes in a young man's face—so young he was practically a boy rather than a man—and I read the terror and righteous determination in them. The car was meant for us, and I didn't think he planned on running us down.

I aimed my weapon and squeezed off a couple of shots, putting holes in the windshield. Tom did the same but still the vehicle kept coming. Only seconds had passed, but felt like minutes, and all I could think about was the new father at my side.

4

"Get out of here," I yelled, shoving him to one side. I squeezed off another bullet and this one met its mark, the car suddenly veering to one side, the same direction in which I'd just pushed Tom. But the vehicle was now on course for hitting the outside wall of the building instead of directly at us, and even though Tom was closer to where the car would smash into the wall, he wouldn't get hit.

A second later, the vehicle crashed with a bone-jarring bang and screech of metal. The car instantly burst into a ball of flames, but it was far enough away from us to not cause us any harm.

I allowed myself to exhale a breath ...

Then my world exploded.

COLE–PRESENT DAY

I hauled a trash bag out of the bin, the muscles in my forearms popping under the strain. I'd learned the hard way that a professional kitchen created a lot of two things—garbage and dirty dishes.

I glanced down at the multitude of tattoos covering my lower arms. Hell, they were covering most of my upper arms and torso, too, but were hidden beneath the white sleeves of my work shirt. The tattoos were surprisingly good considering the vast majority had been acquired while behind bars. They were just another way of fitting in, of acting like I was part of the gang. Though I hated having to blend in with the crowd, I did what I needed to do in order to make it out of jail in one piece. That, and fighting. As soon as people realized you were handy with your fists, they tended to leave you alone. I figured that out in foster care before I'd ever seen the insides of the prison walls.

Turned out the two institutions weren't all that different.

I'd spent most of my days in and out of the system, but I'd been lucky to end up in foster care in this town. My foster parents had been good to me, but things hadn't quite gone the way I'd planned.

Being released from prison was never the way I'd wanted to be reintroduced to Willowbrook Falls. I would have liked to have ventured somewhere else—a Caribbean island, perhaps—but I had to go into the halfway house initially for my probation officer to make contact with me, and then I'd been given this job. It might not be much, but I knew how hard it would be to find other work in a different town. Thank God my old foster parents hadn't completely disowned me, and had managed to find me a position in the restaurant. It was owned by a friend of theirs, Frankie Kilhorn, and they'd put in a good word for me. The money wasn't great, but it was enough to allow me to rent a small, rundown house on the outskirts of town.

I understood why Frankie wanted to keep me out back, away from the watchful eye of the rest of the town. I would be bad for business, and I didn't want to cause Frankie any trouble when he was helping me out. I was a grade A screw up, and I'd given up trying to prove any different to anyone else in this town, or even to myself. Even when I tried to do the right thing, it always went wrong, so what was the point? Now I was just keeping my head down and living for myself. I was never born to be a crowd pleaser anyway.

Trying to ignore the stench of old fish permeating from the trash bag, I hauled it outside to throw into the large industrial container located in the alleyway which ran alongside the back of the building.

As I stepped out, two voices were speaking in low tones, and I just caught the end of the conversation.

"—moved in with her alcoholic father, from what I've heard."

"No shit. How's that going to work? One old booze hound and Hopalong Cassidy."

They erupted into laughter, but as I stepped into view, the laughter faded.

Two of the other kitchen hands, Deano and Ben, were out on a smoke break. The two men were also longtime residents of Willowbrook Falls, and though they'd been a couple of years above me at school, they knew my background.

"Ah, shit, man," said Deano when he caught sight of me.

My mild curiosity about what they were laughing about suddenly deepened to concern. "What's going on?"

Ben nudged Deano and gave his head a slight shake.

I looked between them, the strange sensation in my gut solidifying. "What's up? Seriously."

They exchanged a glance and then Ben said, "Gabi's back."

The words hit me like a punch in the chest, expelling the breath from my lungs and making it hard for me to take another. The ground suddenly felt a long way away, no longer right beneath my feet, as though I'd distanced myself from reality for a fraction of a second.

"Gabi?" I managed to say. "When?"

He shrugged. "Not sure. A few days ago, I think."

"Holy shit. Any idea what's brought her back to town?"

I'd done my best over the last ten years to forget Gabriella Weston ever existed. I'd never succeeded, not really. I'd always held her at the back of my mind, wondering what she was up to, if she was married and with a young family by now. Being behind bars helped to prevent my desire to look her up again, but any time a young woman had walked in at visiting hours, with the same kind of wild corkscrew curls Gabi had, the same curls I used to love twisting around my fingers while she lay with her head against my bare chest, my heart and stomach always lurched with ridiculous hope.

She would never have visited me. Not after what I did. I didn't blame her.

I realized the two other men still hadn't answered my question, and were both distracting themselves, Deano flicking cigarette ash and scuffing a butt around on the floor with his foot.

"What the fuck is going on?" I demanded, squaring my shoulders. There was something they weren't telling me, and I needed to know.

"You should go see her, man," said Deano. "She might appreciate a friendly face."

Ben scoffed. "More like she'd want to bash his face in."

"Yeah, thanks for that," I said, jerking my chin in mock amusement.

"We've got to head back in," said Deano. "Smoke break's over."

They finished their cigarettes and moved to head back into the building.

"Hey, wait up," I called after them, and Deano turned back. The sadness I saw in his eyes shocked me.

"Seriously," Deano said, "just go see her. Even if she smacks you in the face, I reckon she'll be happy to see someone she knows. It's been a long time since she left. I think she's been through a lot."

He walked back into the restaurant's kitchen, leaving me shell-shocked and playing the conversation over in my head.

What were they talking about? I already knew she'd been through a lot—after all, I was the one who'd put her through it—but, for some reason, I felt like they weren't telling me something important.

Gabi, back again. I almost didn't want to believe it.

I couldn't allow myself to hope for anything. She'd still hate me, I had no doubt about that, and I deserved her hatred. I'd dragged her heart through the dirt and then stomped on it several times for good luck. She'd left, and I'd never made any attempt to contact her again.

I didn't think she could hate me as much as I hated myself.

THREE

GABI—ELEVEN YEARS EARLIER

"You know," a male voice said from above, a shadow falling over me, "I've always liked a girl with big boobs."

I was sitting in the park reading and generally trying to avoid going home, when I was so rudely interrupted.

My head shot up, my eyes wide and cheeks flaring with heat, to find a boy with jaw-length blond hair, a leather jacket, and one hand stuffed into the pocket of his jeans, regarding me with blue eyes.

"Excuse me?" I managed to stutter.

"Big books," he said, holding back a laugh and nodding to the novel I held in my lap. "I said I've always liked a girl with big books. Shows she's not afraid to take on a challenge."

I wished the ground would open up and swallow me. I didn't believe for a minute that was what he'd actually said, but there was no way I was going to mention my chest area in front of him.

"Gabriella, isn't it?" he said, dropping onto the grass beside me. "I think we used to have a trig class together last year."

10

"Err, yeah, I recognize you, too."

"Cole," he said, putting his hand out to me. A silver ring hugged his thumb. I shifted my book to shake his hand, feeling weird at doing something so formal. His skin was warm and he held onto my fingers for a fraction too long before releasing them. "Cole Devonport. I also play drums in The First and Last."

"Is that a band at school?" I didn't recognize the name, though everyone seemed to be making up a band at the moment, thinking they were going to be the next big thing. It was as though they all thought their coolness would be elevated a couple of notches, and therefore their chances of getting laid, just because they picked up an instrument. I mean, anyone with a couple of sticks could surely play the drums, couldn't they? I kept my thoughts to myself.

"Nah," he said. "I play with some older guys. Are you sure you haven't heard of us?"

I gave an awkward smile and tugged on the hem of my skirt to cover my legs. "Bands aren't really my thing."

"No? How come?"

I shrugged. "Noisy, with a bunch of guys all trying to outdo each other. What's there to like?"

"You're missing the atmosphere—energy and fun."

I wrinkled my nose. "Hormones and boy sweat. I'll pass, thanks."

He leaned back and cocked an eyebrow. "Did you just imply I stink?"

My cheeks heated again. Jeez, what the hell did this guy want? "No, no, I just—"

He clutched his hand to his chest. "Well, now you hurt my feelings, so you have to come. Bring a couple of your friends, if you want. We'll be on the corner of Tamworth Street and Jackson from seven."

With that, he hopped to his feet, stuffed his hands back in his pockets and sauntered away.

Bring friends. Now that made sense. He must be crushing on one of my girlfriends, though I wasn't sure which. Either of my friends could be easy crushes.

As though my thoughts had conjured them, both Taylor and Jasmine came hurrying across the grass toward me.

Taylor's eyes widened at me. "Did I just see Cole Devonport talking to you?"

"Oh, yeah. I think he was trying to invite you guys somewhere."

She perked up even further, if such a thing was possible. "He was?"

"Yeah, he invited us along to see his dumb band practice."

"You've got to be kidding me. I hope you said yes."

"Well, I didn't exactly get a chance to say anything. He just got up and walked off."

"Where?" asked Jasmine. "What time?"

I told them.

Taylor let out a squeal and clapped. "Oh, my God. This is so exciting. I know you're kind of immune to the opposite sex, but you know he's hot, right?"

I rolled my eyes. "Hot? No. I know he's totally full of himself."

"You can't blame him." She widened her eyes again. "Like I said, he's hot."

"You guys go. I've got better things to do than hang out in a noisy garage all evening."

Jas's eyebrows lifted. "Err, no you don't."

"And he invited *you*," continued Taylor. "We're just the tag-alongs. If you don't go, we don't go."

Jas regarded me. "And if we don't get to go, we are never speaking to you again."

I laughed. "Okay, okay. We can go, but don't expect me to enjoy it. And FYI, I'm pretty sure he only invited me knowing I'd be inviting you two along. No way is a guy like Cole Devonport interested in someone like me."

"Stop being so down on yourself," said Jasmine, elbowing me in the ribs. "You're gorgeous, Gabi."

My cheeks heated. "Whatever."

"Anyway," said Taylor, "you know he's trouble. He doesn't even live with his parents, but with Mr. and Mrs. Cowen, who take in problem kids."

Jas shoved her friend's arm with her hand. "It's foster care, dummy."

"Whatever. His parents couldn't even handle him, so they had to give him up."

"You don't know what you're talking about!" I blurted.

Her mentioning not being wanted hit a nerve. My mom walked out when I was only little, something that hung over me every day. I tried to tell myself it hadn't been about me—that I'd only been two, and no real mom abandons her daughter—yet the idea I hadn't been enough for her wormed its way through me. I hadn't been good enough to keep her. I hadn't been cute enough. I hadn't been well-behaved enough. I hadn't been loved enough.

Taylor caught the expression on my face and reached out to touch the back of my hand. "Oh, shoot. Sorry, Gabs. I totally forgot."

I shrugged, trying not to look bothered. "Forget it. I was just saying we don't really know what the story is, so we shouldn't make stuff up."

"Yeah, you're right. And it doesn't take away from the hot factor. A little danger is exciting." She shot me a wink. "It's not like I'm thinking about marriage material."

So she *was* thinking about him.

I didn't want to admit it, even to myself, but the fact Taylor was interested made my heart sink. She was everything I wasn't—cute, blonde, confident. A perfect match for Cole.

You're not even interested in Cole, remember? I scolded myself. The last thing my life needed was to be complicated even more by boys.

We heard the music before we'd even reached the address Cole had given me, the muffled thump of drums and the scream of an electric guitar.

"Jeez, their neighbors must love them," said Jasmine, raking her fingers through her silky dark hair as she walked beside me in her heels. I'd opted for sneakers, and felt even shorter than I normally did.

Taylor laughed. "I don't think they're the kind of guys who give a crap about the neighbors."

She was right. The front of the garage was swung up onto runners overhead, exposing the band, and their noise, to the street.

Nerves churned in my stomach, and I told myself not to be stupid. Cole had only invited me because he liked one of my friends, and he probably wouldn't even notice my arrival.

We came to a halt in front of the open garage. My eyes sought out Cole, and I found him sitting behind the drums at the back, rapping on the set with a couple of sticks. He caught sight of us and jerked his chin in greeting. I gave a nervous smile in return.

The guys finished their song, and the older one who'd been singing called to the others to take a break. Cole hopped out from behind the set of drums and ambled over to us.

"Hey, ladies," he said. "What did you think of the song?"

"It was loud," I replied, and he grinned.

"Let me introduce you to the band." He turned back to the other band members—older kids—nineteen maybe even twenty years old. "Hey, guys, this is Gabriella, Taylor, and Jasmine."

They all turned to look at us, and I gave an awkward wave.

Cole continued. "The guy with the voice is Ryan, Mikey is on guitar, and on bass is Adam."

Ryan had greasy-looking, dark, spiked hair and had a hand-rolled cigarette tucked behind one ear. He gave us a nod, and then turned back to his friends, not seeming to care that three school kids had turned up. I quickly assessed the other two. Adam had buzzed short, light brown hair, and a scraggly goatee. Mikey had longer curtained hair, like Cole, but his was a similar shade to Adam's. All three of them wore jeans and t-shirts with various band names scrawled across the front.

Cole turned his attention to Taylor. "So what did you think so far?"

She tossed her silky blonde hair. "I loved it. I'm a real rock chick at heart."

His face brightened, and Jasmine and I exchanged a glance.

In the garage, the older guys had lit up a couple of cigarettes and were sharing something from a bottle.

Cole put his hand on the garage wall beside Taylor's head, half boxing her in, and she gave a smug smile. "So what other bands are you into?" he asked her.

I exhaled a sigh. Yep, I'd been right. He was definitely into Taylor. I'd have to amuse myself by watching her fumble around her knowledge of rock bands, which was limited.

"Hey, Cole," shouted Ryan. "You want some of this?" He held up the cigarette he was smoking. It smelled strange, herbal, perhaps.

Cole glanced back and laughed. "I'm kinda busy over here, guys."

When I turned my head, I caught Cole staring at me. He flashed me a quick smile and then focused his attention back to Taylor.

I decided to ignore them. This probably wouldn't be the last time a guy would choose Taylor over me.

I should probably start getting used to it.

GABI—PRESENT DAY

I woke to the sound of a rocket falling somewhere deep in the house. The noise catapulted me from sleep, my heart racing, a flurry of panic and confusion. For a moment, I had no idea where I was, the adrenaline coursing through my veins telling me only to take cover. But then, as I untangled myself from my bed sheets, which clung in a sweaty mess to my body, the realization of what was really happening dawned on me. I wasn't in Iraq anymore. I didn't need to take cover, but I'd brought a little piece of the war home with me, and no amount of hiding would ever let me escape it.

I was back in my own room, the same room I'd grown up in, as though the last ten years had never happened. Only they *had* happened, and I had a permanent reminder of the fact. I wanted to fade back to oblivion, but my sleep was plagued with dreams, so I also didn't want to sleep. But I knew if I didn't get some rest, the pain would be worse, so I couldn't win. My whole life was caught in a cycle of avoiding fear and pain. I wanted to be strong, wanted to remember the person I was before all of this happened, but she felt so far away now, like another woman entirely. I tried to tell myself it could have been worse. I could have been Tom and not lived to see my baby girl grow, or hold my partner again.

It could have been worse. And yet somehow I felt like it couldn't be.

The sound from my dream had followed me into my waking world, and I froze, my ears straining.

What the hell?

The loud rumble and ending whine that had penetrated my sleep and transformed into that of approaching artillery was actually my dad snoring loudly from across the hall. I recognized that snore. It was the one where he was completely out of it, normally the result of a half a bottle of whiskey before he'd fallen into bed.

"For goodness' sake," I grumbled under my breath. The noise was enough to wake the dead.

Pushing my hair back from my face and taking a deep, shaky breath, I tried to compose myself. The t-shirt I wore to bed was pasted to my skin with sweat, and I wrinkled my nose as I pulled the material away from my body with my thumb and forefinger. Ugh, I stank, too.

I glanced at the red glowing letters of the LED clock. It was just after five a.m. Part of me was thankful. At least it was late enough to get up and take a shower. Then I remembered showers were off limits to me now. I couldn't risk slipping and falling. I had to settle for a bath instead.

I reached down to the side of my bed, my fingers searching for my prosthetic leg. I snagged the rubber sleeve and pulled it up onto the bed with me. My sigh came from the bottom of my lungs. There were so many things now I wasn't able to do which I'd always taken for granted before. They weren't the big, active things people might think of when considering their lives as an amputee, but the little things, such as being able to hop out of bed to use the bathroom, without having to go through the hassle of attaching a limb first.

Before pulling the sleeve up and over my stump, I took a moment to assess how it felt this morning—how much fluid retention had caused it to swell, and to make sure I hadn't suffered any scrapes or bumps overnight. To a certain extent, I guessed I was lucky. My amputation was below the knee, so at least I still had the range of movement that joint offered. But I still hadn't gotten used to the stump, and I wasn't sure I ever would. My brain also hadn't cottoned to the fact there was no longer a leg, and I was plagued by strange sensations when my brain tried to communicate with a limb that didn't exist.

The pain was always there. It came and went, faded and rose again, but it was never truly gone. I could never forget about it. Never. Certain things made it worse, such as not getting enough sleep, which was kind of ironic as, because I was in pain, and I struggled to sleep anyway.

I also worried about things all the time. I tried to avoid the news, but with social media, it was everywhere. Seemed like every day some crazy person was walking into a school, or a mall, or a movie theatre and shooting up innocent people. I worried for my own safety, and that of my father, but also for every single stranger I saw on the street. I'd thought my time in the Army would have hardened my heart, but instead it felt as though someone had removed my skin and ribcage, and exposed the organ to the world. I'd been offered the opportunity to return to service after I'd been rehabilitated, especially since I'd been so close to promotion, but I couldn't even think about it. The moment my thoughts drifted in that direction, my heartrate climbed, and I felt sick and panicky.

That part of my life was done now. I just needed to figure out what to do with the rest of it.

After my bath, and swigging a cup of coffee and grabbing something to eat, I still hadn't seen an appearance from my father.

I needed to head to the drugstore and pick up a prescription of the nerve medication I took to try to keep the phantom limb pain at bay. It didn't control it completely, but for the most part I had it under control now.

I was thankful to have my car. I was lucky—as far as lucky can be—in that I had lost my left leg so I could drive a regular automatic and didn't have to have any expensive alternations made. When I was driving I almost felt normal. No one could tell I was the girl with one leg when I was cruising down the highway. Getting in and out of the car, however, was a completely different story. I'd never before noticed just how useful having an ankle was when it came to movement, and with the current prosthetic limb I wore, I didn't have an ankle joint. That would change in later months when I got a new prosthesis with an ankle, but for the moment it was an absolute pain in the ass.

At the drugstore, I pulled into a handicapped space. I needed plenty of room to the side of the car in order to maneuver myself in and out of the car door. All these things I took for granted before. Now the frustration of doing something as simple as getting out of the car drove me insane.

Grunting and sweating in the early heat of the day, I wished I had the guts to wear a skirt or shorts, but I was still hugely self-conscious and didn't want people to stare. I managed to get out of the car, slammed the door shut, and pressed the button on the key fob to lock the doors. I started toward the drugstore when a female voice stopped me.

"Hey, you! What do you think you're doing?"

I turned in confusion to see a woman in her sixties hurrying toward me.

"I'm sorry?" I said, baffled.

"I asked you what you thought you were doing. I can't stand people like you, parking your big expensive cars in the handicapped spaces, thinking you're entitled just because you have money!"

I blinked in shock, gob-smacked. I didn't have money—far from it. The payout I'd received upon my discharge from the Army had gone on my car because I'd needed to be mobile. The small sum I had left over was now my income, as I wasn't working, and I didn't know when I would be again. I hoped I would receive compensation for my injury at some point in the future, but the amount hadn't been decided yet.

Shocked and embarrassed, I couldn't deal with the confrontation. Going on auto-pilot, I turned away from her and headed toward the drugstore as I'd planned.

"Hey!" the woman shouted again, her voice rising to a screech.

Other people were looking now, and my mortification deepened. Who the hell was this woman?

"You need to move your car!" she continued.

She wasn't going to just let me go about my business. I wished I still had a bit of the old Gabi about me—the one who went into a warzone and commanded a company of soldiers. This was one woman in a parking lot, not an enemy in a warzone, and yet here I felt more panicked and out of control than I had in Iraq.

"I'm allowed to park there," I managed finally, though my voice sounded small and meek, not like me at all.

"What?" she screeched. "No, you're not."

"Just because you can't see a disability doesn't mean it's not there."

"Stop making excuses. Just move your damned car."

I pointed toward the car. "I have a badge hanging from the mirror. You can check."

"It's probably your elderly parents' or something. Just because it's in the car doesn't mean it belongs to you."

I just wanted this to stop. We'd created a small crowd now, people loading their cars, or messing with shoelaces, trying to pretend they weren't watching when they couldn't take their eyes off us.

"Yes, I can," I hissed, and, in desperation, bent and grabbed the cuff of my pants leg. I hauled it up, exposing the titanium steel rod that now made up my lower leg.

I wished I could take more satisfaction in the expression on the woman's face, but I was too humiliated at this point. My cheeks burned and I knew I must have been glowing—the heat of the day and the altercation causing me to sweat profusely. I just wanted to grab my meds and get the hell out of there.

The woman lifted her hands in defense. "Oh, my God. I'm so sorry."

"Just forget it, please."

Clearly now mortified herself, she turned and hurried away from the scene she'd caused. I did my best to hold back tears as I turned, my head down, to continue on my way.

"Gabi?"

The male voice behind me made my heart stop. Did I recognize it after all these years? Surely not.

With my heart pounding, I turned to find Cole Devonport standing in the lot. He was older, obviously, his jaw length, blond hair cut short. The stubble across his jaw was a few days over just being stubble, but wasn't quite yet a beard. A blur of tattoos ran up both forearms, though I couldn't see any farther beyond the rolled up sleeves of his shirt. A couple of bird tattoos flew up the side of his well-muscled neck. His face looked harder, more rigid, with cut cheekbones and a sharp jawline. But his blue eyes were still exactly the same, except now they regarded me with sorrow, and what? Regret? He must have witnessed the whole thing with the woman, and seen me pull up the leg of my pants to expose my prosthetic limb. I didn't know how he felt about seeing me like that—probably horrified and embarrassed for me all at the same time—but I knew one thing.

Cole Devonport still looked like trouble.

COLE–PRESENT DAY

Like everyone else in the parking lot, I knew I was staring, but I couldn't quite bring myself to stop.

"Gabi?" I repeated, not knowing what else to say.

"Cole," she replied, appearing as shocked as I felt. "What are you doing here?"

"Here as in Willowbrook Falls, or here as in the parking lot?"

"Umm, Willowbrook, I guess."

"I was released three months ago. I didn't have anywhere else to go."

She nodded and pushed her hair from her face, the roots damp with perspiration. Her hair was still the mass of spiral curls I'd always remembered, though she wore it shorter now than she had when we were teenagers. Other than that, she looked exactly the same to me—hardly a day older.

Well, except for the missing limb, of course.

I nodded down at her leg. "What happened?"

Her lips thinned. "I don't really want to talk about it standing on the sidewalk, Cole. I think people have seen enough of my business for one day."

"Okay, so let me buy you a coffee. We can talk then."

But she shook her head and my heart sank. "No. I don't want to talk about it, full stop. I just want to get what I came for and go home."

She glanced over her shoulder, as though, as though I was trapping her somehow just by standing here and she was checking for an escape route.

"So you're back, then," I continued, wanting to drag out what little time I had with her. "Are you staying with your dad?"

"Yeah, for the moment."

"How is he?"

A shadow fell over her face and she shrugged. "Same as ever." She glanced back toward the drugstore. "Look, Cole. I have to go, okay?"

"Sure, but I'd really like to take you out for that coffee sometime."

She shook her head again. "I don't need your pity, Cole. Just get on with your life, and I'll try to get on with mine."

Gabi turned and walked away, and I tried not to focus on the way she lurched slightly, favoring one side.

I waited until she'd disappeared inside the drugstore and then went back to my car. My shift started soon—I was on food prep for the lunchtime rush—though I would have risked being late if Gabi had agreed to coffee.

Even though I'd known she was back in town, seeing her had still been a shock. It was like being punched in the chest, having her so close again. And she was right, I did feel bad for her. More than that, my fucking heart broke for her. I couldn't even imagine the sort of pain she must be in, how much this must have affected her life. I had so many questions, but I didn't know how to ask a single one without sounding exactly how I felt—shocked, horrified, morbidly curious, and absolutely gutted for her.

And like the selfish son-of-a-bitch I was, I also felt devastated by the loss of one of her beautiful legs. I'd admired every inch of her when we'd been together all those years ago, but perhaps I'd loved her legs the most. The first day I'd managed to get up the courage to speak to her, she'd been sitting in the park, propped up against a tree, reading a book. Her already short skirt had ridden high on her thighs, and I could tell she'd been aware of how much leg she was showing by the way she'd kept tugging at the hem, trying to make the skirt longer. I'd gotten to know those slender calves and smooth thighs a lot better in the months that had followed, and my heart cracked at the idea a part of them no longer existed.

What does the remaining stump look like? How high had the amputation gone? I pushed the thoughts from my head. It wasn't any of my business—not anymore. I'd seen to that ten years ago.

She was obviously still angry with me, and I didn't blame her. Perhaps she was just angry with the world, and I didn't blame her for that either. I wondered what had happened. A car accident, perhaps? I had deliberately tried not to learn anything about her over these last ten years, stopping anyone from even speaking her name if they tried to broach the subject with me. The pain had been too great, and I hadn't wanted to learn that she was happily married with a houseful of children. Maybe I should have wanted to discover she was happy after what I put her through, but maybe part of me had worried I'd learn she wasn't happy, and that would make me feel even worse.

But I'd never wanted this for her. I wouldn't have wished what she must have gone through on my worst enemy.

I lingered beside my car, hoping Gabi would come back out of the store and be forced to talk with me again, but she didn't make a reappearance. I couldn't lurk like this for much longer. I was attracting curious glances, and besides, I was going to make myself late for work.

Not wanting to be leaving Gabriella yet again, I climbed into the car.

She didn't leave my thoughts for a single second for the rest of the day. All I could think about was her being back, and when I would get to see her again.

SLY

I sneaked into my foster family's house and carefully closed the front door behind me. I'd stayed out past my curfew, but I hoped everyone had gone to bed already.

"Cole?" A man's voice.

Damn it. I froze, somehow hoping if I kept still for long enough he'd forget he'd heard me come in. But then the figure of my foster-father appeared in the open doorway of the living room, his arms folded across his chest.

"What time do you call this?"

Busted.

"Yeah, sorry," I muttered. "Me and the guys were practicing and I forgot the time."

"It's almost midnight, Cole. You're supposed to be back by eleven on a school night, and to be honest, I think even that is too late. If you can't stick to your curfew, I'll have to stop you going out during the week altogether."

I hated being told off as though I was a little kid. "I said I was sorry."

Even I could hear the sulky, petulant tone to my voice. It wasn't something I was proud of.

He exhaled a sigh. "Okay, just go straight to bed. I'll see you in the morning."

Happy to escape without punishment, I kept my head down and ran up the stairs.

Emily and Stephen Cowen were good to me, but I'd never consider them to be my parents. Perhaps I was just too old by the time I'd come to live with them a little before my sixteenth birthday. I'd been in and out of so many homes by that point, I hadn't wanted to make any kind of emotional connection with someone, knowing they'd probably get sick of me within a few months. I didn't blame my previous foster families. I knew I wasn't easy to have around. I wasn't exactly the cute, lovable toddler or baby they'd probably hoped for. I had issues, and even though I'd gotten better with age, I'd been an absolute shit between the ages of thirteen and fifteen. Drinking, smoking, shoplifting. Name it, and I'd probably done it. I'd already been kicked out of several schools for fighting or truancy.

I pushed open the door of the bedroom I shared with another foster kid, Danny. I wasn't surprised to find him still awake, sitting on his bed with his back leaning against the wall, headphones clamped to his ears as he listened to his portable CD player.

Danny was almost a year younger than me, and a good foot shorter, but he didn't let that hold him back. He reminded me of a scrappy little terrier, who, aware of his size, went into everything with his teeth bared and hackles raised. I liked to think I was a little more chilled out about things than he was, but Danny had a way of winding me up.

I noted the stack of CDs beside him on the bed weren't his own.

A couple of strides brought me over to his side of the room, and I grabbed for the CDs. He hadn't even bothered to look up when I walked in, but, as I lunged, he reached out and shoved my arm away.

"What the fuck, dude?" he blurted, wrenching off the headphones.

"Those are my CDs. Don't take my stuff without asking."

"Jeez, man. I was only borrowing them."

"Yeah, right. Borrowing something without asking is basically stealing."

"You'd know all about that, wouldn't you?"

My rage boiled. "Are you calling me a fucking—"

The bedroom door burst open, and Stephen stood in the doorway, his expression thunderous.

"Are you trying to wake the whole damn house? What's going on in here?" He raised a hand. "No, actually, I don't want to hear it. You're already in my bad books, Cole, for breaking your curfew, and then you come back in and start a fight?"

I tried to defend myself, but the hand lifted again, silencing me. "I said I don't want to hear it. Go to bed, and if I hear another word, I'll ground you for a month."

Fuming, I dragged off my clothes and climbed under the covers of my bed. I rolled over so I faced the wall, my foster-brother at my back. Danny still had my CDs. They might only be things, but I didn't have much stuff that was my own. In a few months I'd turn eighteen and would finally be free from the system that had pushed and pulled me in every direction since I was twelve years old. When that happened, I wanted to be able to take the few things I had with me.

I couldn't stew over Danny for long. My thoughts left my foster brother and went to Gabriella Weston instead. She'd shown up at my band practice that night, when I'd been certain she wouldn't turn up. I'd chatted to her friends, trying to make her see me as an amiable type of guy. They did all the things I'd taken for granted girls did around me—

the giggles and eyelash fluttering—but Gabi hung back, leaning against the garage wall and ignoring me. I'd stepped up the flirting, being deliberately louder, even touching her friend's hair to try and get her to glance in my direction, but she'd only looked bored.

I wasn't sure what fascinated me so much about Gabriella. She seemed different than the rest of the girls at school. She was smart, and while she had a couple of close friends, she didn't appear interested in fitting in with the crowd. While the other girls all sidled up to me, flirting and twirling their hair around their fingers, Gabi acted as though I barely existed. When I spoke to her, she looked at me as though she couldn't quite believe I'd had the nerve to engage her in conversation. That might put some guys off, but not me. I'd like a challenge. Plus she had the cutest nose I'd ever seen—the way it tipped up slightly at the end—big brown eyes, and dark curls I imagined sinking my hands into. She wasn't quick to smile, but I bet when you eventually coaxed a smile from her, it would be like she'd given you the greatest gift on earth.

I was determined to get that smile, and I always got what I wanted.

GABRIELLA—PRESENT DAY

I got back to my dad's house, still reeling from the altercation with the woman in the parking lot, and from seeing Cole again. I hated that he'd gotten even hotter with age. If the universe had been kind to me just the once, he would have had a beer gut and a receding hairline by now. But no, instead he was even better looking—a grown man now instead of a boy. Tattoos and muscles, and a hard edge to his jawline. I didn't know what he'd been through in prison, but he appeared to have lost the playful, relaxed air I'd loved so much about him. Sure, he'd had a temper back then, and even at eighteen had been quick to fight, but I'd always believed that had been an act so he could survive in the world in which he'd been raised. I'd always resented only having one parent—especially as the parent who'd been left behind wasn't exactly a functioning member of society anymore—but I couldn't imagine having grown up feeling like no one wanted me. My dad had plenty of faults, but, other than the drinking, he'd never made me feel like he didn't love me. If anything, I was the one who probably made him feel like the unloved one.

I pulled my car up in the driveway and began the awkward process of climbing out with my prosthetic limb. The position always reminded me of a dog cocking its leg—something that didn't do much for my self-esteem. To be fair, no part of the last six months had done anything for my self-esteem. Here I was, twenty-eight years old, out of work, and living with my alcoholic father. Oh, yes, and missing a limb, and now an ex-boyfriend on the scene who looked better than ever, and who'd witnessed me arguing with a woman in a parking lot, while bright red and dripping with sweat, all before flashing my prosthetic limb at half of town. As far as I could tell, I had absolutely no reason to feel good about myself.

Trying not to think about it, and failing miserably, I let myself into the house. Immediately, I caught the waft of bacon cooking, and my stomach grumbled with hunger. I'd only grabbed a banana before leaving the house, and though I suspected my dad had only just managed to get out of bed, I'd already been up for hours.

I walked into the kitchen to find him standing at the stove, flipping rashers. He smiled at me as I entered, and I tried not to notice his bloodshot eyes and puffy complexion.

"Hey, sweetheart. There you are. I wondered where you'd gotten to."

I gestured to an envelope on the countertop on which I'd scribbled him a note before I'd left. "I wrote you a note, Dad. Didn't you see it?"

"Obviously I didn't, or I wouldn't have asked you," he grumbled.

He got frustrated with himself in the same way I did. His drinking made him miss things, and he wasn't as sharp, mentally, as he used to be. He got frustrated, and then he got angry. He wasn't a mean drunk, by any means, and had never hit me, though he'd shouted plenty. I knew he was angry at himself for not being able to control his addiction—especially now I was home and in the condition I was in. He wanted to be able to do more for me, but the drink was stronger than he was.

"I just went to the drugstore to pick up my meds. It's no big deal."

"Okay, good. Sit down and I'll bring you some breakfast. Got to keep your strength up."

I did as he suggested, though it was closer to lunch than breakfast now, and slid into a chair at the dining table.

He placed a cup of coffee in front of me, and I knew without tasting it that the beverage was full of sugar. I'd told him multiple times I didn't take sugar in my coffee anymore—I hadn't since shortly after I'd left home—but he kept forgetting and I didn't have the heart to remind him again. A bacon sandwich—thick white bread, dripping with butter, and half a pigs' worth of bacon—slid onto the table beside it.

I forced a smile. "Thanks, Dad. Looks great."

I knew I would barely eat half of the food, and would have to dispose of the uneaten part without him noticing so I didn't hurt his feelings. I had to watch what I ate now I wasn't so active. I'd been told I would be fitted for a blade once my stump had settled down, but that wouldn't be for another couple of months or so yet, and that was only if the funding for the blade came through. I was desperate to get back to running—I'd run six miles almost daily for most of my adult life—and the loss of this ability to do what I loved, and allowed me to de-stress, was as hard as the loss of the limb itself.

"So ..." I started, unsure whether or not I should broach the subject, but finding myself unable not to talk about it. "I bumped into Cole Devonport while I was out."

His head whipped around to face me, his thick, bushy eyebrows lifting. "Cole, as in the teenage boyfriend?"

"Well, he isn't a teenager anymore."

He scowled. "No, obviously not. You know what I meant."

"Yeah, sorry." I twisted my coffee cup in my hands and then lifted it slightly to take a small sip, trying not to grimace at the cloying sweetness. "He asked how I was."

"So he should," he said, gruffly. "That boy was ultimately the cause of … this." He gestured to my leg.

I sat up straighter. "Cole was not responsible for me losing my leg, Dad. I haven't even seen or heard from the guy in over ten years."

"He was the reason you ran off and joined the Army."

"He didn't drive a bomb-laden car into my post in Iraq." I could feel my tone getting heated, my body tensed. Why did I still feel the need to defend Cole to my father, even after all this time? "And he wasn't the only reason I left town."

His head lowered, his shoulders dropping. Immediately, I felt bad, a wave of guilt swamping over me, and not only because I'd brought up my leaving. Hearing that Cole had spent the last ten years in prison twisted my insides. I couldn't begin to imagine what his life had been like.

"I don't want to have this conversation, Gabi," my dad said, standing from the table and picking up his untouched sandwich.

"What about your food?" I replied, keeping my tone softer.

"I lost my appetite." He threw the sandwich into the trash and then walked from the room.

"Where are you going, Dad?" I called after him, frustrated once more. That seemed to be what my life revolved around now—just dealing with one frustration after the other.

"I'm going to take a shower," he called back.

I didn't reply, but my thoughts went to the bottle of vodka I knew he had hidden in the top of the toilet cistern. I figured his shower might take a while.

I gave a sigh and turned my attention back to my breakfast. I ate a couple of mouthfuls, though my appetite had all but deserted me. My thoughts kept flicking back to Cole. Suddenly the boy—who'd been my whole life when I'd been seventeen, but whom I'd tried not to think about for the past ten years—was back in my head again. How could a pain I'd believed I'd let go of suddenly rise up back inside me as fresh as though it had happened yesterday? I'd thought I'd gotten over everything he'd done, but perhaps I'd simply buried it, like a long forgotten object, only to be unearthed again and dusted off.

No, I couldn't start thinking about Cole again, not after everything he did back then, and what had followed. Besides, I had bigger things to worry about. I had an appointment that afternoon to be assessed for a new limb, which would be a big upgrade on what I was currently wearing. At the moment, my leg was effectively strapped onto the lower half of my body with rubber right up to my groin, and not only was it uncomfortable, when the weather was hot like it was, I sweated something awful. On top of that, I also had to wear numerous socks over my stump to try and make the stump fit into the top of the prosthesis, and the number of these had to be changed during the day as the stump would grow and then shrink again due to fluid loss, and make the prosthetic fit badly. The new leg would be a pin lock leg, so would hopefully fit a lot better, and I'd be done with the rubber.

The appointment was never a done deal that I'd get my new leg, though. First of all, my stump would need to fit the end of the prosthetic, which was never a guarantee, as it changed size and shape so much. The stump I had now looked nothing like the one I had when my leg was initially amputated after the bombing. Secondly, if I managed to get the slightest scratch or sore I wouldn't be able to wear my leg at all. The risk of infection was high in amputees, and if I suffered a bad infection, more of my leg could be amputated. The thought of this terrified me. I'd only just started to come to terms with what was left of my leg, and the possibility of losing more and having to start all over again was a living nightmare.

I spent a couple of hours reading on the couch, before readying myself for my hospital appointment. My dad hadn't reappeared, and when I went to check on him, I discovered he'd taken himself back to bed. I wished I could do something to fix him, but he'd been a heavy drinker for as long as I could remember, and nothing I'd ever said or done had made any difference. I knew I hadn't helped by taking off all those years ago, but the truth was I hadn't even considered him at the time. I'd been filled with so much hurt and betrayal, I hadn't had the space in my heart for anyone else. My heartbreak had been like a kind of madness, taking over my every thought. Leaving Willowbrook Falls, and Cole Devonport, far behind had been the only thing I'd been concerned with back then. I'd started over where there was absolutely nothing to remind me of the boy I'd loved.

Over the years, as the pain started to fade, I'd begun to worry about my dad more and more, but he appeared to get by—a functioning alcoholic—until the day he wasn't anymore. Someone had grown suspicious of his behavior. Perhaps they smelled alcohol on his breath once too often, or he'd made one too many mistakes, but he was asked to take a breath-test, and it came back twice the legal limit. He was suspended right away, and then later lost his job at a hearing. I came back when I had time on leave, but I couldn't stay. I loved my dad, but why did I have to give up my life because of his illness? I'd tried to ask him to get help so many times, but even now he was still in denial. He convinced himself his way of living was normal.

It would have been good to have my dad accompany me to my appointments, but I didn't want him with me when he was drunk.

Instead, I was resigned to the fact that, like most of my life, I would be doing this on my own.

I drove to the hospital and, after giving my name to the desk, took a seat in the waiting area. Glancing around at the couple of other people in the waiting room—an older man in his fifties, who was an amputee from the upper thigh and was in a wheelchair, and a younger man in his early twenties with no obvious disability—I offered them a smile. They both smiled and nodded back in recognition.

"Gabriella Weston?"

I turned at my name. An attractive man in his mid-forties stood in the doorway of one of the rooms which led onto the waiting room. He was a different professional than the one I'd seen previously.

"Hi, I'm Doctor Merryweather. Would you like to come through?"

I nodded and did my usual ungainly attempt at standing. I'd never realized before just how much having a calf muscle helped to be able to stand from sitting. The result was me looking like an old lady trying to get to her feet. The doctor made no attempt to help me, knowing this was something I needed to practice on my own. This was my life now. I couldn't have people helping me all the time.

"So how have you been getting on, Ms. Weston?"

"It's Gabi, please," I said. "And I've been getting on okay."

He glanced at his notes. "You still have the support of your father? You're staying with him?"

I nodded. "That's right."

"Good. It's important you have a good support system right now."

I just forced a smile. What more could I do?

"And how about dealing with the emotional side of everything you've been through. Have you been talking to anyone about what happened in Iraq?"

"I had a counselor for the post traumatic stress disorder. It did help."

"And now?"

I gave what I hoped was a reassuring smile. "I'm better now." I glanced at my leg. "Well, mentally, anyway. Obviously, this is never going to grow back. I'm not part salamander."

"No, of course not."

My cheeks heated and I wondered when I'd learn how to control myself in public. Apparently flashing my leg and cracking jokes was the way I dealt with my disability.

"Well, I have your new leg here to try on. We'll assess it for size, and then make any adjustments, and you should be able to come back in a week for a final fitting."

I resisted the urge to clap with excitement. I was desperate to get rid of the hideous rubber which went right up to my groin and held my current limb in place. In this heat, it was so uncomfortable, there were moments when I'd considered going back in the wheelchair rather than dealing with the sweaty, horrible material. The new sleeve didn't come anywhere near as high up my thigh, and had a type of screw attached to a disc at the end. When I pushed it into the prosthesis, it would just click into place. Being able to take my leg on and off would get a whole heap easier.

I removed my prosthesis, and tried not to stare at my stump. It looked very different than when I'd first woken up from the explosion and discovered I'd lost my limb. Back then it had a much blunter ending, and the wound sticking my skin together had been raw. Now the stump was more pointed in shape, and the scar had faded to a red line. I still found it difficult to look at, but not as badly as I had in the early days. Back then just acknowledging what had happened sent me into a full-blown panic attack. I'd not wanted to come to terms with the fact the hideous sight was now a part of me. Plus my mind played tricks on me—

and still did—making it so I could still feel my limb, especially when I was about to fall asleep, or just upon waking, so I'd have to bring myself back to reality every time I opened my eyes.

Doctor Merryweather smiled as he examined my stump. "This is looking great," he told me. "Some people wouldn't be ready for this type of prosthetic for another six months, but you've healed brilliantly. Being young and physically fit has definitely helped you with that."

A warm glow expanded inside me at his praise.

The doctor showed me how to attach my new limb, and I smiled at him as this time he put out his hand and helped me to my feet.

"Have a walk up and down the corridor for five minutes," he told me. "Make sure it feels completely comfortable. If there are any niggles or anything rubbing, just say, because what feels like something tiny after five minutes, will feel like a rock caught inside the sleeve after you've worn it all day."

"Thanks. I guess I'll be back in five minutes, then?"

His smiled widened. "See you in five."

I did as he suggested, walking up and down the hospital corridors, focusing on how the new leg fitted and if there was anything causing me any discomfort. As far as I could tell it was far superior to the other one, and I loved the freedom of not feeling like half of my lower body was encased in rubber. Some people might get their kicks from that kind of thing, but I wasn't one of them.

I went back to the doctor's office and told him I was completely happy with the new prosthetic.

"That's great," he replied, scribbling something on the notes in front of him. "We'll schedule you an appointment for the same time next week, and then you can take your new leg home."

"Thank you so much."

"You're very welcome."

He left me alone to put my old leg back on, and then I gathered my purse and made my way out of the hospital and into the parking lot. The idea of my new leg had put me in a great mood, and I planned on treating myself to a drive-thru Starbucks on the way home. Since losing my leg, I had begun to truly appreciate the genius of a drive-thru *anything*.

My car was in the other handy thing I'd learned to love—the handicapped spots, right next to the entrance.

As I fumbled in my purse for my keys, I lifted my head and a figure across the parking lot made my heart stop.

I'd only ever seen him one other time as an adult, but despite this, I recognized him instantly—the newly tattooed sleeves, the broad shoulders, the buzzed short blond hair. My heart leaped into my throat, my body tensing. Absurdly, my first instinct was to throw myself onto the ground between the two cars I was standing beside, and hide until he had gone, but I knew if I did that, I'd never get up again.

Keep walking, I willed him. *Don't turn around.*

And yet, as though my thoughts had caused him to do so, Cole threw a casual glance over his shoulder and his line of sight landed directly on me.

He smiled at me, and then turned directly around and strolled toward me. I stood, rooted to the spot, my cheeks already burning.

"Gabi," he said as he approached. "Are you stalking me?"

My eyes widened. "No! Of course not." I gestured wildly behind me. "I had an appointment."

"It's okay. I was kidding."

The burning in my cheeks grew hotter. "Sure. I knew that."

His eyes were so blue, and exactly as I remembered them. He'd always had a way of seeing right inside me, his eyes able to search my face and know exactly what was written on my heart. I didn't feel like that had changed at all.

"So, is everything okay?" he asked.

I nodded. "Yeah, I was just seeing my specialist. I'm going to be getting a new leg soon." I felt ridiculously awkward and embarrassed talking to him about my amputation. This guy had once upon a time used his tongue to trace every inch of my skin, and now a massive part of the skin he'd loved—or at least had said he'd loved—no longer existed. Was it weird for him, too? Or did it completely gross him out and he was trying not to think about it?

"So you get a new leg?" he asked, appearing genuinely curious. "Do you have more than one?"

"Well, I have two legs, but only one prosthetic leg."

I was pleased to see his cheeks color in return. I had gotten to him, and for some reason, I liked that. This was certainly an area where I had one over on him. Annoyingly, the blush made him look even more handsome, the pink in his cheeks a contrast to the ice blue of his eyes and hardness of his jawline.

It suddenly occurred to me that he'd made a joke about me stalking him, but what was he doing at the hospital? I asked him the question.

"Oh, I'm mentoring a kid. He's not doing so well."

"What?" There was so much in those two sentences that threw me for a loop. "A kid? Not doing well?"

"Yeah, he's got issues with drink and drugs. Actually, he's got issues with pretty much everyone and everything. I'm trying to help him, but it's not going so well."

"Why would you be helping him?" Considering Cole's background, I was amazed he'd be allowed anywhere near another kid who was trouble.

"It's part of my program to get me back into society. I'm volunteering to try to help youngsters not to make the same mistakes I did."

He studied me again, and my whole insides lifted and tightened. I hated how he had such an effect on me.

Cole ran a hand over his head. He used to do the same thing when he was eighteen and had long hair to push back. "Look, Gabi. We don't have to talk about all of this stuff in the parking lot. Let me take you for a coffee."

I physically backed away. "Oh, no," I said, even though I'd been promising myself coffee—ideally iced, with vanilla syrup—only moments earlier. "I don't think that's a good idea."

"We have a lot to talk about, though. Surely that deserves at least one coffee."

All I could think about was the pain he'd caused me, how long it had taken me to put myself together again. I'd managed to do it back then, but now I was literally not the same person—not all of her, anyway. I didn't have the strength to let him back in only for him to break my heart again.

Don't be stupid, Gabi. He's not going to want you again. Look at him. He's ridiculously hot, and you don't even have both legs anymore. The idea of being with you in any way other than fully clothed would totally gross him out.

I hadn't even been able to bring myself to think about what sex would be like with a missing limb. I couldn't imagine it—especially not with Cole.

"I'm sorry, I just can't."

"Gabi, I know you still hate me for what happened, but we both live back in the same town again, and we're going to keep running into one another. Can't we make this whole thing a lot easier on both of us and at least try to be friends?"

Sudden anger surged up inside me. "So you just want me to sit and drink coffee with you, smile nicely, and chitchat about the good old days."

His forehead pulled down in confusion. "No, I just want to talk to you, that's all."

42

"Yeah, to make you feel better about all the shit you put me through when we were kids. So you can go home and sleep better in your bed, without having to worry about the poor girl who you're now living in the same town with, and who is missing a fucking leg."

It was his turn to step away. "I promise, there was no ulterior motive in asking you for coffee. I honestly just wanted to spend some time with you."

"Sure, I know how that works. Then you'll go and share all the juicy gossip with your buddies over beer, and you can all have a good laugh about how Gabi Weston is now hopping all over town."

He shook his head, looking to the ground. "I'm sorry you think that."

"Yeah, sure you are. You proved to me just what kind of person you are ten years ago."

With tears burning the backs of my eyes, I fumbled for my keys again. I secured my fingers around them, and without looking back at Cole, I walked at a quick pace to my car.

I got in, and sat, trying to breathe without crying. I was too old, and had been through too much, to sit in my car crying over a guy I hadn't seen in over ten years. Besides, my outburst at Cole hadn't been all about what he'd done to me. I had my own guilt to live with, and deep down I was worried that if I had to hear too much about those years he'd spent behind bars, I'd find myself confessing.

Sniffing, blinking back the tears, I put my car into reverse and started to pull out of the space—

Hands slammed down on my rear windshield, and I jumped, jamming on the brakes. "Jesus Christ!"

A figure appeared at my car window and tapped with knuckles. I rolled it down and Cole's face appeared in the space.

"What the hell is wrong with you?" I demanded.

"I didn't want you to leave without giving you this." He held out a slip of paper. "I know you'll probably burn it, but I just wanted to say that if you ever need me for anything, you can call me, okay?"

I stared at him, not taking the slip, so he leaned in and placed the paper on my dashboard. "Take care of yourself, Gabs."

And he stepped away, allowing me to pull out of the parking lot.

COLE—PRESENT DAY

I shouldn't be surprised Gabriella Weston hated me.

What had I been hoping for—that the years would have faded everything I did, and she would come rushing back into my arms? She'd been my one and only real girlfriend, but that didn't mean I'd been hers. She could have been married and divorced again for all I knew. Hell, she could still be married, though I hadn't heard any rumors about a husband, and I was pretty sure if there was someone special in her life, they would be with her during a time like this. The same couldn't be said for me. Gabi was the only girl I'd ever loved. I'd been in prison for the past ten years. I hadn't exactly had much opportunity to create new relationships. Not that my location made much of a difference. Even if I'd been a free man, I didn't think I'd ever find a love that would burn as strong and bright as the love I'd had for her when I was seventeen, going on eighteen.

How different would things have been if I hadn't screwed everything up? We might be married by now, have a couple of kids of our own. She might not have gone through whatever trauma had cost her her leg.

I had a shift later that day, the evening shift, which meant I wouldn't be getting off until the early hours of the morning. I wouldn't mind the later finish if I could just figure out a way to sleep in the next day. After spending most of my adult life under prison rules, my body was trained to wake at six a.m., and even when I didn't collapse on my bed until after one, I still found my eyes pinging open right before six. I was conditioned, that was for sure, but I wanted to leave my prison life behind me. The future I'd dreamed of when I was eighteen had never materialized. In fact, I'd been forced to put it off for another ten years, but now I had a second chance and I didn't intend on fucking things up again.

I took a shower, got dressed, and headed out to my shift. As usual, the kitchen was busy and hot, and I nodded my hellos to the guys working their asses off to make sure customers got their meals on time. I was on prep for the start of the shift, and would move to pans later in the night after most of the meals had gone out. It wasn't exactly classy work, but I was allowed to keep my head down and get on with things without being forced to interact with too many people.

As I worked, my thoughts kept drifting to Gabi. Both times I'd seen her had felt like a punch to the chest. It was like stepping back in time, and I had to physically stop myself from reaching out and touching her as we spoke, just as I always had when we were teenagers. She looked exactly the same to me, though I knew I must appear brutish to her. Ten years behind bars would harden a guy up. I wondered if she hated my tattoos, and that my hair was so much shorter now. Did she feel nostalgic in any way for the boy I had been back then?

The kitchen was always a noisy place, pans crashing and banging, meat sizzling, and people shouting orders to one another, but, beneath it all, a commotion sounded from the front of house. I glanced over my shoulder, wondering what was going on. It was normally a pretty chilled out place to work, but something was definitely up. I heard shouts, and a plate crashed.

One of the waitresses burst into the kitchen, her gaze flicking across the space until it landed on me.

"Hey, Cole," she yelled. "We need you out front. Some asshole is having a fit about his meal."

"Can't you handle it?"

"No, we need you."

I was never asked to be front of house. The owner didn't think I would be good for business. But most of the people working out front were women—the hostess and waitresses. Perhaps they just needed someone who appeared a little intimidating. I figured I fit that bill.

I dropped the potatoes I was peeling, the vegetables splashing into the muddy water, and barely stopped to wipe my hands on the apron I wore.

Shouts filtered through to the kitchen, and, as I pushed open the door, they grew louder. A small group had gathered in a circle around someone who was standing at the end of a table, a clutter of broken crockery at his feet. *Asshole.* Who the hell came into a restaurant to start a fight?

I squared my shoulders, fully planning on grabbing this guy and throwing him out of the door. I couldn't afford to get myself in any more trouble, but I figured there were enough witnesses around to explain how I was the one trying to put this to an end, not start it. I sensed Deano at my shoulder. He'd also been working in the kitchen, and I knew I had backup. As I pushed through the small crowd, one of the waitresses—a tiny woman in her fifties—tried to placate the man.

"Stupid bitch," said the guy. "If my meal is tasteless, I ain't gonna pay for it!"

"But you ate the whole thing ... " She was still trying to reason with him.

The man must have noticed the movement in the crowd as I approached, and his head whipped toward me. The moment he locked eyes with me, I froze in surprise. What was it with people crawling out of the woodwork at the moment? Or perhaps it was just that I'd been away for so long. Everyone else had been around this whole time.

Ryan.

He straightened, his eyes widening. "Fuck me, Cole Devonport."

To my astonishment, he apparently forgot the scene he'd created and strolled toward me. With me stunned into inaction, he grabbed my hand and shook it, smacking me on the shoulder with his other hand. I could feel everyone staring, trying to connect the two of us. Plenty of people knew about my prison stay, and I didn't want to be associated with the likes of Ryan Becks. My reputation was bad enough as it was.

I dragged my fingers out of his hold and took a step back. "I think you need to leave, Ryan."

"Now is that the way to greet an old friend?"

I scowled. "We're not friends. We never were."

He barked a laugh. "No? You could have fooled me."

"Leave, Ryan, or we'll call the cops."

He gave a smug smile. "You know the police pretty well by now, don't you?"

I balled my fists, resisting the urge to lunge for him and break his face. I kept my tone even, though anger bubbled beneath the surface. "This is your last chance. Turn around and walk away, or the police are going to be called."

He gave a nonchalant shrug. "No problem. I didn't want to stay in this shit hole any longer, anyway." He turned, and for a moment I thought he was going to leave without any more trouble, but then he spun back to me. "Hey, how's that piece of skirt you used to hang out with? Gabriella, wasn't it? Is she still as fit as she was back then?" He chuckled. "I remember how she was always gagging for it."

A red haze descended over my vision, and I was no longer aware of any of the people around us, or how I was supposed to be protecting my already ruined reputation. With a growl, I lunged toward Ryan, my shoes crunching on the smashed crockery. Hands grabbed my arms from behind, holding me back. I shook them off, but the delay had given Ryan just enough time to turn and saunter from the building, the little bell above the door ringing as the door swung shut behind him. I could make out his figure walking into the night. A part of me—a massive part—wanted to race after him and smash his head into the sidewalk, but I knew I couldn't. Going after him now would be viewed as assault, and it would put me right back behind bars.

What the hell was he doing back here? As far as I was aware, Ryan had left town not long after I'd been incarcerated. I wondered if he'd seemed as surprised about seeing me as I'd been about him. Had the shock in his eyes matched my own, or had he been a little too confident about approaching me again for the first time in ten years?

I didn't know, but the last thing I needed right now was the likes of Ryan back in my life.

NINE

Cole Devonport was walking down the school corridor, directly toward me. I ducked my head, holding my books closer to my chest, and kept going, hoping he'd somehow not notice me.

But as he got closer, I realized he was the one trying not to catch my eye, and despite the way he walked, with his head down and his blond hair hanging over his face, it was impossible not to notice his black eye and split lip.

Before I'd had the chance to think through what I was doing, I'd reached out and caught him by his forearm, pulling him to a stop.

"Hey, Cole. What happened?"

"Gabi," he said, his gaze flicking to me. "Hey, how are you doing?"

"I'm fine. What happened to you?"

He gave his head a slight shake and glanced away again, his cheeks heating. "I got into a fight with my foster brother. It was stupid."

"Your foster brother? Does he come to Willowbrook High?"

"Nah, he goes to Blackdown," he said, mentioning another high

50

school across town. "He'd already been going there for a few years before he moved in with our foster family, so they figured there was no point in moving him."

"And he did this to you?"

"Would you believe me if I told you he came off worse?"

I could hear a teasing tone to his voice, but I felt like he was using it to cover how he really felt. I couldn't imagine having to live in a house that didn't even belong to one of my parents, and then getting in a fight with someone I lived with—a fight so bad it left me with injuries every kid at school would surely notice and be gossiping about.

"Did he?" I asked.

Cole pushed his hair back from his face and grinned. "Nah, not really, but only because I knew I'd end up in more shit than he would. He's younger and smaller than me, so handing him his ass wouldn't exactly go down well with the couple who've taken me in."

My eyes widened. "So you let him hit you instead?"

"I don't know if *let him* is exactly the right way of putting it, but he definitely got in a couple of swings before I managed to pin him down."

"And why did he want to hit you in the first place?"

"He took some stuff of mine, so I figured it was only fair I took some of his things in return." He shrugged. "He wasn't exactly happy about it."

I wrinkled my nose. "I guess not."

As we spoke, he gradually lost the slightly defeated atmosphere he'd had as he'd walked down the hall, the cocky attitude returning. Before I knew what was happening, he'd slung his arm around my shoulder and I discovered we were walking side by side down the corridor, him propelling me along.

Other students cast us curious glances as we walked, people stopping chatting at their lockers to raise eyebrows at us. I'd always been someone who was quite happy to be invisible at high school, but all of a sudden I felt a little spark of excitement, of confidence, at walking through school with Cole Devonport's arm around me. It didn't mean anything. If anyone else had stopped him, they'd be the one walking with him now, but for the moment I allowed myself to soak in the ounce of stupid pride I felt at Cole paying me attention.

I checked myself.

No, I wasn't like that. I didn't need the attention of a boy to make me feel better about myself.

I ducked and slipped out from under his arm. "Actually, Cole, I was kind of headed in the other direction. I have an English Lit class."

"No problem. Meet me for lunch."

"Sorry?"

"Lunch. You know, that meal between breakfast and dinner. I'll meet you on the benches outside the gym."

"But I'm supposed to—" I started. Only Cole had already turned and walked away. He looked over his shoulder and shouted, "Later!"

My face burned, but a smile tugged at my cheeks. I was supposed to be meeting Taylor and Jasmine for lunch. Was I really considering ditching my friends to eat lunch with a guy? I wasn't the type of girl to do that, and anyway, I didn't know how Taylor would react if she found out I ditched her to go and eat lunch with the guy she was crushing on. I'd seen how much she'd loved being around Cole, and she'd been pissed at him for not calling her already. I wasn't so surprised. Sure, he'd been flirting with her, but guys like him flirted with anyone with a vagina.

No, I decided. *I won't go.* It wasn't as though I'd even be standing him up, as I hadn't agreed to lunch in the first place. He'd just told me to turn up and expected me to do so.

The idea made me bristle—I didn't like being told what to do by presumptuous jerks. It would serve him right to be sitting by himself for a few minutes before he clocked onto the fact I wasn't going to show.

I tried to ignore the dip of disappointment in my stomach at my decision.

The last thing I needed was to get involved with someone like Cole.

Besides, he probably only wanted to use me to get more juicy bits of gossip about Taylor or something similar.

Guys like Cole were nothing but trouble.

I got home after school, fully expecting the house to be empty. My dad was working the late shift that week, which made me a latch-key kid. Not that I minded. I was seventeen, and perfectly capable of making my own dinner, and putting myself to bed. Besides, it was sometimes easier when he wasn't around. At least then I didn't need to worry about saying the wrong thing or upsetting him in some way. It wasn't that he was mean or violent—nothing like that—but he had a way of flying off the handle about things I hadn't even thought were a big deal. I knew what the problem was—I saw all the crushed cans and empty bottles in the trash—but there was no way I'd dare say anything to him. He was the parent and I was the kid. He was the one supposed to be telling me off for behaving badly, especially considering his job. But I knew things had been getting worse recently, and I just wasn't sure how to approach it. I guessed I'd been hoping things would get better by themselves somehow, that he'd magically grow out of it, but the problem had been going on for years now, and recently his drinking had escalated. I didn't know if it was because he'd been under more pressure at work, or if it was the idea of me leaving to go to college in the not so distant future, and him being left on his own, but gradually more cans and bottles had started to appear.

I turned the key in the lock and pushed open the front door.

Immediately, something felt different.

I paused and frowned, realizing I could hear something where normally the house would be in silence. It took me a moment to place the sound, but when I did I hurried into the living room to find my dad asleep on the couch, his hands folded across his chest, snoring.

I glanced at the floor. A couple of empty beer cans were sitting on the carpet. Dammit.

Crossing the room to the couch, I took hold of his shoulder and gave him a quick shake. "Dad?"

He didn't wake. The snoring stopped momentarily, but then started again.

"Dad!" I said, louder, giving him another shake that felt harder than I'd have liked.

This time, he startled awake. "Huh, what?" He blinked at me and then rubbed his face. "Jesus, Gabi. What are you shouting at me for?"

"Aren't you supposed to be at work?"

His eyes widened and he sat up straight. "Ah, hell. What time is it?"

"Four-thirty. Don't you start at three?"

"Damn. I fell asleep. I've got to go."

I glanced back down at the beer cans. "Go? You're still going to work?"

"Of course I am, Gabi," he said, exasperated as though it was somehow my fault he'd fallen asleep. "Where else am I going to go?"

"But …" I hesitated. "Haven't you been drinking?"

I looked pointedly at the empty cans, lifting my eyebrows and widening my eyes, hoping to get my point across without needing to say much more.

He shook his head. "I had a couple of beers with lunch hours ago. I don't need you telling me I've been drinking. It's not like I work regular hours like most people. If I don't get a bit of down time, this job will run me into the ground."

I held up both hands in defense. "Okay, okay. I was only asking."

I held my tongue as he got up and went upstairs to change into his uniform. I was worried about him driving, but I knew I wouldn't be able to say anything—he'd only make excuses and defend his choices. Perhaps what he was saying was right and he had only drunk a couple of beers hours ago? I doubted it, and I thought if I looked hard enough I'd find an empty bottle of vodka hidden somewhere in the house, but I didn't intend on searching. He was the responsible adult, and I was the kid. Nothing I said would make any difference.

Wanting to help, I brewed a pot of coffee while he was getting changed and then put it in a thermos mug for him to take with him.

He reappeared within ten minutes.

I handed him the coffee, and gave him a smile, wanting to build bridges. I didn't want him to go to work still angry with me. He smiled back and leaned in and kissed me on the cheek, a waft of mint overlaying the stale alcohol flowing over me.

"Thanks, sweetheart," he said.

"No problem, Dad. Stay safe, okay?"

He threw me a wink as he turned away. "Always."

GABI—PRESENT DAY

I woke filled with the desperate need to pee. I'd been having one of those dreams where I was searching for a toilet, and I knew I wasn't going to hold on much longer.

With an aching bladder, I swung my legs out of bed and hopped to my feet.

In a moment of complete disorientation, the floor rushed up and smashed me in the face.

I found myself in a crumpled heap, jarring my neck, my teeth cracking together. For a split second, confusion filled me, trying to work out what had happened to make me fall, and then it all came tumbling back over me. Of course, I had completely forgotten about the amputation.

I let out a scream of frustration and pounded my bunched fists on the floor. "Fuck, fuck, fuck!"

I hurt from the fall, and tears pooled in my eyes and then streamed down my cheeks. I didn't like giving way to self-pity, but right at that moment I didn't care. I didn't want to be someone who couldn't even get out of bed at night without falling on her face. My dad had slept through the whole thing, just as he always did, and I felt stupid, and helpless, and utterly alone.

This wasn't the first time I'd forgotten and done exactly the same thing. It had happened more in the early days and I'd thought I'd gotten over it. But when I dreamed I had two legs, and then I still felt that leg when I woke, there never seemed to be enough time between waking and remembering to stop me falling down when I got out of bed.

I couldn't stay on the floor, crying. I still needed to pee, badly. The last thing I needed was to have an accident on top of everything else. That would be the ultimate kick in the teeth.

Pushing myself to sitting, I angrily brushed the tears from my cheeks with the back of my hand and reached for my prosthesis. I wished I'd been allowed to take my new pin lock leg home, but for the moment I had to deal with the awkwardness of the rubber sleeve again. I attached the leg to my stump, and then used the side of the bed to pull myself to standing.

Through the drapes filtered the first light of morning, and for that I was relieved. At least I wouldn't have to try to get back to sleep again.

I hobbled to the bathroom to relieve myself, and then came back into the bedroom to grab my robe. My eyes settled on the small slip of paper on my nightstand.

A couple of days had passed since I'd last seen Cole.

I should have thrown his number away, but instead it sat on my nightstand, drawing my eye every time I walked into the room. When I finally managed to sleep, it was the last thing I stared at before my eyes slipped shut, and it was the first thing I saw when they opened again.

I didn't want to want to see Cole again. If anything, I wanted to hate him so deeply that nothing would ever break through my hate—not the intense blue eyes, or the full lips, or the stubbled jaw. But more than how he looked now, I found it was my memories I battled with more. The time we'd spent as a couple had been the happiest, most intense time of my life, before it had all crashed and burned. Cole had brought me to life all those years ago, when I'd believed there had been no more to living than reading and trying to manage my dad's behavior. I'd loved him, and I didn't think a love like the one I'd had for Cole Devonport when I was seventeen years old ever went away. It faded, sure, especially because of the way it had ended, but any kind of emotion that powerful created who we were as adults. It had shaped and molded me, and at the time I'd believed he and I were going to spend the rest of our lives together. He obviously hadn't felt the same way, but now here he was as an adult, asking to spend time with me again, and still I was drawn to him.

I needed to remember that the only reason he wanted me around was out of guilt. He felt guilty for what had happened back then, and he felt guilty because he was probably grossed out at the idea of my stump. He certainly didn't want to be around me out of any kind of romantic notion, and I wouldn't be able to handle it if he was.

Who the hell wanted to date a girl who only had one leg?

Later that morning, my dad took an unexpected trip out to the store, so I had the house to myself. It didn't happen often, and I was enjoying the peace and quiet. It wasn't to last, however, as my doorbell sounded. My heart did a stupid little skip and hop. Would Cole come to the house to see me? No, I chided myself. Why did he seem to always be at the front of my mind lately?

"Coming," I yelled toward the front door, knowing it took me longer than normal to haul myself out of the couch, and then get to the front door. Like an elderly person, I managed to stand, using the edges of the seat to half pull, half push myself up. I did my lurching walk, hoping whoever it was hadn't given up and left already.

I opened the door and my mouth dropped in surprise.

Two women and a boy of about seven stood on my doorstep. Both women plastered on wide smiles as they saw me.

"Gabi, hi!"

My gaze moved from one to the other in surprise. "Jasmine," I said. "Taylor. I wasn't expecting to see you."

Jasmine gave an apologetic smile. "I know. Sorry for dropping by unannounced. We should have called first, but we heard you were back in town and we just happened to be in the area." She held her hands out either side of her. "So here we are."

"Yeah, so here you are." I stepped back, freeing the doorway. "Please, come in."

"Oh, only if you have time," she chirped. "We wouldn't want to interrupt."

I silently observed that they already had interrupted me, but I didn't say anything. I also noticed how Taylor had remained silent so far. I guessed she wasn't sure how to figure out the situation yet either.

"Mom?" the boy said suddenly. "Is this the lady who only has one leg?"

Taylor's perfect lips parted and she clamped her hand over the boy's mouth. "Oliver!" Brushstrokes of pink painted her throat.

Mom? So Taylor was a mother now? She must have gotten pregnant young. I did the math and relaxed slightly. She hadn't been *that* young.

I forced a smile at the boy, Oliver. "Yes, I'm that lady who only has one leg."

"Cool!" he mumbled from behind Taylor's hand. "Can I see it?"

"Oliver!" she exclaimed again.

I laughed. "It's fine, honestly. Though I'd rather not start flashing on the doorstep. The neighbors might complain."

Taylor laughed a little, too, and I felt a fraction of the awkwardness dissipate between us.

"Come in, please," I said again.

I led them into our compact living room, and they both took seats on the couch, Oliver perching on the armrest.

"Can I offer you a drink? Coffee? Something cold, perhaps?"

"Oh, no, we're fine," said Jasmine, but I could tell what was behind her words. She probably didn't want the invalid shuffling around after them.

"So, how have you both been?" I asked, sitting in the comfy chair opposite them. "It's been a long time."

"Yes, it has."

I'd kept in touch with Jasmine sporadically over the years, but I hadn't had any contact with Taylor, and Jasmine had known not to mention her.

I turned to Taylor. "So, you've been busy." I glanced at her son.

"Umm, yeah, Ollie has definitely done that."

"I'm bored," the boy complained. "There's nothing to do here."

"Sorry," I said, wrinkling my nose. "I don't have any kids' toys or anything. I glanced out of my window. "You're welcome to play in the yard, though. My old treehouse is still out back. Hopefully it isn't completely rotten by now."

Taylor looked relived. "Yes, that would be great, thanks."

She shooed the boy out the back, and then, after making sure he wouldn't fall through the floor of my old treehouse, came and sat back down again. "That's better. We can actually talk now."

"So, really," Jasmine said. "How are you?"

I shrugged. "I've been better, I guess."

"So the rumors are true?"

I nodded and lifted the leg of my pants. Both women grew pale. Taylor put her hand to her mouth. I was shocked to see tears in Jasmine's eyes.

"Oh, my God, Gabi," my old best friend said.

"It's okay." I didn't know why I felt the need to reassure them, but I did. "I'm alive, and that's the main thing. The soldier I was stationed with when this happened didn't make it. He had a young family and everything."

Taylor shook her head. "That's awful."

"Yeah, it was, but I'm a lot better now." The truth was I'd used the thought of Tom's death to pull me through the hardest times. Even in the early days, when I'd felt like there was no point in fighting any more, I reminded myself of him, and how he would have given anything to have survived with only a lost limb. If our positions had been reversed, he would be here now, holding his baby daughter and kissing his wife. He'd have been able to see his little girl grow into a woman, and would have happily walked her down the aisle on her wedding day, thankful for his prosthetic leg.

The thought of him caused tears to threaten, so I glanced away, not wanting them to see my weakness, and knowing they would never truly understand.

"So what about you guys?" I threw back to them. "You have a kid now, Taylor. That's amazing."

"Yeah, he is. Ridiculously hard work, but wonderful. Boys are a different species, I swear."

"So, are you married?" I asked, sneakily trying to find out who Oliver's dad was without directly asking the question.

She laughed. "Oh no, thank God. I hooked up with Lawrence Knight when I came home on Spring Break in my last year of college, and managed to get pregnant."

"Lawrence Knight?" I remembered the slender, dark haired boy from school.

She must have heard my surprise in my tone.

"Yeah, he filled out some during his late teens—shot up and out like a football player. When I told him I was pregnant, he took off, and his parents moved not long after. I could probably have tracked him down if I'd tried, but I wasn't going to chase him. He knew how to get hold of me if he wanted, but he didn't even bother. Oliver doesn't miss what he didn't know, though I do wish he had a father figure around at times, especially now he's getting older. He could do with someone to rough and tumble with, you know?"

I nodded, as though I did. "So did you drop out of college?"

She shook her head. "Nah, I managed to graduate, though I did so with a bump. Then I moved back home with my folks, and I've stayed ever since."

"What about you, Jasmine?"

She smiled. "I'm still running Mom and Dad's business. They couldn't keep it up after Mom had her stroke, and I couldn't leave them like that anyway."

"Wow, so much responsibility, both of you." Who would have thought my beautiful, carefree friends would have ended up back in the same town, both living normal day-to-day lives. I'd been sure Taylor would have ended up in Los Angeles, living the life of a movie star or model, and Jasmine would have ended up in New York, doing something cool like fashion designing or editing a magazine.

I wasn't sure why I was surprised. It wasn't as though my own life went to plan. What was it I had wanted to do, anyway? I was sure I'd entertained dreams of studying English and writing, but they now felt as airy-fairy as the dreams I'd held of being a princess when I was five.

"So," said Jasmine, shifting in her seat and glancing toward the floor. "Have you seen Cole since you've been back?"

I stiffened. "Only in passing."

Her eyes widened, focusing on me now. "Did he talk to you? What did he say?"

"Nothing, really. Just being polite."

"I hear he's working at Frankie's now."

I gave a nonchalant shrug, trying to pretend I didn't care. "It's none of my business what he does with his life. He screwed it up enough when he was eighteen. I didn't intend on letting him drag me down then, and I certainly don't intend on allowing him the chance to do the same now."

I looked over to Taylor, who had taken a sudden interest in Oliver still playing outside. She got to her feet and wandered over to the window, watching him the whole time, though I knew it was only an excuse so she didn't have to look at me. I was tempted to ask if she'd seen Cole at all, if she'd been to visit him, even, when he'd been in jail, but honestly, I didn't want to know. All of that was in the past now. By the fact she had Oliver, she'd obviously moved on. It was only a stupid teenaged crush. We all made mistakes back then. I couldn't hold hers against her.

Could I?

"It's okay, Taylor," I said, addressing the elephant in the room. "We're both grownups now. There are far more important things than us fighting over Cole Devonport when we were kids."

She spun to face me and bit her lower lip. "Oh, are you sure, Gabi? I've been feeling horrible all these years, and then when I found out what had happened to you ..." Her gaze flicked down at my leg, and I knew the real reason for her concern. She probably hadn't given me a second thought since high school, but now I was back and with a leg missing, that busy old train called *The Guilt Trip* had taken her on a ride.

But I'd meant what I'd said. Life was too short to hold ten-year-old grudges. We'd been kids, and I was sure we all would have done things differently with a little more life experience in the bank.

So you're willing to forgive Taylor for how she acted back then, but you won't forgive Cole?

I shoved the annoying voice which had piped up in my head to the back of my mind.

"Of course," I said with a smile. "Let's start over fresh. I know I could still use some friends in this town."

Her face brightened and she brought her hands clasped against her chest as though she hugged herself with pleasure. "Thanks so much, Gabi. You always were the one who had her head screwed on."

The front door clicked open and everyone turned to the sound. A couple of seconds later, my dad's head poked around the door. His eyes widened as he saw us all there, and then he stepped into the room.

"Girls," he said, as though we were all still teenagers. "How good of you to come and visit Gabi."

Jasmine smiled. "It's our pleasure, Mr. Weston."

"Look at you, all grown up. I know you've been around town, but I never really knew what to say."

"No problem, Mr. Weston."

He waved a hand. "Oh, call me Bill now. You're all grown women. I can't have you talking to me as though we're not equals."

A yell and a cry came from the back yard.

"What on earth was that?" I exclaimed.

Taylor jumped to her feet. "Shit, Oliver!"

We all rushed to the back door. Oliver was on his feet, but clutching his arm.

I bit my lower lip. "Is he okay?"

Taylor had rushed over to her son, and had her arm around him. "Yeah, he's okay. Just slipped as he was climbing down." She gave a tight smile. "Guess that was our cue to leave."

"Sure he's going to be all right?"

"Yes, it's only a bruise. He's a boy. A day doesn't go by where he's not injuring himself in some way." Taylor ruffled her son's fine blond hair, so like her own.

I saw them all to the front door.

"Well, I hope we'll see you around," said Jasmine. "Maybe we could meet for coffee sometime?"

"Or wine?" said Taylor, and we all laughed.

"Sounds like a great idea," I said. And it did. Though I'd had comrades during my time in the Army, and we'd been close, it wasn't the same as having girlfriends. There was always a certain amount of watching what you said, being a woman in the Army, joining in with the banter, while still wanting everyone to take you seriously.

I liked the idea of having friends again.

GABI–ELEVEN YEARS EARLIER

"What the hell is going on with you and Cole?"

The accusation chased me up the school hall as I was hurrying to get to my next class on time.

I blinked in surprise and turned to find Taylor behind me, her hands on her hips, her lips pressed together in a hard line.

"Sorry?"

Her nostrils flared as she stared at me. "You know exactly what I'm talking about."

I glanced either side of me, as I noticed other students had started to get an inkling that something was about to go down. They were like piranha fish—just a hint of blood being spilled was enough to get them circling. "Seriously, Taylor. I have no idea."

"Then why have I got people telling me that you two are acting cozy as anything, walking around with your arms around each other?"

The penny dropped. Someone must have told Taylor about Cole putting his arm around me in the hall the other day.

"He put his arm around me while we were walking. He was just being friendly—I promise there's nothing going on."

"Really? So he doesn't call me, and then he's seen all over you? What am I supposed to think?"

I was starting to get exasperated now. "Taylor, I haven't done anything wrong. He even asked me to meet him for lunch, and I said no partly because I was already meeting you guys, but also because I didn't want to upset you."

I'd said the wrong thing. Her expression dropped. "He asked you to eat lunch with him?"

"Err, yeah, but just in a friendly way. There's nothing going on," I said again, sounding like a broken record.

"I thought you said he'd asked us to the band practice the other day because he liked me?"

I realized I'd given her the wrong idea then, too. "Well, no, not exactly. I said he'd invited me to band practice and told me to bring some friends if I wanted. I assumed he was just using me to get to you. I mean, all the guys at Willowbrook High try to hit on you."

Her eyebrows shot up her forehead. "No, they don't!"

"Yeah, they do. What's not to like?"

"I could say the same thing about you."

I rolled my eyes. "Oh, please."

"Anyway, I'm not talking about lots of guys. I'm talking about one guy who I thought liked me, and now apparently likes my BFF instead."

I threw up my hands. "He doesn't like me! He just invited me somewhere, and then I stopped him and asked him a question, so he put his arm over my shoulders while we walked. None of that is definitive proof of someone liking someone else."

She didn't look convinced, and I had to admit, a thread of doubt had even started to weave its way inside me. Why had he invited me to his band practice if it hadn't been to hit on either Taylor or Jas? Was it just that he'd spotted me sitting on the grass, with my skirt too short and riding up my thighs, and I'd looked like an easy target?

My face heated. Shit. Did he think I was easy? Had someone else said something?

The total opposite was true, but you never knew what sort of stories were going around the rumor mill. But yet, if that was the case, why did he barely acknowledge me at practice the other night? Did Cole think flirting with a girl's friend was one way of getting her attention?

"Hello?" Taylor said, continuing our argument. "I think you're kidding yourself. But if you don't even like the guy, maybe you can move out of the way for someone who actually does?"

What was she asking me? That I shouldn't have any contact with Cole so she could step in? There wasn't even anything to step into, yet for some reason the thought of giving Taylor the green light made me uneasy. Taylor always got what she wanted, and the idea of her getting Cole suddenly twisted me up inside.

She must have noticed my hesitation or recognized the expression of doubt I felt sure was on my face.

"You *do* like him, don't you? Jeez, Gabi. So you're going after my leftovers now? How about coming over to my house and going through the trash as well?"

I felt like she'd slapped me. "What?"

"You heard me. These aren't exactly the behaviors of a best friend, Gabi!"

And with that, she spun on her heels and stormed off down the hall.

People were sniggering behind their hands, exchanging glances and whispering to each other. I'd just about had enough of being the hall gossip for the time being. I'd spent most of my high school life being invisible, and I didn't want that to change any time soon.

It seemed as though if Cole Devonport was in my life that was exactly what would happen.

GABI—ELEVEN YEARS EARLIER

To delay going home, I'd spent most of the evening studying in the library.

When eventually I forced myself back to the house, I discovered the front door wide open. I paused, my heartrate instantly picking up, climbing into my throat. It wasn't like my dad to leave the door open. Did we have an intruder? I knew he was off tonight, and I thought he'd be catching up on some sleep after working nights for the last few shifts.

Then I realized his vehicle was missing from the driveway. He must have gone out, but then why would he have left the front door wide open? Security was normally one of his things.

"Hello?" I called out, not sure if I wanted a response or not. If a burglar was currently trashing our house, it wasn't as though he was going to answer me.

I entered into the entrance hall. "Hello?" I called again. "Dad?"

The place felt empty, no sense of life coming from within its walls. I hurried into the living room, every inch of my being alert for any sound.

Ears straining, nostrils flared, muscles tensed for fight or flight. Even my skin felt as though it were hyper-sensitized, as though I might be able to feel the movement of someone in the air before I heard it. This was a safe neighborhood, and rarely did we hear of a break-in, but there was always a first time.

I entered the living room and my heart sank. Beside the couch lay an empty bottle of vodka and several empty cans of beer, crumpled up and tossed.

"Ah, shit."

Dad had gone on another binge.

That, in itself, wasn't unusual. It was like him to have a couple of days off work and then have a heavy drinking session. It was as though he was able to restrain himself while he was working, and keep a handle on things, but then as soon as he didn't have the responsibility of going to work, all his restraints went out the window.

What was unusual, however, was the fact the front door was open and the car was gone.

I prayed someone else was driving, and the door had swung open in the wind. Even letting someone else drive would get him in trouble, but not half as much trouble as if he was driving drunk out of his head. I dreaded the thought of him being on the road, with the innocent people he might be putting in danger. If he ran someone down, he'd never forgive himself, and I'd never forgive *myself* for not doing something about his drinking sooner.

Clinging to some final threads of hope, I raced around the house, praying I'd find him slumped in a drunken stupor somewhere. I took the stairs two at a time, but when I checked all the rooms, including my bedroom and the bathroom, it became clear he was nowhere in the house.

I wanted to cry, but I couldn't. There would be time for self-pity, and anger, and frustration later. Right now, I just needed to find him. I wished

I could call Taylor, but she was still mad with me because of the whole Cole Devonport thing, and anyway, I couldn't call her, because that would mean having to tell her the truth about Dad's drinking, and I couldn't risk doing that. Word got around too quickly, and if someone got wind he was drinking too much, it would be the end of everything for him. I couldn't say a word to anyone.

One thing I knew for sure, the house was empty. Wherever my dad was, he wasn't here.

I grabbed my purse and keys, and ran back out of the house. I hesitated at the door, wondering if I should lock it behind me or not. If Dad returned and didn't have any keys on him, he wouldn't be able to get back in. Then I reasoned that he must have his house keys on the keychain for the car. Hell, he could just sit in the car for all I cared. At least it would mean he'd gotten home safely.

I knew I wouldn't be able to cover much ground on foot, so I set off at a jog. There were a few places I knew my dad liked to go—the cliff-face overlooking the cove, or down at the park. I prayed he hadn't gone to a bar. Even smashed drunk, I hoped he had enough sense to stay out of the center of town.

I checked all the usual places, the dread inside me thickening to a sludge which seemed to trickle through my veins. I was exhausted now, my jog slowed to a walk, and I was barely dragging my feet off the ground. I was so angry with my dad for doing this to me—he was so selfish when it came to booze—and I was frustrated by my own lack of action. I'd tell him, I decided. I'd tell him he needed to get help, and we couldn't go on living like this. I wished I could give him some kind of ultimatum to push him in the right direction, but then I remembered how people only got help when they wanted it themselves. I had a feeling my dad was lying to himself as much as he was to me about how much he drank.

Above my head, the sky rumbled ominously.

I glanced up to realize I hadn't even noticed the thick grey storm clouds which had rolled in while I'd been so desperately trying to find my only parent. I'd been stupid, really, thinking I could find a man in a car, when I was just a girl on foot. I had no idea where he was, but at least I hadn't noticed police car sirens or seen a multi-car pileup anywhere.

A fat, warm droplet smacked me on the forehead, then another, and another. In my rush, I hadn't even thought to bring a jacket. The sky opened up in a deluge, soaking me to the skin within seconds. My t-shirt clung to my skin and my skirt slapped around my thighs as I walked.

"You have got to be kidding me!" I cried up at the sky, my face upturned.

Did everyone just want to dump on me? When was I going to catch a god-damned break?

A couple of vehicles passed me. The light was fading now, headlights shining in the gloom. I suddenly became aware I was a young woman, out walking alone when it was almost dark. I was also soaked and my clothes stuck embarrassingly to my skin. I used my thumb and forefinger to pinch my t-shirt away from my chest. I literally looked like a contestant in a walking wet-t-shirt competition.

A truck pulled up alongside me and I squeezed my eyes shut briefly, my body tensed, willing the person to go away. The last thing I needed right now was to be cat-called and hassled by a car full of jocks who thought they were being funny.

"Gabi?"

A male voice shouted at me from out of the driver's open window.

My name, someone who knew me.

I glanced cautiously to one side, a combination of rain and tears dripping from my eyelashes, so I had to blink to clear my vision. I didn't recognize the truck, and I picked up my pace, close to breaking into a run. Could my day get any worse?

"Gabi, hey, it's Cole. Hang on a minute!"

I drew to a halt. Cole?

Turning to the truck, I pushed my sodden hair out of my face and squinted at the vehicle. He leaned across the passenger seat and pushed open the door. "Get in, will you? It's pouring."

I glanced up at the sky as though I hadn't noticed, blinking as fresh raindrops hit my eyes. "I'll get the seat all wet," I said, stupidly.

"It'll dry. Just get in."

I didn't have much option, did I? So far this evening, all of my choices were wrong anyway, so I might as well make another stupid one. Cole Devonport wasn't about to abduct me and have his wicked way with me—not looking like this, anyway. Drowned rodents came to mind.

I climbed into the truck and slammed the door shut behind me. I dripped onto the floor, water running into my face. He reached behind the passenger seat and pulled out a hooded sweatshirt.

"Here," he said, handing it to me.

I looked at him dumbly and he gave it another gentle push into my hands. "You can dry yourself with it."

"Oh, right, thanks."

I took his sweatshirt and used it to dry the rain from my face and hair. The material smelled of him, Lynx deodorant, and musky boy smell. It was a good smell—comforting—and I found myself pressing the sweater against my face for longer than was probably suitable. I didn't want him to notice I'd been crying. When people thought something was wrong they asked questions, and right now I didn't have any answers.

When I removed his sweatshirt from my eyes, I found him staring at me.

"What?" I said.

"Are you going to tell me why you're wandering around in the rain at almost ten at night?"

Crap. Was it really that late? I'd completely lost track of time.

I shrugged. "I was taking a walk and got caught in the rain."

"Seriously? Who even takes walks these days?"

I bristled. "I do!"

"Okay, okay," he replied. "Whatever you say."

"I do like to walk," I muttered.

Cole's lips twisted as he regarded me. "Yeah, well, you don't have to tell me what's going on. That's your business, and believe me, I know how it feels when everyone wants to know your business. But if you ever need someone to talk to, you know where I am."

I appreciated him not pressuring me. "Thanks, Cole."

"So you want me to drive you home?"

"Yeah, I guess so."

A smile quirked his lips. "You don't want to walk?"

I smacked him on the arm. "Don't tease."

He laughed. "Sorry, I couldn't help myself. Are you going to tell me where home is?"

I gave him my address and then settled back in the seat as he pulled the vehicle away from the curb and headed toward my house. "Who does the truck belong to?" I asked, realizing I hadn't seen him driving it before.

"My foster parents. The guys I play in the band with needed some gear moved and I offered to help."

"They don't have cars of their own?" I inquired, thinking as they were older they'd be more likely to have their own transport.

"Yeah, Ryan does, but he said it was in the shop." He gave a shrug. "I don't mind helping out."

"How long have you been playing in the band?"

"About six months now."

"And you enjoy it?"

He laughed. "Of course. I wouldn't do it, otherwise. The band is the one thing I have where I don't have to worry about all the other shit in my life. The guys can come off a bit cocky at times, but they're all right, really."

I didn't intend on telling him about my instant dislike of the other band members. Maybe it was just because they were older, but they'd given me the distinct impression they looked down on us, Cole included.

He glanced over at me as he drove. "Aren't your parents going to be worried about where you are?"

I shrugged. "It's only my dad, and he doesn't pay much attention to me. My mom took off when I was two, so I don't even know where she is, and I doubt she's given me a second thought."

He gave a slow nod. "I know all about parents being screw-ups, seriously. My folks didn't even want me around. Apparently I was off the rails because I snuck out a couple of times, and got drunk." He shrugged. "They were just looking for an excuse to be free of me."

"I'm sorry. My dad stuck around, at least, though there are days when I wonder if life would be easier if he hadn't." Immediately guilt swamped over me in a wave. Of all people, I shouldn't have said that in front of Cole. He'd probably love to have a parent around, even if they were an alcoholic who embarrassed themselves in front of the whole town.

But to my surprise, he reached out with the hand not holding the wheel, and his fingers covered mine. His eyes appeared closer to grey than blue as he regarded me with a depth I'd not felt about him before. "Sometimes we just have to make the best of what we've got. None of it is ever easy."

Surprise tears sprang to my eyes and I blinked them away, pulling my hand from his.

As we approached my house, my heart lifted with relief to see my dad's car parked back in the drive.

Cole also spotted the vehicle. "Your dad's home."

"Yeah."

I didn't know what else to say.

"Are you okay going in there alone?" he asked me.

I forced a smile. "Of course I am."

His blue eyes focused on mine, studying my face. I felt like he could read all my secrets as though they were tattooed upon my skin.

"You can tell me if you're not, Gabi," he said. "I've been in the position plenty of times where I haven't wanted to go home."

I appreciated his honesty. I could hear the pain in his words, saw the flash of discomfort across his face as he confessed this to me. I felt awful that I couldn't be honest with him in return, but it wasn't just my life I'd be messing with if I told him the truth.

A sudden impulse overtook me, and I leaned over and planted a kiss on Cole's cheek.

His eyes widened, his lips tweaking in a grin. I had caught him by surprise.

"Thanks for the ride, Cole." I opened the passenger door and slipped from the seat.

"Hey, Gabi," he called to me, before I'd had the chance to slam the door shut.

I turned back to him, and he threw his sweatshirt at me. I snagged it from the air.

"So you don't get cold." He smiled at me.

I couldn't help but smile back. He leaned across the passenger seat and pulled the door shut behind me.

I pulled the item on over the top of my still damp t-shirt and wrapped my arms around my torso as I headed toward my house. The truck idled in the road until I'd walked through the front door, and then it pulled away. I was touched he'd waited until I was safely inside before he'd left.

I didn't want to lose the warm glow that being with Cole had created inside me, but I had to deal with my dad. Exhaling a sigh, I walked into the living room to find him asleep in his spot on the couch.

The relief I'd experienced upon seeing his car in the drive vanished, replaced by raging anger. I stalked over to him and whacked him on the foot, the smack jolting him awake.

"What the hell, Dad!"

He gave a grunt and rubbed his hand over his face. "Huh? What?"

I balled my fists and glared at him. "I've been out half the night looking for you!"

He sat up and shook his head slightly. "What on earth would you do that for? I'm a grown man, Gabi. I can take care of myself."

He appeared genuinely baffled by my actions, and once again, I started to doubt myself. Then I noticed the empty bottle and cans I'd come home to that afternoon had been disposed of, and I wondered if I'd find them in the trash or if he'd been more careful with where he'd disposed of them.

That was the trouble with addiction. It was sneaky and manipulative, and if you weren't careful it became every single part of you.

"If you're the adult," I snapped back, "how about you start acting like one, and at least let me know where you're going to be. If I come home and find you not here, I'm going to worry. I'd like to think you'd do the same for me, but I'm starting to wonder if you care about me at all."

His expression softened. "I love you, Gabi. Of course I would care about where you are."

"Really? Because you didn't seem to care too much tonight. Or did you not notice I wasn't even in the house?"

He sighed. "You're almost eighteen. I figured you were with your friends."

"Well, I wasn't. I was out looking for you. But like you say, you're the adult and I'm the kid, so I guess I didn't think before I acted. Next time, I'll stop myself even caring."

I knew I was being huffy, but I was feeling alone and unloved. I turned and stormed from the room, stamping up the stairs to my bedroom. I peeled off my wet clothes, but took Cole's hoodie and bundled it into a ball to use as a pillow. I climbed beneath my sheets and allowed the scent of him to lull me to sleep.

GABI—PRESENT DAY

My days were filled with various appointments—doctors, physical therapy, my psychiatrist—and between those I read, and cooked, and generally allowed life to pass me by.

I got back from another torturous physical therapy appointment to find my back door wide open. My dad hadn't told me he was going anywhere that day, so I figured he was out back on the deck. I'd planned on making some iced tea, so I headed out to ask him if he wanted a glass. It would be nice to sit out in the sun with him for an hour and catch up on things.

When I stepped outside, it took me a moment to spot him. He wasn't sitting on the deck, or pottering around in the flowerbeds. Instead, he was on all fours right at the back of the yard, his head pressed up against the bars of the gate which closed our yard off from the alley behind.

I frowned, my stomach twisting in anxiety.

"Dad?"

Something was wrong. All thoughts of iced tea vanished as I hurried toward him.

"What the hell, Dad!" I exclaimed, trying not to notice the way his pants had slid halfway down his backside, exposing a far too large expanse of plumber's crack. He grunted and struggled, and it suddenly dawned on me that he wasn't able to move. Panic surged up inside me, and I stepped closer to get a better look. My mouth dropped open. I had no idea how he'd managed it, but his neck was trapped between two of the metal bars of the back gate. Rolls of fat squeezed both sides of the bars, and his already pink face was gradually turning crimson.

"Jesus Christ." I crouched beside him and tried to take hold of his neck through the bars on either side—the ones not holding his neck prisoner.

"Gabi," he slurred. "Leab me alooo..." *Leave me alone...*

Ugh, he was drunk. Way too drunk.

"I can't leave you alone," I said, exasperated. "You'll end up choking yourself or breaking your god-damned neck."

"Wanna go sleep."

I was starting to lose my patience, plus I was scared and worried, which are never a great combination. "For fuck's sake. You're in the back yard and it's four o'clock in the afternoon. What do you think the neighbors are going to say?"

I didn't think any of the neighbors would actually be able to see what was going on from this position, but if I ended up having to call nine-one-one to get him out, I could guarantee every single one of them would find out about it quickly enough. In fact, they'd all be standing around with drinks of their own, watching the whole scene go down and having a good gossip about how far Bill Weston had fallen while they did.

No, I couldn't call the emergency services. It would kill him to have everyone standing around him in this position.

I wracked my brains for what to do. I needed something slippery—

soap, washing up detergent, olive oil?

"Wait here, Dad," I said, and then realized what a stupid thing that was to say. It wasn't as though he was going anywhere.

I hurried back into the house, as much as my leg would allow me to, and went straight for the kitchen. Figuring I'd save myself a couple of trips if the first option didn't work, I grabbed the hand soap, detergent, and olive oil from the cupboards. With them all clutched against my chest, I went back to where my dad was still embarrassingly stuck. What had happened to the big, strong man I'd grown up with? How had he ended up like this? I blinked back tears, knowing I didn't have time to pity either of us. From an outsider's point of view, this probably looked hysterical—the one legged woman attempting to free her drunk father from a gate. The reality was far more sobering.

Dad had started to sober up a little, but it didn't help. He was starting to panic, yanking his neck backward and forward. "Gabi! Where are you?"

"Dad, stop it, keep still. You're going to make the area swell, and it'll be even harder to free you."

I used the soap first, wrinkling my nose as I tried to smear it between the bars and his skin. "Christ, I can't believe I'm even doing this," I muttered.

When he didn't budge, I tried the oil and then the detergent. I was making one hell of a mess, but I was getting desperate.

I attempted to move him again, taking his head in both hands now, and angling it in different directions, but my leg was starting to hurt, and I wasn't able to put enough strength behind what I was doing, or get the angle right.

"Ah, Gabi, you're hurting me."

"Well, what the hell were you thinking?" I snapped.

"I dropped my keys and I was trying to reach them."

"What with? Your mouth?"

This was insane. I couldn't do this on my own. I simply wasn't strong enough, or able bodied enough. I couldn't call the emergency services; it would kill him. But I didn't trust anyone else.

My mind went to the little slip of paper on my bedside table and my stomach flipped. Cole would help me, and he knew how to keep his mouth shut. Did I dare call him? The thought of doing so deeply embarrassed me—I hated he would learn my secret about my father this way, even though most of the town already knew why he'd been dismissed from his job. But I didn't have any choice. I didn't know anyone else in town strong enough physically to be able to help. And I hated to admit it, but part of me desperately wanted to be in his company again.

I touched my father on the shoulder. "I need to get help. It'll be okay."

"No, Gabi." He started sobbing. "I'm sorry, I'm so sorry."

"I won't be long. Just try to keep still."

I didn't have any option but to leave him. I raced into the house, as much as my leg would allow me to race, and went upstairs to my bedroom. Cole's number was right where I left it, and my heart thudded hard as I picked up my cell and dialed his number. My mouth had run dry from the adrenaline of finding my dad in such a way, and now calling Cole had only made things worse. I listened to the rings, my lips sticking to my teeth, my tongue to the roof of my mouth. Last night's glass of water still sat, untouched, on my bedside table, so I picked it up and took a gulp.

He wasn't going to answer, and what would I do then?

But then he picked up. "Hello?"

He sounded out of breath.

"Cole, it's Gabi."

"Gabi?" His tone brightened. "Hey, Gabi. It's so good to hear from you. Sorry I almost missed your call, I was out running."

"You were running?" I almost forgot my poor father as the surge of a combination of hope and jealousy rose up inside me. I missed the sport with a physical pang, almost like the loss of a loved one, though I hoped I'd get back to it one day.

"So, what's up?" he asked me.

"Actually, I'm sorry to dump this on you, but I need your help. Can you come over to my dad's house?"

"Sure. What's going on?"

"Honestly, it's kind of hard to explain. Can you come over quickly?"

"I'm on my way."

"Thank you, Cole."

I went back out to the yard, and waited for Cole beside my dad, listening out for the sound of the door, or a car pulling up. My dad slipped in and out of consciousness, or perhaps it was sleep. I wasn't sure I knew the difference. I sat with my hand on his back, worrying I'd done the right thing by calling Cole. What if my dad was badly injured and I should have called an ambulance?

A figure walked out of my back door, still sweaty from his run, his t-shirt molded to his torso, his blond hair a shade darker.

Cole.

"Hey, I knocked but no one answered, so I let myself in. Hope that's okay?"

I forgot he knew his way around this house almost as well as I did. He caught sight of the person half lying, half crouched on the ground beside me, and a couple of lines appeared between his brows. "What ... ?"

I had no choice but to explain. "My dad's drunk and somehow he's managed to get his neck stuck between the bars. I don't have the strength to get him out myself. I need your help."

He didn't ask any more questions—and I was reminded of how that was something I'd always loved about him, that he'd never pressed me into revealing anything to him I hadn't wanted to—and came toward me at a jog. When he reached me and my dad, he crouched as well, frowning slightly as he studied the scene.

My dad made a noise and tried to pull out of the bars again.

"Hey, Mr. Weston. It's Cole Devonport." He spoke slowly and calmly. "I'm going to get you out of there, okay?"

Utter thankfulness that he was here to help swelled inside me. I had no idea what I would be doing if he wasn't. The sudden urge to fling my arms around him and give him a hug took hold of me, so I bunched my fists and pressed my arms to my sides to stop myself.

This is Cole, I reminded myself. *He hurt you so badly you changed your entire life course. This is not a man you want to hug.*

Cole's gaze landed on the bottles of various liquids which I'd brought from the kitchen. "Which of these have you tried?"

"All of them," I admitted. "But I couldn't get a hold of him enough to try to work him out again. My movement's kind of restricted with my leg."

"Sure."

Cole reached through the bars, one hand either side of my dad. Gradually, he manipulated my dad's drunk, dead-weight head to the correct angle. "This is probably going to hurt your ears a little, Mr. Weston," he warned.

My dad gave a gurgled grunt as answer, but at least he was conscious. "When I push, I'm going to need you to pull back. Can you do that, sir?"

"I can do it," came his slurred, anger-filled answer.

Cole didn't appear perturbed. "Okay, ready. One, two, three ... "

I wished I could help more, but instead stood by, every muscle in my body tensed, wincing as Cole worked my dad's head back through the bars, and my dad pulled back on him like a cow trying to get out of its milking equipment. For a moment, I didn't think it was going to work, but then he popped free and fell backward onto his ass in the dirt.

"Oh, thank God," I breathed, so relieved this horrible, embarrassing incident was over. "Dad, can you walk?"

"It's okay," said Cole. "I've got him."

I smiled. "Thanks, Cole."

Deciding I didn't want to leave the collection of soap and oil bottles around my back yard—yet another thing for the neighbors to gossip about—I stepped toward them. The heel of my prosthetic limb hit an oil patch, and before I could even yelp my shock, the ground vanished from under me. I felt the twist on my leg as the sleeve attached to my stump wrenched in the opposite direction to my actual limb. My knees hit the floor with a bone jarring smack, my teeth clacking together, and I cried out, partly in pain and partly in shock. Cole reached for me, but he had his hands full with my dad. I squeezed my eyes shut, remaining on my hands and knees, biting the inside of my lip to stop myself crying out. The intense brightness of the pain softened to a throb, and I was able to open my eyes and reconnect with the outside world.

Cole stared at me. "Shit, Gabi. Are you all right?"

I nodded briskly. Not only was the fall painful, it was also embarrassing. *Like father like daughter.* "Yes, just get my dad inside."

His gaze flicked between me and the house, clearly debating in his head if he should dump my dad and help me instead.

"Please, Cole," I insisted.

He exhaled a sigh through his nose and hoisted my dad higher on his shoulder. My dad muttered something unintelligible.

"I'll be right back," Cole said.

I forced a smile. "I'm fine."

Even so, I waited for him to return before I attempted to stand again. I couldn't risk going over in all the slippery liquids on the ground again.

Cole ran back to me. "I put your dad on the couch. He's snoring."

I rolled my eyes. "Typical."

He crouched beside me and put my arm around my waist. "Can you walk at all?"

"I think so."

He hesitated, and then said, "Screw it." His other arm reached beneath my legs, and before I had a chance to argue with him, he lifted me up, cradled against his chest. "Cole, I can walk!" I protested, though honestly in that moment, I wasn't completely sure I could. I wasn't averse to dragging myself across the ground, though. It wouldn't have been the first time.

"Stop talking, Gabi," he told me.

I opened my mouth to protest some more, and then shut it again. Being carried by Cole, feeling his big, strong biceps bunched up beneath my body, was certainly preferable. His body felt completely different than how I remembered. Though he'd always been strong, back then he'd been lean and wiry. Now he was physically bigger, his shoulders and chest thick with muscle. From my position, I could see more tattoos crawling up from beneath the neckline of his shirt and up the back of his neck. The thought of seeing what Cole looked like now with no shirt on suddenly flashed into my head.

It was just curiosity, I told myself. It didn't mean anything. I just wanted to compare what he looked like now to the body I had known off by heart as a teenager. I told myself this, but it didn't stop my heart from fluttering and set my insides squirming.

He carried me into the house and set me down on the seat of one of the chairs at the kitchen table.

"Thanks," I said, and tried not to miss the feel of his body against mine. "Do you think my dad is all right?"

Cole gestured with his head. "Yeah, he's still asleep in the other room."

I wrinkled my nose. "How does his neck look?"

"Pretty sore and bruised, but he'll survive. What the hell was he doing?"

I sighed and shook my head. "He said he was looking for his keys, but who the hell knows. He might as well have been searching for fairies, he was so out of it."

Cole frowned. "Does he get like that often?"

I hated talking to Cole about this. Even when we'd been teenagers I'd done my best to hide my dad's drinking, almost even more than he had. Since my dad had been fired, I figured there wasn't much point in making a secret of it anymore.

"Too often for my liking," I admitted.

"Jesus. I'm sorry, Gabi. Like you don't have enough to deal with."

I sighed and ran my hand over my face. "Yeah, my life's just a fucking bed of roses right now."

"I know the feeling."

No, I wanted to say. *You asked for what happened to you, or at least a large portion of it. I never asked for any of this. You can carry on and live a normal life, but I'm stuck with my disability forever.*

He must have noticed my silence. "What's wrong?"

I didn't want to throw a whole heap of accusations at him now, especially not after he'd just helped me. Plus I carried my own guilt about what had happened back then, and I didn't want to bring it all up again. I was still bitter from the past, there was no doubt about it, but what I hadn't realized was that I was also bitter about the future.

"I have an appointment to get my new leg in a couple of days," I said instead, "but my doctor is never going to fit it with an injury."

"It might be better by then," he suggested.

I shook my head. "Even if it's the slightest scrape, he won't allow me to even wear my old prosthetic, never mind fit me for a new one. The risk of infection is too high, and if there's swelling, it won't even fit."

"When is it?"

"Eleven on Friday morning."

Cole frowned. "I'm supposed to be working the lunch shift, but I'll get it changed."

"Why would you do that?"

"So I can take you, of course."

I shook my head. "I don't need you coming with me, Cole."

"It doesn't have to be a need. Sometimes you're just allowed to just want something."

I let his words sink in. I hadn't allowed myself to want anything in a very long time.

Cole walked over to our refrigerator and pulled open the freezer section, and started hunting through it.

"What are you doing?"

"Looking for ice to help with any swelling, and then I'm taking you upstairs and making sure you're comfortable before I leave you again."

Leave you again. I tried not to read too much into his words.

"You don't need to, Cole. You did everything I asked."

"I'm not leaving you here like this." He paused and pulled out a cool pack I'd kept in there for exactly this kind of swelling. "Ah-ha. Here we go. Right, now I'm going to carry you upstairs. I assume you're still in the same bedroom?"

I nodded, my cheeks heating from the memories of all the times we spent in that bedroom. There was nothing quite like that passion of a first love, of exploring each other's bodies, and for me, my sexuality for the first time. We hadn't been able to get enough of each other back then. I wondered if he was thinking the same thing, or had the fact I was now an invalid put any kind of thought like that from his mind.

As though we were a newly married couple, Cole scooped me back up, and then balancing me on one knee, he reached out, picked up the cool pack, and dropped it onto my stomach.

I squealed and snatched it back off again. "Hey, that was cruel!"

He laughed, his eyes creasing at the corners in a way they hadn't when he was eighteen. "Sorry, couldn't resist."

I caught him staring at me, and my heart flipped. "I thought you were taking me upstairs." Why did everything I say make me think of him in that way?

He grinned. "Of course."

With me clutching the cool pack in one hand, the other hand around his tattooed neck, he carried me up the stairs to the bedroom. I tried not to focus too much on the soft hairs at his nape and the warmth of his skin beneath my fingers. He pushed open the door and placed me carefully on the bed.

"Wow, this place doesn't look any different."

I kept feeling as though we were slipping through cracks in time, brief flashes of how things had been all those years ago. Then I'd be back in the present with a sickening jolt, remembering how things were now, and how they would never go back to the way they'd been. Ever.

He stood back, his hands on his hips. "Right. Tell me exactly what you need."

"I'm fine, Cole, thank you. I might have lost my leg, but I can still take care of myself."

The truth was, I needed to remove my leg and see what the damage was, but I had no intention of doing so in front of Cole. The process was ungainly and embarrassing, and I wasn't about to show him what my stump looked like, especially not if it was swollen and possibly scraped up, which I suspected it was.

"Can you just check on my dad again on the way out?"

"Sure."

"Thanks, Cole."

He gave a regretful smile. "Any time." He looked like he was hesitating, considering something, but then he turned and left.

Unexpected tears filled my eyes, my heart clenching. *No, no, no.* I couldn't still have feelings for Cole Devonport. There would only ever be heartbreak in store for me if I allowed myself to go down that route. The feelings would never be reciprocated, and even if I allowed myself to believe for a moment that they were, there was nothing to stop him screwing everything up all over again.

I lay in bed that night, trying not to worry about my appointment. Wrenching my stump today might set me back weeks, and I could even end up back in a wheelchair, temporarily, at least.

Would Cole really come to drive me? It would mean he'd see my stump, and the thought filled me with anxiety. No, if he did turn up to take me, he would just wait outside. There was no reason for him to come into the office with me.

My phantom limb sensation was driving me crazy. I knew it was partly because of my anxious state that it was worse tonight, my brain sparking off too many nerve endings and trying to communicate with a limb that no longer existed, but that didn't mean I could stop it. As I lay in bed, I had the horrible feeling I still had my leg, but instead of laying flat in a normal position, it felt as though it was bent at the knee, and my leg and foot were hanging through a hole in the mattress. I'd experienced the sensation plenty of times before, but it didn't make it any less unnerving or distressing. I tried to shift onto my side, but now it felt as though the leg would have been bent at an unnatural angle. Even though I knew the limb wasn't even there, never mind bent weirdly, I couldn't get the thought out of my head and my heartrate increased, panic clutching my chest. If I continued to lie there, I'd end up with a full-blown panic attack—something that I'd started to get a handle on in recent months. I needed to distract myself, and that meant giving up on sleep.

I should probably go downstairs to check on my dad. His neck was most likely swollen and bruised from getting it stuck in the gate—my mind still boggled at how he'd managed to get himself in that situation—and I hoped it wouldn't swell enough to affect his breathing in any way.

Sudden bitterness rose inside me. I shouldn't be worrying about him right now. He should be here, taking care of me. I hated how selfish his addiction to drink had made him. He didn't even know I had taken a fall, never mind actually care if I was hurt. If it wasn't for him and his stupidity, I would never have slipped in the first place.

Anger filled me. Next time, I'd leave him out there. I'd let the neighbors see, and I'd call the emergency services.

I was done protecting him.

COLE—ELEVEN YEARS EARLIER

I approached the garage where The First and Last practiced, muffled rock music already thumping from behind the closed door. I frowned and broke into a jog.

They'd started without me.

I guessed Ryan was trying to make a point that I hadn't been around much lately. I was only ten minutes late, but I hadn't seen the guys as much as normal. Since the night I'd found Gabi wandering the streets in the rain, I'd done my best to spend time with her, 'accidentally' bumping into her in the mall, and sitting with her at lunch. She treated me with the kind of tolerance someone might have at finding a stray but cute dog suddenly following them around everywhere, but I was desperate for her to see me as something more.

I was still annoyed with myself for making a mess of things on that first night when I'd invited her to band practice. I didn't know what I'd been thinking, strutting around like a god-damned peacock, trying to get Gabi's attention by flirting with her friend. I'd totally misjudged her, thinking she'd be like other girls—just happy to be in my company. What an idiot I'd been. I felt especially bad as I was now the cause of her falling out with her friend, though I couldn't help thinking Taylor wasn't much of a friend if that was all it took to ruin their friendship. Maybe I didn't understand the fairer sex at all.

Gabriella was constantly on my mind lately, her wide smile and big eyes always willing to jump into my head. I hoped I was wearing her down. Breaking down those defenses she'd built so high around her. I could still feel the imprint of her lips against my skin, how I'd caught a waft of her perfume—something sweet and citrus—as she'd leaned over and kissed me after I'd driven her home. I knew she was hiding something, but I didn't know what. The thought her dad might be hurting her bothered me, though I'd never seen any unusual bruises on her, and she didn't dress to hide her skin. It wouldn't be unusual for a guy like him to be easy with his fists—a power thing—not that I was one to talk, though I'd never laid my hands on a woman. I wondered if that might have been the reason Gabi's mom had taken off when she was small. Though I knew it wasn't a good thing to have in common, I liked that Gabi understood how it felt to not be wanted. Selfish, I knew, but I'd always been a selfish son-of-a-bitch.

How could I be anything else when I'd never had anyone to care about other than myself?

But now, for some reason I couldn't explain, I cared about Gabi. Our relationship was currently as innocent as a newborn baby, but she'd somehow woven herself into my heart. I took hope in the fact she'd kissed me on the cheek the other night. I needed to get her alone, take her on a real date, but nothing I came up with felt good enough for her. I didn't have much money, and the thought of taking her to the movies or just to the diner for something to eat didn't feel adequate. For some reason, getting Gabriella Weston to notice me felt like the most important thing in the world.

We were just kids and I was dreaming to think we might have something together—we barely knew each other—but I couldn't help fantasizing about the future. I imagined I would have a place of my own, and we would spend some real time together, cooking meals and cuddling up on the couch to watch boxed sets of DVDs. I'd never had my own space before, where I could do whatever I wanted, and to have Gabi at my side made the fantasy perfect. In fact, I realized, if she wasn't by my side, I feared the loneliness that had been at the center of my soul since I'd been a small child would only deepen.

Each day that passed brought me another day closer to my birthday.

I knew my foster parents wanted me out. I'd been fighting with Danny again, and they'd now separated us, so I was sleeping on the couch. I could tell they were counting down the days until they'd be rid of me, and I didn't blame them. Life would be easier for them with me no longer around, but they were too good people to just throw me out or try to get me placed with another family when I was so close to being free from the system.

Though I was looking forward to being independent, the prospect gave me sleepless nights. I didn't have many opportunities ahead of me. I hadn't had much of an education, no job, no family to give me a helping hand. I was in this on my own. Sure, I had the band, but even I wasn't dumb enough to think we were going to hit the big time. We weren't exactly mainstream. The only thing I knew anything about in the world was how it felt to be an unwanted kid raised by the state. I didn't think there was much I could do with that—it wasn't as though anyone was going to stump up money for my college education any time soon.

Perhaps someone would take me on as an apprentice, though I had no idea what I could be an apprentice at. I wasn't particularly good with cars, having never had a dad or older brothers to show me my way beneath the hood of a vehicle. My skills in a kitchen were limited to toast, and I knew nothing about plumbing or electrics.

Besides, I didn't even know if an apprentice's wage was enough to rent a room, never mind an entire apartment. But I *did* want to work, and I was willing to do anything. I wanted to get out of the system and start to build a life for myself, off my own back. I'd been floating around for so long, all I wanted was to create some roots and anchor myself for a while.

I bent down and hooked my fingers beneath the old style garage door and hauled it up to send it backward across runners overhead, revealing my bandmates, still jamming. My drum set sat empty and silent in the corner.

Ryan jerked his chin at me, and Mike gave me a half smile, but Adam just stared at the ground as he continued to pluck the strings of his bass. I forced a smile back and then wove between them to take my seat behind the drums. I picked up my sticks and was about to beat out a rift, when the song came to an end.

"Break time, guys," Ryan called.

Shit.

I didn't know if he'd done that as a deliberate slight, but already my back was up.

"You coming, Cole?" he said as he walked past.

A door on the back led out behind Ryan's house, which the garage was attached to.

I hadn't expected the invite. "Oh, yeah. Sure."

I got to my feet, leaving my sticks beside my drum set, and followed them out. They sat in a patch of sunshine, rolling cigarettes from papers. I didn't smoke—I tried it a few times, but I just didn't like it. I wasn't averse to a couple of drinks if they were being offered, but I would avoid the tobacco.

Except this time I noticed they were dropping more into the hand-rolled cigarettes than tobacco. I was used to smoking weed on the odd occasion, but this was something else.

"What you got there?" I asked.

"Just a little extra something to perk us up." He held lit the cigarette and took a toke and then held it out to me. "Want some?"

I lifted a hand. "Nah, I'm good, thanks."

"You don't have to smoke it. You can snort some if you want."

"Seriously, I'm fine."

He shrugged and handed the cigarette over to Mike. "Suit yourself."

I sat awkwardly with them while they passed the smoke around. Before long they were laughing together, making me feel like a total outsider. I'd never felt uncomfortable in their company before—well, maybe occasionally, but not like this. If I'd felt like I was on the outskirts of things when I'd walked into band practice, now I felt like I was practically on a whole other continent. Was this still some kind of punishment for having Gabi around? Or did they not even give a shit, and this was just something that was going to have been around anyway?

I got back to my feet and shoved my hands in my pockets. "So, are we going to jam, then?"

They'd been laughing with their heads together, but looked around as I spoke, as though they'd forgotten about my presence altogether.

"Yeah, sure, dude," said Ryan. "Let's jam."

I tried not to let my relief show as we headed back into the garage. Everyone took their positions and I slid onto the stool behind my drum set. I was glad to be back on comfortable ground, and as soon as Ryan counted us in, we were all playing together just like usual. I tried to put the memory of whatever they'd been smoking out of my mind. It wasn't my business. They were adults and could do whatever the hell they liked.

I felt sure I didn't have anything to worry about.

FIFTEEN

COLE–PRESENT DAY

On the morning of Gabi's hospital appointment, I arrived at her house a half hour earlier than needed. I'd been ready to leave by eight a.m., and had done my best to make the hours go faster, but still I'd left way too early and then driven around town with the radio on loud. Despite driving to the opposite side of town, I'd still ended up sitting outside of her house stupidly early.

I was nervous, and maybe that was stupid, too.

Once upon a time I'd known this woman—though then she'd been a girl—even better than I'd known myself. I'd held her when she'd been sad, and brushed away her tears with my fingers. I'd fought with her when she'd been angry, and laughed with her when she'd been happy. I'd kissed her mouth, and her eyes, and run my tongue over every inch of her skin.

Yet here I was now, nervous to even sit in the same car with her.

I wondered if she'd forgotten about my offer to drive her to her appointment. Perhaps I was being ignorant again. I hadn't thought that she might need specialist transport if she was back in a wheelchair because of her injury. I didn't know how these things worked, and now I wished I'd asked the right questions instead of pulling the macho-hero stunt with her and all but bullying her into allowing me to come. I was in unknown territory, and I didn't like it.

The front door opened and Gabi appeared, wearing her prosthetic, but aided by a pair of crutches. Her corkscrew brown curls were wild around her face, and she wore a maxi-dress, which covered her prosthetic leg, but showed off her cleavage. God, she was so fucking beautiful, always had been. No missing limb would ever change that for me.

Immediately, I threw open the driver's door and jumped out to help her, but she'd juggled both the crutches, her purse and the front door, and turned to face me with a smile. "Just how long were you planning on sitting out here?" she said.

"Not long enough to get the courage to come and knock," I admitted.

Gabi frowned. "What are you nervous for? I'm the one with the appointment."

Her words made me realize how different our head-spaces were now. While I was worrying whether she was ever going to want to see me again, she was worrying about whether or not she would be able to walk.

Fuck, I was such a shallow bastard at times.

"How's your dad" I asked instead, wanting to change the subject.

She shrugged. "Much the same. Seems no worse for his experience, apart from maybe a bruised ego."

Gabi headed to the passenger side of the car. I nipped around quickly to open the door for her.

She lifted her eyebrows at me. "I'm capable of opening a car door, Cole."

"I know that. I'd still open the car door for you whether you were on crutches or not."

I thought I saw a hint of a smile on her lips, but I didn't want to push my luck.

She got in the car and I took the crutches from her and slid them across the back seat. I slammed the door shut and then got back behind the wheel and pulled the car out into the light traffic.

"How has your … leg been?" I asked as I drove.

She glanced over at me. "It's okay, you can say stump. That's what it is."

"Okay … stump." The word sounded ugly and awkward from my lips.

"It's been all right," she said, answering my question. "I think getting the ice on it so quickly really helped, so thank you for that."

I gave her a smile. "You're welcome." I hesitated, wanting to ask her something, but not wanting to upset her. But my curiosity got the better of me. "What happened to your leg?"

I glanced over at her, but she stared directly ahead. For a moment, I didn't think she was going to tell me, but then she started to speak, her voice remaining even throughout her story.

"It was a bomb in Iraq. A car drove directly toward me and a soldier I was stationed with. I thought the vehicle was most likely driven by a bitter local who wanted to mow us both down. I pushed the other soldier out of the way, and shot the driver, but it made the car veer off course, toward the soldier I was with. I thought the car was still too far away from us to cause any damage, but as soon as it hit the wall of the building where we were on lookout, the vehicle exploded. Turned out there were explosives on board. The soldier I was with died. He was the father of a newborn baby girl. I escaped with only the loss of my leg."

I tried not to let my shock show on my face. Of all the possibilities I'd considered, for some reason Gabi being a veteran had never occurred to me. Was it just because she was woman? If she'd been a man who had returned to town with a missing limb, I thought that would have been the first thing that would have jumped into my mind. Or was it just that I'd never considered the sweet, bookish girl I'd fallen in love with would have ever joined the Army? A wave of guilt washed over me. Had she enlisted just to get away from me? Was her missing limb ultimately my fault?

"I'm so sorry, Gabi," I managed to say between the barrage of thoughts jumbling around my head.

I couldn't even imagine the things she'd been through.

"I should have pushed him the other way," she said. "He'd still be alive then."

"It wasn't your fault," I said.

She shook her head. "You weren't there."

For once, I was at a complete loss for words.

Within ten minutes we reached the hospital, and Gabi hooked a blue disabled parking placard onto the rearview mirror of my car. She seemed to have shaken off the morose atmosphere which had settled over her during recounting the events that had led to her injury, and she flashed me a smile.

"Not many perks of losing a leg," she said, "but that's one of them."

"I hadn't considered a parking placard to be a perk before."

"Well, they are. I also lost about eight pounds in one go, so there's that, too."

My eyebrows shot up my forehead, and she laughed and pushed her hair from her face. "Got to look at the bright side of things."

That was my Gabi, right there. The girl I remembered—fun and feisty, and incredibly sexy. A sudden urge to plunge my fingers into those tight curls and kiss her hard took over me, but I didn't want to ruin the delicate bridge of friendship we'd created.

"Thanks for letting me drive you today, Gabs." I risked reaching out and touching her hand, but she pulled away from me.

Her brown eyes studied my face, and a couple of faint lines appeared between her eyebrows. She didn't appear angry, more curious. "What's your game plan here, Cole? Why do you even want to drive me? Is it a guilt thing?"

"No, of course not. I mean, I do feel guilty about what happened between us …"

"Nothing happened between us," she said, quickly. "We were young, and clearly you were stupid."

I couldn't argue with her.

"Don't worry," she said, "it's not like I think you're going to hit on me, or anything."

Her words surprised me. That was the exact thing I thought she might have been worried about.

"You're not?"

She laughed but there wasn't any humor in the sound. "It's not like I've got men lusting over me these days. I mean, no one wants a woman who only has one leg." She snorted. "Actually, that's not true. You wouldn't believe the number of guys who have a thing for amputees, but honestly, I'm not interested in being someone's fetish."

My mouth dropped. "You're kidding me, right?"

"Nope. They're a real pain in the ass, especially with social media these days. They stalk the forums and befriend any young woman who fits the bill. They even pretend to be amputees themselves to try and create a bond with real amputees. They're known as devotees. "

"I had no idea."

She shrugged again. "Why would you?"

We got out of the car and made our way to the assisted mobility department in the hospital. I lurked awkwardly as Gabi let the receptionist know she was there.

"You can wait in the car," she told me, after the receptionist had told her to take a seat. "Or go and grab a coffee. I'll probably be a little while."

"I'm happy to wait."

She shook her head. "I need to do this on my own."

"Oh, right. Sure. I'll see you back by the car, then?"

Gabi gave me a small smile. "See you in a while."

I turned and walked away, my stomach in knots, feeling like I'd just been dismissed.

SIXTEEN

GABI—PRESENT DAY

Watching Cole's broad back as he walked away, I tried not to let myself think about how he hadn't argued with me when I'd said no man would want a woman with one leg. Why had I been expecting him to?

It was a stupid and insulting thing to say anyway—there was no reason why someone who'd become an amputee would suddenly become undesirable. I felt sick and guilty that I'd allowed my own insecurities taint other people. What I had meant to say was that *Cole* wouldn't want me now I was missing my leg.

I didn't know why I kept letting myself think there might be something more between us. Was it just because of how close we'd been in the past? I wished I could stop thinking of him like that. No matter how many times I reminded myself of how badly he'd hurt me, and of the fact I would never let him see my stump, or that he would even *want* to see my stump, my heart kept longing.

Movement came at the door of my doctor's office and I glanced up.

"Ms. Weston," said Dr. Merryweather, "do you want to come through?"

Using my crutches, I got up and followed him through to his office. He gestured for me to take a seat opposite him, which I did.

He crossed one leg over the other and leaned forward slightly, nodding at my crutches. "So, Gabi, how have things been since last week? Problems?"

I was almost tempted not to tell him about my fall, just in case he refused to fit my new leg because of it. Even if he couldn't see any damage, he might decide it was better to leave it for another week or two. But I couldn't risk *not* telling him. The idea of infection and a new amputation terrified me more than anything else. I also had the crutches with me. It wasn't that I really needed them to walk, more that I hadn't wanted to put any unnecessary pressure on my stump without having to resort back to the dreaded wheelchair. I hated that thing.

"It's not been great," I admitted. "I had a fall, and the prosthetic felt like it went one way, and my stump the other."

He winced. "Doesn't sound good."

"I got some ice on it right away, and elevated it. I haven't had any more pain since."

"You shouldn't have been wearing your prosthesis at all," he chided me.

"I know, but it felt okay. If it hadn't, I wouldn't have worn it, I promise."

"Okay. Well, let's take a look."

I sat with my remaining foot on the floor to steady myself, and removed my prosthesis. Dr. Merryweather edged closer, frowning slightly as he inspected my stump. My heart lodged in my throat, dreading what he was going to say. To distract myself, I glanced around his office, noting the posters on the walls advertising different prosthetics. In particular, my gaze landed on one which asked if I'd ever served in the United States Army. Just seeing the words made my heart thump, and I averted my eyes. I knew I was lucky my injury was funded from the government, when many others would have to use insurance, or even worse, lose their homes to pay, but I couldn't stand to even see the poster.

Within a minute, I became aware of the weight of my residual limb pulling me down on one side. When I'd had two legs, I'd never given any thought to how much having two feet came into day to day comforts. Now I couldn't get away from it.

Dr. Merryweather slid his chair away from me again.

"Looks like you were lucky," he said. "I can't see any signs of swelling, and there are no scrapes or grazes, so you got away with it this time."

I breathed a sigh of relief.

"You must be careful, though, Gabi. You can't risk having falls. It's too dangerous for you. You must take care of yourself."

I wondered what he would say if he knew exactly what I had been doing to cause the fall.

Something must have shown on my face because he frowned in concern. "You've still got support in place, haven't you?"

I nodded.

"Your dad," he continued. "Is that right?"

I nodded, though my stomach twisted with anxiety. "Yes."

"Did he come with you today?"

I shook my head, glad I didn't feel like I was lying this time. "No, a friend brought me."

"That's good. While I want you to be independent, it's still important you remember to ask for help when you need it, understand?"

"Understood."

"In that case, shall we try your new leg again, and make sure it's still a good fit?"

I grinned. "That would be wonderful, thank you, Doctor."

Twenty minutes later, I walked out of the hospital with my new leg, feeling like I was walking on air. It was such a relief not to have the awful wetsuit-like material right up my thigh, especially in this heat. It had been almost unbearable. Only my desire not to end up back in a wheelchair had made me put up with it, but now my new, foam lined sleeve only came up just past my knee, and I felt so much more comfortable. I walked with a smile on my face for the first time in a long time, and carried the crutches rather than using them to walk. I still had a slightly awkward gait, but at that point I honestly didn't care.

Back in the parking lot, I spotted Cole sitting behind the wheel of his car, tapping the fingers of both hands against the steering wheel to music I couldn't yet hear. As I watched, he lifted his hands and air-drummed to the beat, and I laughed. Teenaged Cole obviously still lay beneath the surface of the hardened, tattooed skin he'd developed.

He turned his head slightly and caught sight of me laughing at him. He grinned in return and my traitorous little heart did a flip.

Cole jumped out of the car to meet me. "Hey, how did it go?" He took the crutches from my hands. "Doesn't look like you need these anymore."

"It went well. The new leg is so much better."

He nodded, though there was no way he could understand. "That's good." He paused, "Since you're mobile and everything, I wondered if you had plans for Thursday yet or not."

"Thursday?"

"Yeah." He lifted his eyebrows expectantly and then prompted. "July fourth?"

"Shit, really?" I'd completely lost track of the significance of the date. For me, recently, the only important dates were hospital ones.

"I take it that means you don't have plans."

"No, I hadn't even thought about it."

"I'd love to take you to the display at the beach."

In our area it was illegal to let off backyard fireworks. With the weather so hot, and everything so dry, they were a fire hazard.

"I don't know, Cole. I mean, my dad might want to do something with me." I almost added, *if he's sober enough*, but managed to hold my tongue.

"He can come, too," Cole added.

"Seriously?"

"At least then you won't have to worry about me trying to seduce you." He gave me a wink and my cheeks flushed.

"Okay, but if I bring my dad, it's definitely not a date."

He held up his hands. "Just old friends catching up. Definitely not a date."

But after he drove me home and I checked with my dad, he said would make some plans with some buddies, and that Cole and I should just go together.

Looked like it was going to be a date after all.

SEVENTEEN

GABI—ELEVEN YEARS EARLIER

Saturday morning for me always consisted of hanging out on the couch, in my pajamas, reading, or watching crap television. This morning was no different. My dad had gone to work, so I'd made myself a stack of pancakes, which I'd devoured, and then settled on the couch. I'd just started to become immersed in my latest book when the doorbell sounded.

I sat up, looking in the direction of the door, as though I might be able to work out my visitor's identity by psychic abilities alone. I wasn't expecting anyone.

A delivery man, perhaps?

The bell rang again and I dropped the paperback I was reading onto the coffee table and got to my feet. I hurried over to the living room window and peered out, my cheek pressed against the cool glass, to catch a glimpse of my visitor.

My jaw dropped.

Cole stood on my doorstep, the truck he'd been driving the other night sitting in the place of my dad's car in the driveway.

Oh shit.

What the hell was he doing here?

I suddenly became aware of the mess I was in, my hair scraped back into a ponytail, and wearing my baggiest, holey pajamas. I couldn't answer the door to him like this.

Shit, shit, shit.

I raced to the mirror hanging above the living room fireplace and yanked my hair out of the band, hastily dragging my fingers through my curls. I used a lick of spit on my finger to scrub away any traces of yesterday's mascara from under my eyes.

I would have loved to run upstairs and get changed, but I was worried he'd decide I wasn't in and leave. The only other option was to strip down to my underwear and meet him at the door like that, but I didn't think our relationship had quite reached that point yet.

My line of thought made me realize two things. One, I didn't want Cole to leave, and two, I was starting to think of not only being naked around him, but about us actually having some kind of relationship.

He might think differently when he saw me in my PJs though.

The doorbell rang again and I ran to the front door. Positioning my body behind the door, so he couldn't see what I was wearing, I managed to open it with only my head poking out.

"Cole!" I said, giving him a wide smile, and then remembering I hadn't brushed my teeth yet, and clamping my mouth shut again.

His eyes narrowed quizzically at my strange positioning, but he didn't mention it. "Hey, Gabi. I hope you don't have any plans for today."

"Umm, no, not really. Why, what's up?"

He grinned and pushed a hand through his blond hair. "I'm taking you on a date. With me," he clarified. "Our first date."

A bubble of happiness rose inside me, but with it came uncertainty.

"You are?" Taylor still wasn't speaking to me, and I was worried that by accepting I would only widen the void between us. But at the same time, nothing had ever happened between him and Taylor, and I felt like she was being unreasonable by acting in such a way. I had to admit that, despite the annoying, cocky attitude he'd first presented me with, Cole had gradually been growing on me.

"Yes, I am," he replied, and then hesitated uncertainly. "So ... are you coming?"

"Where are we going?"

"It's a surprise."

My lips twisted. "I'm not so good with surprises."

"You'll like this one, I promise."

I decided I wasn't going to say no. "Okay, but I need to get changed. Can you give me ten minutes?"

A cheeky grin cracked across his face "You mean I don't get to take you out in your pajamas?"

Damn, he had noticed.

I stuck my tongue out at him. "Ten minutes!"

I partially closed the door so he wouldn't see my flannel-clad backside running up the stairs, and then turned and raced to my bedroom. I'd never been one to care much about my clothes, but all of a sudden what I wore seemed vitally important. Damn, I should have asked him where we were going. The beach? A movie? Fancy restaurant? They each required a different outfit.

A sudden noise came from downstairs, something thumping. I paused, listening. Was that Cole? I thought he'd have waited in his truck. The horrific thought that my dad might be home early went through my head. I'd die if he found Cole waiting for me and decided to have one of his fatherly talks. I would literally die of embarrassment.

But everything remained quiet.

Knowing I didn't have much time, and not wanting Cole to think I was the kind of girl who spent ages picking out an outfit, I opened for a pair of skinny jeans, a looser, floral top, and a pair of sandals. I quickly scrubbed my teeth, and applied a little mascara and lip gloss. My heart was pattering, my hands shaking with excitement. I needed to chill out and calm down, or Cole was going to think I was way too eager.

I liked him, I realized, I actually, really liked him. And if he was turning up on my doorstep taking me out on surprise dates, I was pretty sure that meant he liked me, too.

I guessed Taylor had been right all along.

With an extra bounce in my step, I hurried down the stairs, grabbed my purse and keys, and left the house, locking the door behind me.

Cole was waiting beside the truck. He opened the passenger door for me, and I hopped in, and he slammed it shut. He walked around the vehicle and climbed behind the wheel.

We grinned at each other, warmth and excitement blooming inside me. Had I ever felt this way before—suddenly so alive?

"So, are you going to tell me where we're going?" I asked.

He shook his head and slung his arm behind my head, across the back of the passenger seat, as he backed the truck out of the drive. "Now where would the fun be in that?"

"Did I mention I hate surprises?"

He cast a glance over at me as he drove. "You won't hate this one."

I was excited, and my excitement grew as he took the road heading out of town and got onto the freeway. "Can you at least tell me how long it'll take us to get there?"

He shrugged. "Couple of hours."

My mouth dropped. "A couple of hours?"

For the first time, he lost the cocky attitude. "Yeah, that isn't a problem, is it? I mean, you don't have to be back for your dad or anything?"

"No, he's working until late. He won't even know I'm gone."

"Do you like having your freedom?"

"Do you?" I threw the question back at him. "Your foster parents have been good about lending you their truck."

"Yeah, they're all right. My foster dad, Stephen, taught me to drive, too. They've done everything they can to make sure I'm able to be independent when I leave them."

I noticed the drop in his tone. "Is that soon?"

"Yeah, in a few months. I stay with them until after I graduate, and then I'm free, baby." He gave me a wide grin, but I felt like something was hiding behind the smile.

"Free? Wow. What are you going to do?"

"Get a job and a place of my own, I guess. What about you? What are you going to do after graduation?"

"College."

I realized that would mean we'd be separating before we'd barely gotten started. I pushed the thought away. I seriously shouldn't be worrying about stuff like that. We hadn't so much as kissed, apart from my peck on his cheek, which didn't really count.

"You've been accepted?"

"Yeah, acceptances from all three I've applied to."

He smiled at me, and my heart flipped. "Congrats."

"Thanks. I've just got to graduate now."

"You must have it in the bag."

"As long as I don't do anything to royally screw up, I hope so."

"You won't. You're the sensible type."

I bristled. "I'm not that sensible!"

He cocked an eyebrow. "No?"

"No!"

Cole didn't look convinced. "Anyway, I'm not saying that's a bad thing. You're going to have a great future, Gabi. I can tell."

My cheeks flamed. "Thanks."

We settled into the drive, chatting about school, music, what foods we enjoyed, and places we liked to go. When he drove, studying the road, it gave me the opportunity to snatch glances at his profile. He seemed so much older to me than his almost eighteen years. Perhaps it was because of everything he'd been through in his life that he seemed more mature. I didn't know, but I knew just the sight of him caused butterflies to dance around my stomach. The defined jaw, the full mouth, the long blond hair and piercing blue eyes. He was a teenage girl's wet dream. I could understand why Taylor was jealous, though I still didn't understand why he'd chosen me over her. I was tempted to ask him, but I wasn't sure I was ready to hear the answer.

Less than two hours had passed when Cole signaled to take the next exit. I sat up in my seat, interested in where we were headed.

The town was only a little larger than our own, and didn't appear to be anything special. As we drove through the wide, quiet streets, I wondered what we'd driven two hours to get here for. I couldn't see anything unique about the place.

"Are you going to tell me where we're going yet?" I asked.

"We're going here, a little town called Livingstone."

"Any reason why?"

"Yep. I'm taking you to a bookstore."

"A bookstore?" I was pleased, but I still didn't understand. "You know we have one of those back in Willowbrook, right?"

He chuckled. "Sure, but there's something special going down in this one."

"But you're not going to tell me what?"

"Not a chance."

We drove through town, and Cole found a place to park. "It's over there."

I looked in the direction he'd nodded. A line of people had gathered in the street. What was going on?

"You're going to need this," he said, and handed me a book.

I glanced down to find the same novel I'd been reading in the park the first day he'd spoken to me. "How did you get this?" I exclaimed.

"I came into your house when you were getting changed."

"You did what?"

"Yeah, I was hoping I'd find it."

"What if it had been in my bedroom?"

He gave me a wink. "Then I guess I would have figured out a way to get into your bedroom." A little thrill went through me, but Cole gave a laugh. "No, seriously, I would have just bought you a new copy here, but I thought it was better for you to have your own book."

"Why do I need my own book?"

"How about you stop asking questions, and go check it out for yourself."

My curiosity was at an all time high. I gave him an excited, hyped-up grin, and then hopped out of the car and hurried over to join the people outside the bookstore. In the shop window, numerous posters were inside the glass, the display filled with the same book I held in my hands.

Realization dawned. "Oh, my God."

Cole had followed me. "The author is doing a signing today."

I spun to face him. "I could actually kiss you right now!" The words were out of my mouth before I'd had a chance to think about them.

He grinned, his cheeks heating with pleasure. "I won't stop you."

Acting impulsively, I stood on tiptoes and planted a kiss against his soft lips. It was quick, fleeting, but it was enough to get my heart racing even more than it already was. This was quite possibly the most exciting day of my life.

We joined the line, and within a few minutes, they started letting people into the store.

I thought of something. "It's a good thing I liked the book," I said, teasing him.

"I knew you were enjoying it."

"How?"

"That day I first spoke to you, I'd been watching you for about fifteen minutes before I came over. You didn't look up once."

That he'd noticed such a thing, and that he'd been watching me for long enough to notice, warmed me inside.

As we waited, the line gradually grew shorter, until I was finally at the desk to get my autograph. Audrina Lane, a British author with wild red curls, smiled up at me as I approached.

I didn't want to gush, but I couldn't quite help it. "Oh, my God. I can't believe I'm actually meeting you. Your books are amazing."

She smiled, reserved, but still warm. I figured she must hear this a hundred times a day. "Thanks so much. Who can I make the book out to?"

"Oh, just to Gabi—with an 'i.'"

She scribbled her signature and handed the book back to me. I hugged it to my chest. "Thank you!"

I turned to grin at Cole, who was waiting in the wings, and then skipped over to him. "I can't believe you did this for me," I said.

His blue eyes studied my face, and he grew serious. "The first time I met you I made myself a promise."

His words surprised me. I was quickly discovering I was easy to surprise, or perhaps he was just good at it. "You did?"

"Yeah. I promised myself that one day I'd get a real smile from you, and I think I just came good on that promise."

I smiled again. "Yes, you did."

He took my hand. "And I think I just got another one."

"Yes, it was. Thank you, Cole."

"Anytime."

I lifted my eyebrows. "Well, now, that would mean you driving me to book signings all over the country if you really meant that."

His gaze focused on mine, intense, trapping me in the connection we had. "Gabi, if it meant I got to spend time with you, I'd happily drive you anywhere you wanted, every single day of your life."

GABI—PRESENT DAY

Cole would be picking me up for our July Fourth date at any moment, and I still hadn't decided on my choice of outfit.

It was another unforgiving hot day, and the evening was proving to be more of the same. I knew all the other women would be wearing shorts and t-shirts, or little summer dresses, and even though I wanted to not have to feel like I had to hide myself, I just didn't have the courage. I didn't want the attention or the sympathy—children pointing and staring, and the adults assuming I must have lost my leg through diabetes or some kind of vascular disease. I especially didn't want all the extra attention with Cole there, too. It would only serve to remind him I was damaged goods now.

So is he, I reminded myself, and a wave of guilt swamped over me. Neither of us had gotten out of the past ten years unscathed, only Cole's scarring had been more to his reputation than his body.

The doorbell rang.

Shit, I still wasn't ready.

"Gabi," my dad called up the stairs. "Cole is here."

"One minute!" I yelled back. I stared at the small mountain of rejected clothes which now sat on my bedroom floor. My closet was practically empty. "Shit, shit, shit." I'd run out of time to be fussy, and decided I wasn't brave enough to parade around with my leg on show just yet—no matter how proud I was of my new pin-lock sleeve. I grabbed a long white skirt and a black sleeveless top, and then opted for some slip on sneakers. Open-toed sandals or high heels simply weren't going to work for me.

Knowing Cole was waiting, I raked my hands through my curls in front of the mirror, and slicked on some lip-gloss. I would have to do.

This isn't a real date.

No, but then why did it feel like one?

I made my way downstairs to find my dad standing with Cole on the porch. I'd never felt more like a seventeen-year-old again as I did in that moment. What the hell were they talking about? Considering our past, I didn't dare think. I hoped my dad wouldn't say anything that would send Cole running. Both he and I knew there was a strong possibility of that happening. But with relief I heard the mention of runs and pitchers, and realized they fallen onto that topic all men seemed able to converse about—sports.

They both turned as I stepped out of the door.

"Hi, sweetheart," said my dad with a smile. "Cole and I were just catching up." My gaze shifted between them, but stayed longer than it should have on Cole. He wore a short sleeved, white shirt, his tattoos emerging from the sleeves to cover the rest of his arms, and the light blue jeans he wore fit far too well around his thighs.

"You ready to go?" Cole asked.

I'd been staring. "Oh, sure," I said, my voice too bright.

He leaned in and kissed my cheek, and a waft of his aftershave, something modern and fresh, washed over me. "You look beautiful, by the way," he murmured, his mouth so close to my ear I felt the heat of his breath against my skin. Something inside me, which I thought was long dead, tightened with a low throb.

I took a breath. "Thanks."

My dad was watching us with a knowing expression and I glared at him, trying to warn him not to say anything. "So, you sure you're going to be okay without me, Dad?" I asked. "I feel bad us not spending the Fourth together when it's my first year back home."

"Nah," he said, with a shrug. "Me and the guys have a bit of a tradition going anyway, and trust me, you're not going to want to hang out with a bunch of us oldies drinking beer, farting, and complaining about life."

I laughed. "As long as you're sure."

"I'm sure. You kids go and have fun."

I wasn't sure how anyone could think of Cole—with his six-feet-something frame, tattoos, and muscles—as a kid, but I guessed my dad would always see us as the teenagers we had once been.

We left the porch, and Cole opened the car's passenger door for me. I climbed in, and he slammed it behind me, and then got behind the wheel.

I was strangely nervous, butterflies flitting around in my stomach. Was it just being in such close proximity to Cole again? I wasn't sure, but something was setting me on edge.

He glanced over at me as he drove toward the beach. "You okay?"

I nodded and smiled. "Of course."

"So I hope that skirt has a stretchy waistband?"

I balked. Did he think I looked fat? "You do?"

"Sure. There's going to be hot dogs and burgers, and I believe we can literally eat our own body weight in s'mores. There's also going to be a parade and then the fireworks when night falls. I don't know about you, but I've missed the last ten years of this, and I plan on making the most of this one."

I laughed. I'd missed a fair few when I'd been stationed. We'd always made the most of things, but fireworks definitely weren't allowed. In fact, if there was a bang on those Fourth of Julys, we'd have all been running for cover.

That strange, uneasy sensation turned over inside me again.

Within ten minutes, we reached the beach. The parking lot was already filled with vehicles, and we drove around until we found a spot. People wove between the traffic, carrying picnic hampers and blankets. Cole parked, and we headed into the throng. Music blasted, and even though it was only early evening, the party vibe was certainly underway. Bodies swayed and jiggled, holding plastic cups of beer in the air. Those with families remained on the outskirts, barbequing while their children ran around clutching treats of ice cream and cotton candy.

"This is great, huh?" Cole looked down at me with a grin. I didn't want to spoil things for him, knowing how much he was looking forward to his first July Fourth in years, but the crowds were making me nervous.

If something happened, how would we get out of here?

I didn't want to think of people running and screaming, pushing each other and trampling friends and strangers alike to get out of the way, but the image forced itself into my mind. God, I was such a freak. Everyone else was out to have a good time, and my thoughts were morbid.

"Let's grab a drink," said Cole, dragging me to one of the beer stands. I wasn't going to argue with him. Hopefully a beverage or two would help me relax. We queued up at a drinks stand, and Cole bought up a couple of plastic cups of cold beer. I took a sip and smiled at him.

"It's really great being here with you, Gabi." He glanced down. "I know we don't want to live in the past, but I really wanted to be able to talk to you about what happened when we were teenagers."

I shook my head. "I don't, Cole. Let's just leave it in the past."

"But that thing with—"

"No." I cut him off. "I don't want to rehash what happened. We were really young, both of us, and we both did things we ended up regretting."

"We did? You mean joining the Army?"

I shrugged. I didn't want him to probe any deeper. "It wasn't the direction I thought my life was going to go. I mean, no one is ever going to factor this," I gestured to my leg, "into their life plan."

"No, of course not."

Silence settled uncomfortably between us, and I took another sip of my beer and glanced around at all the happy, carefree faces. Families sat on picnic rugs, their children running around, playing. Younger couples kissed and laughed. I wanted that to be me one day, that carefree attitude, but instead I felt as though my youth had been crushed out of me, and I was forever worrying about the worst possible scenario. A black cloud didn't just hover above me. Instead it surrounded me, suffocating me, and making it impossible to see a way out.

"You hungry?" Cole asked.

I was relieved to have a distraction. "Sure," I said, even though I wasn't.

"Hot dog or burger?"

"Hot dog, thanks."

We got our food and settled on the grass. The parade went by, and we chatted about what school had been like, both of us deliberately avoiding certain names and incidents. We were treading on fragile glass, and neither of us wanted to break it.

Dusk began to fall, and sparklers burst to life around us.

Though having Cole at my side again felt wonderful, I wasn't able to shake the dread that had been following me around since we'd arrived, and the uncomfortable fluttering in my stomach had nothing to do with the sexy, masculine man beside me. I caught people glancing over, a few recognizing us, and nudging each other and whispering. The feeling of air closing in around me.

The first firework shot into the air above the ocean with a fizz and a long *wheeeeeh*, and then a massive bang.

My heart jackknifed into my throat, strangling my breath.

A second firework followed, and another and another. Tears of fear filled my eyes and though I was already sitting, I slowly folded into myself, my knees drawing into my chest, my back curling over, my head going down. Uncontrollable shakes clutched my whole body, the trembles vibrating right down to my soul.

Cole slipped his arm over my shoulders, perhaps absentmindedly as he watched the display, but he must have felt my shaking and noticed something was wrong. "Gabi?"

I couldn't answer him. The whizzing and banging continued, while everyone around us *oohed* and *ahhed* at the beauty, and all I could think of was the explosion where I'd lost my leg. The same exact terror of that moment clutched me now, and with it came the intense pain I had experienced when I'd woken up in hospital and been told about the condition of my leg from the blast. I'd still had the limb at that point— my foot and toe mangled, the tibia and fibula both shattered. I'd been given the option of them trying to save it, but was told I would most likely never walk again. Or else they could amputate the limb and I would be able to learn to walk, and even run again one day.

How had that even been a decision? I was an active, strong woman. I couldn't spend the rest of my life in pain and in a wheelchair.

The same pain I'd experienced back then began to creep up the limb which no longer existed, and I gave an involuntary cry of fear. I knew this pain. I'd suffered with it for months after the amputation. Most would recognize it as phantom limb pain, but it was so much worse than that. It wasn't just pain, it was agony, and no amount of pain medication could help because this was a hurt my brain was creating all by itself.

"Gabi," Cole's voice came to me again, reaching into the cloud of hurt and terror I'd found myself in. Still the fireworks kept exploding, each massive bang making me flinch and cower. "What's wrong?"

"My leg!" I managed to gasp. "My leg hurts."

Those three words barely brushed the surface of what I was experiencing. I knew what was happening—the banging from the fireworks had set off my post traumatic stress disorder, which in turn had set off the phantom limb pain. I needed to get away from the fireworks, but I was in too much pain and too frightened to move. I had resorted to sitting, curled over, with my arms over my head, trying to block out the sound.

I could hear the worry in Cole's voice. I couldn't even bring myself to be embarrassed at my reaction, or be worried if people were staring at me. I only wanted this all to be over.

"The fireworks. It's the fireworks."

I guess he pieced together what was happening. I suddenly found his arms beneath my body, and then he lifted me. I cried out at the sudden movement, tears streaming down my cheeks. I buried my face into his chest, dampening his shirt, and his big biceps crushed the side of my face, covering my ear and muffling the bangs. He turned from the crowds and the fireworks, and strode away. I could feel the determination in his steps, in the squared stance of his body.

"It's okay, Gabs," he muttered above me. "It's going to be okay."

I clutched to him like a drowning man on a life raft. He reached the car, and gently set me down to open the door. Then he helped me into the passenger seat, where I resumed my curled up position, the shaking continuing.

I only wanted everything to stop.

COLE—PRESENT DAY

I jumped behind the wheel, turned the key in the ignition, and had us out of there with a screech of wheels on asphalt. I was probably driving too fast, determined to put space between Gabi and the fireworks, though the whizzes, bangs, and pops continued as though they were chasing us. I had no experience of what she was going through, but every single fiber of my being was desperate to help her. I reached out and switched on the radio—not because I wanted any music, but because I wanted to drown out the explosions of the fireworks.

She shook and trembled in the seat, her head bent, tears streaming down her cheeks. Her hands had reached down to clutch at the prosthetic leg beneath her long skirt, and I caught a glimpse of the lightweight metal which vanished into her sneaker.

I wasn't the sort of guy to be in touch with his feelings, but the sight of her in such fear and pain caused my throat to tighten with a sharp pain on its own and my vision grew misty. I'd never seen someone like this before, and the fact it was Gabi made everything worse. I would have sacrificed my own leg at that moment if it meant releasing her from whatever hell she was trapped in.

Her father's house was too close to the beach to offer much protection from the noise of the fireworks. Even through closed windows and walls, she'd still be able to hear the bangs. My house, on the outskirts of town, was a much better option, at least until the worst of the noise passed.

I kept my foot to the floor, and within fifteen minutes, we'd reached my place. Most of the fireworks had already ended, though the occasional rocket still went off—young people setting them off illegally at their own beach parties, I suspected. Every time I heard a bang, I wanted to kill the person who had lit the fuse.

Gabi appeared to have completely internalized what she was going through. I tried to ask her questions, but she just shook her head, and kept her hands clamped over her ears.

I swung into my driveway and hopped out. I went to lift her from the passenger seat, but she put out her hand.

"I can walk," she gasped. "Just help me."

I put my arm around her, helping her from the seat. Together we staggered toward my small rental. I fumbled in my pocket for my keys, located them, and managed to get the door open. With her fingers gripping the material of my shirt, I guided her toward the couch. She was limping badly, sucking air in over her teeth with each step. We reached the couch and I helped her to lie down, and then stood feeling helpless and stupid, much like a man must feel when his wife is giving birth to their first child.

Crouching beside her, I put my hand gently on her shoulder. "Gabi, tell me what I can do to help. Do you need a doctor?"

She shook her head.

"Some pain medication, then? I have some, though it's not very strong. Do you have anything at your dad's I can get for you?"

Again, she shook her head, but this time she lifted her eyes to meet mine. The fear and pain I saw in their dark depths twisted my heart, and again the desperate urge to do anything possible to rid her of that pain came over me.

"Pain meds won't help," she said. "The pain isn't real … I mean, it's real to my brain, but the pain I'm feeling isn't really there. It used to be bad after the surgery, but I got it mostly under control."

"But the fireworks set it off again?"

"It was the bangs. I just felt like I was right back in the moment. It won't last forever. I just have to let it pass." A tear slid down her cheek. "I'm so sorry, Cole."

Her words surprised me. "Sorry? You don't have anything to be sorry for."

"I ruined your Fourth."

"Crazy girl," I said, taking her hand. "I still got to spend it with you."

She forced a smile and I knew it was for my benefit.

I squeezed her fingers. "There isn't anywhere else I'd want to be."

TWENTY

GABI—ELEVEN YEARS EARLIER

After the book signing, Cole took me for a burger and fries, and then we drove back to Willowbrook Falls.

We got back before dark, and I figured my dad would be home already, but when we reached my street, I discovered the drive empty and my dad still not home. Cole pulled into the spot instead and switched off the engine. I was tempted to invite him inside, not wanting our date to end, but I didn't want him to think I was easy.

Cole smiled at me. "I'll walk you to your door."

"You don't have to. It's right there."

He shrugged. "I know, but I want to."

Nerves danced around my insides, sending my blood racing. He was hoping for an invite inside; I didn't doubt it. He had obviously noticed the absence of my dad's car. I knew what he wanted, but he wasn't going to get it.

I got out of the car and Cole walked me up to my front door.

"Thanks so much for a wonderful day," I said, as he waited

expectantly.

"Thank you for coming with me and not telling me to get lost when I turned up on your doorstep."

I laughed. "Were you worried?"

"A little," he admitted. "You can be kind of hard to read."

This was news to me.

He reached out and took my hand. "But seriously, Gabi, I'm really glad you said yes." He was looking at me intently, and my heart thrummed. His other hand slipped around my waist, pulling me just a fraction closer.

This was it.

He was going to kiss me.

Cole Devonport was actually going to kiss me. The cool kid at school. The tough kid. The kid all the girls wanted and none of the guys wanted to mess with.

It wasn't as though I had never been kissed. I had. Of course I had. I wasn't that innocent. But I'd never been kissed by someone I actually liked.

This kiss was going to be epic. I just knew it. It was the kiss I'd be comparing all other first kisses to for the rest of my life.

He leaned in, the space between us rapidly disappearing. My heart hammered, my breath quickening in my chest. I wanted to simultaneously press fast forward to have his mouth on mine, and press pause to capture myself in the moment forever.

Cole locked my eyes with his blue gaze, searching for any hint that I might want him to stop.

I didn't.

A suggestion of a smile played on his perfect lips as they parted slightly, and his hand around my waist pulled me a fraction closer. His head tilted to one side as he moved in, meaning for us to fit together, but his movement made me tilt my head too, only I went the wrong way and our noses bumped.

We both gave a nervous laugh, and moved again, in the opposite direction this time, resulting in exactly the same effect, our noses clashing.

No, no, no! What the hell was I doing? *Just keep still, Gabi!*

I did as I told myself, and his lips finally made contact with mine.

And for a couple of seconds, it was perfect, and brilliant, and everything I'd dreamed, and then we both tentatively opened our mouths, tongues touching, the kiss deepening ...

Our teeth cracked together.

We jerked apart, and I clutched my hand to my mouth, my cheeks flaring with embarrassment. How the hell had that happened? It wasn't as though we both had big, bucked teeth or anything.

Cole stared down at the ground, a frown pulling his eyebrows together. He gave his head a slight shake, as though he didn't quite understand what had happened, and then released me. My heart sank. I was a crap kisser! Oh shit, I was a crap kisser and he was going to go and tell everyone in school how Gabriella Weston tried to chew his face off!

"Look, I'd better go," he said, backing away.

I wished for the ground to open up and swallow me. "Yeah, of course."

He started to turn around to walk away. I risked glancing up and caught his expression. He looked as baffled as I felt, a line between his eyebrows, his lips—lips that had been on mine only moments before— now twisted in confusion.

Holding back tears, a painful lump formed in my throat. This ill-advised romance was over before it had even gotten started.

He drew to a halt, and turned back and stared at me. "No. This is not how this is going to go."

My eyes widened. "What?"

"This is not how you're going to remember our first kiss. You need to pretend like the last couple of minutes never happened, okay?"

"Ooh ... kay," I said, wondering where he was going with this.

"Good," he replied.

Then he marched back toward me, determination in his eyes and the set line of his jaw. I almost ducked as he reached for me, slightly worried by the fierce look in his eyes, but thankfully I managed to restrain myself from doing anything so stupid the second time around.

His outstretched hand slipped around the back of my head, his fingers knotting in my curls. His other arm caught me around the waist, yanking me to him. He held me firm in his grasp, as though worried I might turn and run away. His mouth crushed mine, taking control, owning me. What I'd thought would have ended up being a sweet, tentative kiss was something else entirely. His lips pressed against mine with exactly the right amount of pressure, and as our mouths opened, our tongues met, tasting each other. His hand in my hair, the other hand on my body. I'd never been so aware of my proximity to another person in the whole of my life. I wanted to press myself harder against him, and as our kiss deepened, I found my hands had already made their way around his back. I could kiss him like this forever, and that was how it felt, that we just stood, our bodies pressed together and kissed and kissed, and kissed.

TWENTYONE

It took three days before I started to feel like myself again.

I'd spent the night of the Fourth of July on Cole's couch, with him sitting on the floor beside me, rubbing my back and stroking my hair until the worst of the pain and fear had passed. At first light, he'd driven me back to my dad's house, but, upon finding my dad passed out drunk in bed, and unable to rouse him, he'd said he wasn't going anywhere.

I self-medicated with an antidepressant and an anticonvulsant to treat the pain. I knew my doctor would have told me to come in and see him, but I'd been in this position before, and I knew what worked. My phantom limb pain would get better, but it was hard to remember that when I was caught right in the middle of it.

Cole had to leave me later that morning to go to work, but my dad managed to rouse himself, so Cole left, kissing me on the forehead, and promising to come back later. I used the privacy to apply a heat pad to my stump. Everything I was doing was about trying to change the way my brain was trying to communicate with my missing limb. I needed to disrupt the way my nerve endings were firing, and that would hopefully bring me some relief.

I thought I would never sleep, but managed to fall into a fitful doze, filled with visions so vivid I wasn't sure what was real and what was a dream. One moment I was back in Iraq, and instead of having one leg amputated, I was missing both, and was dragging myself around in the dirt, crying for someone to help me. The next moment I had both legs back again, and I was able to run as I used to, running so fast I felt like I was flying and powering up hills effortlessly.

I didn't know which was the worst part—the nightmare of not having any legs, or the reality of knowing I'd never run like that again.

When I woke, it was dark once more. I'd slept through most of the day. Cole was back, sitting at my bedside, watching me with a concerned expression. I caught a whiff of cooking oil and charred meat, and realized he hadn't even gone home to get changed before coming back to visit me.

"Hey," he said, noticing I was awake. "How are you feeling?"

I sat up slightly, making sure my lower half was covered with the bed sheet. I still wasn't ready for him to see my stump. "Better, thanks. You didn't need to come straight back here."

He edged forward in his seat. "I was worried about you. You were all I could think about my whole shift."

I glanced away. "Sorry."

Cole reached out and covered my hand with his own. "Don't ever be sorry. You have nothing to be sorry for."

"I ruined your July Fourth."

"Fuck July Fourth."

"Cole!"

He shrugged. "Well, none of this is your fault. I don't want you ever feeling like it is."

"And I don't want you to feel obligated to be here. We shared some moments when we were kids, Cole. You don't owe me anything."

He frowned. "I'm here because I want to be."

I couldn't keep arguing with him. I was too tired, and I knew any stress would make my phantom limb pain worse.

"I appreciate you checking up on me, but honestly, I'm still pretty beat. I just need to sleep this off, and I'm sure I'll be back to normal in a few days." I noted the dark shadows beneath his eyes, the lines on his forehead and grooves between his cheeks and mouth appearing deeper. "You must be exhausted, too. You've been working, and you didn't sleep much last night either."

His shoulders dropped and he ran a hand over his head and exhaled a sigh. "Yeah, I'm kind of beat. Your dad said he'd make up the spare room for me, though, if you wanted me to stay."

I gave him what I hoped was a reassuring smile. "Cole, I'm a big girl now. I'll be fine while you go home and get yourself some rest and cleaned up."

He glanced down at his stained white t-shirt. "I'm a bit of a mess, huh?"

I smiled, the first genuine one in a while. "Just a bit."

"So can I call you tomorrow, or swing by?"

"Sure, I guess."

"Okay, great." He got to his feet and then hovered over me, uncertainly. He darted in and placed a kiss to my cheek, his stubble longer and not far off a beard now, the hair a combination between soft and scratchy against my face. The kiss was brief, chaste, the type of kiss you might give your elderly aunt or grandmother.

He backed away and gave me a final smile, before leaving the room.

I placed both hands over my face and sank deeper into the bed.

I felt so torn. I knew having him around was a bad idea in the long run, that this ... whatever *this* was ... wouldn't end well for me. At some point, a young, fit, gorgeous woman who had all her limbs was going to attract Cole's attention, and then I'd be left here, forgotten. I knew his attentiveness to me wouldn't last, and that his motives were all about the guilt he carried rather than any actual feelings for me, but at the same time my heart longed to have him around. I felt better with him by my side, safer, and ironically more secure, even though I knew secure was the last thing I should be feeling.

I was dangling over a precipice, just waiting for Cole to let me fall.

Cole returned the next day as promised.

My pain had subsided, and I'd gotten out of bed and taken a bath. I was dressed and mobile again, and some days I had to be thankful for achieving the small things. I was even more thankful to be dressed when a knock came at my front door.

I opened the door to find Cole balancing a stack of something in a brown paper bag. His biceps bunched either side, and the muscles in his forearms strained.

"Hey, you're out of bed," he said, from around the side of the pile.

"Yeah, I'm feeling much better."

"That's great. I didn't know you'd be up and about, so I brought you something. I guess you can still make use of them, though."

"Cole, what on earth is all this?"

"They're all the books I remember you loved to read when you were seventeen."

I laughed. "My taste in fiction has changed somewhat since then."

The hurt on his face surprised me.

"I still love to read my old favorites, though." I reached out to take the books from him, but he pulled away.

"I'll carry them through. They're surprisingly heavy."

He carried them into the living room and set them down on the coffee table. They almost overbalanced and we both reached for them at the same time, our hands meeting. I looked up at him as we steadied the pile, and caught him grinning down at me. I smiled back and we locked eyes, our fingers touching. My heart flipped in my chest, and I dragged in a breath, forcing myself to pull away from him and stand straight. I needed to stop imagining these little moments of friction between us.

"These are great, Cole" I said, nodding to the books, my eyes skimming down the spines for the titles. "It'll be a real trip down memory lane." I wondered if it was really a good idea to be remembering anything else from when I was seventeen. Just having Cole here was bad enough.

"You're welcome." He glanced around. "So, where's your dad?"

"He's popped out to the grocery store. Knowing him, he'll be a while."

"As long as he doesn't get himself stuck in any more gates."

I rolled my eyes. "Yeah, I know. I still don't understand how he managed to do that."

Cole frowned slightly. "Tell me if I'm out of line, Gabi, but has he ever tried to get any help?"

I shook my head. "I don't think he's even accepted he has a problem. I thought after he lost his job—"

"He lost his job?" Cole interrupted. "I figured he'd just retired."

Of course, Cole wouldn't have been privy to all the town gossip when he'd been behind bars.

"No, he was fired. He was on duty with a blood alcohol level several times above the legal driving limit, and of course he'd been driving as well. He lost his license and was put on suspension that day, and then lost his job during the hearing. I thought that would have been the nudge he'd needed to get help, but he just carried on. If anything, the drinking got worse."

"Didn't you being home with your injury make him want to change?"

I shook my head. "Not a chance. I don't think he ever will change now. The drink will probably kill him in the end."

Cole took my hand, his fingers warm and firm around mine. "Jeez, Gabs. I'm sorry."

I shook my head and glanced down, embarrassed. "Don't be. It's not your fault."

"I know, but I care about you."

"You do?" I risked lifting my eyes back to his.

Cole bit his lower lip, and my insides quivered. "You know I do. I always have."

He stared at me in this dark, intense way, and then his hand lifted and his fingers brushed my cheek. His hand left my face, his knuckles grazing my jaw as they slipped around the back of my head. Then his fingers knotted in the hair at the base of my neck and he dragged me forward, leaning into me as he did so. He kissed me hard. There was no pause to make sure it was what I wanted, or tentative gentleness. No, Cole Devonport kissed me as though if he stopped for one second he would never get to kiss anyone again. His tongue thrust between my lips, searching for mine. I met him with equal hunger, an excitement I'd not experienced in a long time soaring up inside me.

He was kissing me! Cole was kissing me!

But instead of letting me enjoy the kiss, my stupid brain started working. *Why is he kissing you? Does he feel sorry for you? Does he still feel guilty? Cole broke your heart and he'll do the same thing again.* And then the worst thought—*if he wants to kiss you, he might want more, and if he wants more, you'll have to show him your stump ...*

Panic replaced excitement, and I put my hands against his chest, trying to not be distracted by the hard muscle beneath his t-shirt, and pushed him away.

"No, Cole!"

His handsome face crumpled. "I'm sorry …" But he frowned and shook his head. "No, hell, I'm not. I'm not sorry I kissed you."

"Well, I am. I can't do this."

"What? The kissing? Seemed like you were doing it pretty well to me."

"Not the kissing," I corrected myself. "Well, yes, the kissing. But I'm talking about all of it. The time spent together, the touchy-feely stuff. All of it! I haven't forgotten what you did when I was seventeen, Cole. I haven't forgiven, either. You broke my fucking heart, and I'm not about to put myself in that position again. I've got enough shit to deal with without you adding to it."

He put his hands up in surrender. "Gabi, the last thing I want to do is land any more shit on your doorstep. I made the biggest mistake of my life when I—"

"No," I all but shouted. "I don't want to hear it!"

I saw him taking a breath, calming himself, preparing for what he was about to say. "Gabs, we were in love all those years ago—about as in love as I think it's possible to be. Does that mean nothing to you now?"

"Of course it does, but I don't think you should be the one asking if our love meant something. I wasn't the one who screwed it all up."

I winced at my words. That wasn't completely true, but he didn't know about that part, and I didn't intend on ever letting him know.

"Okay, fair point. I just want to understand why you don't want to try again."

"You don't know me anymore, Cole. The girl you fell in love with doesn't even exist. You have no idea what my life has been like all these years that we've been apart."

"What about my life?" he said. "You don't know what my life has been like inside prison either."

"No, and I don't want to know."

I caught the pained expression on his face.

"I'm sorry, Cole, but like I said, I have enough issues in my life. I don't need any more complications."

"Okay, I understand that. But what if I wanted to help instead of complicate anything further?"

"You don't know me anymore," I said. "You don't know what I've been through. You've no way of understanding me or helping me."

"So is that the only way a relationship can work, if the couple has been through everything together? What about a couple who meet later in life, who've gone through a whole life's worth of experiences without each other before meeting? Are you saying that relationship could never work because they didn't go through everything side by side? I think that's bullshit, Gabi. Maybe I don't understand right now, but you can *make* me understand. You can teach me what you're going through. I'm standing here in front of you, begging you to tell me."

Tears filled my eyes.

"Don't we deserve a second chance?" he asked, softly.

I was close, so close to breaking down and letting him back into my heart, but I couldn't. I just couldn't.

I pressed my lips, not wanting to even look at him. "We don't always get a second chance at things, Cole. Sometimes too much damage has been done. Take my leg, for example. I'll never get a second chance at the life I'd thought I was going to live when I had both legs, and I can never go back to that life. Maybe our relationship is the same. Maybe too much damage was done for us ever to recover."

"Gabi ..." he said, reaching for me.

But I stepped away, shaking my head. "You know, I still remember exactly what you said to me in the school hall that day. I should—I must have replayed it a million times over in my head in the months that followed."

"Shit, Gabi. I'm so sorry."

"It's too late for sorry. It's almost eleven damn years too late." I knew he would wear me down. That he would say all the right things and I would melt into his arms. I couldn't let myself do that. I wasn't strong enough to fix myself again. "Please, Cole. Just go, and leave me alone."

He stared at me with pain and longing in his blue eyes, and my heart threatened to crack.

"Now, Cole! I want you out of my life, for good this time."

His chin quivered and he balled his fists, and for a moment I thought he was going to say something else, but then he turned on his heel and slammed out of the house.

I push the front door shut behind him and pressed my back against it. A keening sob escaped my throat and I squeezed my eyes shut, trying to hold back the tears. I wasn't strong enough. I'd never been strong enough. And the worst part of it was that my heart was breaking all over again, and this time it wasn't even Cole's fault.

It seemed I was able to break my heart all by myself.

COLE—PRESENT DAY

With my head reeling from Gabi's rejection, I jumped in my car and took off. I was driving too fast, but I didn't care. She still hated me for how I'd behaved when we were teenagers, still held every word I'd said to heart. I wished I could go back and change everything, but that was impossible. I'd hurt the girl who'd never deserved to have been hurt, and then life had come along and wounded her even more.

I bunched my fist and punched the steering wheel. "Fuck, fuck, fuck!"

With a final growl, I lifted both hands and slammed them back down again, barely keeping control of the car.

Kissing her had felt so good—right, and perfect, and like I'd finally found my way home again after all this time. And then she had pushed me away and told me she'd never forgive me, and my moment of hope that we'd be able to start afresh shattered before my eyes.

I was disappointed, yes, but most of all I was angry. Not at her, though, never with her. I was angry at myself for being so damn weak when I'd been eighteen. I should never have allowed myself to be led astray so easily. I should have grabbed Gabi back then, and taken her away from all of this. We would have created a life together by now. She would be whole and unharmed, and maybe we'd even have a couple of kids running around. Instead, she had an injury she would never recover from, and I'd wasted the last ten years behind bars.

Damn. I needed a drink.

Leaning forward over the steering wheel, I kept my eyes peeled for somewhere I could get one. Within a few minutes, I spotted a place on the outskirts of town, somewhere I doubted anyone would recognize me.

I pulled into the parking lot and climbed out of the car. I headed into the bar and barely noticed my surroundings— the dim lighting, a couple of pool tables, and an old fashioned jukebox positioned against one wall. Behind the bar, a skinny woman in her forties, wearing a tight, strappy white top, gave me a smile as I walked in.

"Hey, darlin'," she drawled. "What's your poison?"

"Whiskey," I told her, positioning my ass on the barstool. "Straight."

I threw a couple of twenties onto the bar and she glanced down at them. "I don't know what kind of whiskey you think we serve here, but that's way too much."

I picked up the glass and downed the shot, and then pushed the empty glass back toward her. "I'm not planning on having just the one."

My rented house wasn't too far from here. I'd be able to leave the car and stagger back. I didn't plan on getting hit with a DUI. With my record, it would send me straight back to prison.

She refilled the glass, and this time I nursed it a little longer before I drained the contents. The alcohol was going to my head now, something I was pleased about. It helped to dull the intense hatred and self-loathing growing inside me. I wanted to think about something other than Gabi, but my brain didn't want to let me. Every thought I had led back to her. I tried to focus on the plans I'd had when I'd been inside. I'd used my time to complete a four-year bachelor's college degree in social work. I'd wanted to use my experiences, both from my time spent in the system, to the stupid mistakes I'd made, to help teach other kids like I'd been not to make the same mistakes. I'd even been allowed to mentor a nineteen-year-old since I'd been released, though things hadn't been going so well for him. Drugs were even harder now than they'd been when I was a teenager, and this boy had gotten himself hooked on crack. I didn't know if I'd be able to help him, but I'd wanted to try.

Drowning in my thoughts, I lost track of time, the minutes slipping into hours.

I'd finished my third whiskey and moved onto a fourth, or was I finishing my fourth and moving onto my fifth? I was losing count. This time I added a beer back to my order; it wasn't as though the liquor was helping to quench my thirst. The barmaid tried to talk to me a couple of times, but my single word answers weren't keeping her entertained, and so she moved onto a couple of older guys who were happy to flirt and laugh at her jokes.

I was pretty damn drunk now, the bar blurring in front of me, the music swirling around my ears as though I was underwater.

"Cole?"

I turned to see a blonde woman standing behind me. She held a pool cue, and wore a tight green dress which hugged every curve. I frowned, not understanding how she knew my name, and then her identity dawned on me.

"Taylor?"

She smiled, revealing a flash of whitened teeth. "Yeah, hi. It's been a while."

I was confused. "What are you doing here?"

"My girlfriend was meeting a guy out here, and wanted me to come in case he turned out to be an asshole."

"And did he turn out to be an asshole?"

"He didn't show, so I'd say that would have to be yes."

"Sorry about that."

"She's not bothered. We're happy just to have a girls' night."

I looked over to where another woman was beside the pool table— curvy, with short dark hair. All the guys in the bar had their eyes focused on the two women. I didn't think they'd be worrying about a date not showing for too long.

"Well, it was good seeing you, Taylor," I said, rising from my spot on the stool. I'd been there so long my ass cheeks were numb. "I'm heading home."

"No!" she said, reaching out to place her manicured fingers against my chest. "The night is young. We've not seen each other for years. Let me buy you a drink and we can catch up."

"Really, I need to be going." I felt like I was getting drunker by the second, feeling slightly detached from the situation.

"I saw Gabi the other day," she said, her tone hitching with hope. "So sad what she's going through."

My heart lurched. "You saw Gabi?"

"Yeah, Jasmine and I went around for a coffee. I think she appreciated having some old friends around. Have you seen her?"

Gabi. My kryptonite.

"Did she mention me at all?" I couldn't help myself.

Taylor grinned. "I'll get us that drink, shall I?"

"Let me get them." And I found myself back at the bar.

We found a seat and talked about Gabi, about the awful thing that had happened to her, and how she was so brave and coping so well. After another drink or two—I had definitely lost track—we both opened up about how it was weird talking to her about her amputation, how we felt uncomfortable and guilty all at the same time. It was good to be able to talk about this stuff, but I could feel my tongue getting thicker, my words starting to slur. My eyelids were heavy, and I knew I needed to get home, though I wasn't sure how I was going to make it. What had felt like an easy walk a few hours ago now seemed like an impossible task.

"Sorry, Taylor," I said, staggering to my feet. "This has been good, but I've got to go."

"How are you getting home?" she asked, blinking up at me with her wide, blue eyes. "You can't drive."

"I know. I'll walk."

"No, I'll drive you. Just let me go and tell my friend I'm taking you home."

I glanced over at her friend who was now cuddled up to a guy, sitting on his lap while she giggled at his jokes. I just wanted to crawl into bed and go to sleep. "Okay, sure."

I got up from the chair and swayed, using my hand on the table top to keep me upright. Taylor laughed, "You okay, there, big guy?"

"Yeah, I'm fine."

I managed to find my balance, and Taylor took hold of my arm to help me keep it. Together, we stumbled from the bar, and she led me toward what I assumed was her car. A booster seat was in the back, a DVD player screen attached to the back of the headrest.

I frowned. "You got a kid?"

She smiled, "Yeah, a boy. He's seven now. My mom is watching him while I have some time to myself."

"Oh, right."

I managed to get into the passenger seat and give Taylor my address. "I know it," she said. "We'll be there in ten minutes."

The car engine started, the sound, vibration, and movement of the car lulling me into a drunken sleep. I sat with my head against the passenger window, bumping it slightly every time we went over a pothole. My drunk, half-dreaming thoughts went back to Gabi. I'd call her as soon as I got in, I decided. I'd tell her I still loved her, and that we needed to start over. I saw her face in my mind, laughing and smiling at me. I remembered our kiss, the taste of her tongue moving against mine. I thought of when we'd been teenagers, of the hours we'd spend making out on her bed, how I could have spent forever buried between her thighs ...

TWENTY THREE

COLE—ELEVEN YEARS EARLIER

"So I was thinking," I said, as I caught Gabi's hand from behind as she walked up the corridor.

She jumped at my touch. "Jeez, Cole, you just about gave me a heart attack." But she smiled at me, that big, wide smile that crinkled her brown eyes, the smile I'd grown to adore, and I felt like I'd been punched by the force of my feelings for her.

I grinned. "Sorry, but anyway, I was thinking that me and the guys are going to be jamming tonight, and I'd really love you to come."

She pulled me to a halt, the smile fading from her face. "I don't know, Cole. I'm not sure the rest of your band will want me there."

"Don't be silly. Why would they not want you there? They always have other people around when we're playing—in fact, I think some of their friends are coming tonight as well, so it'll practically be a party. It would feel weird without you."

She hesitated, and I could see she was thinking about it.

I positioned my body in front of hers. "You should probably know that

149

I am prepared to get down on my knees and beg, if that's what it takes."

Her cheeks flushed and she glanced at all the other students moving in every direction around us. "You wouldn't?"

I gave her a wink. "Try me."

"Okay, okay," she said, giving me a little shove to get me moving again. "I'll come, but if it's weird, I won't stay for long."

"It won't be weird, I promise. We'll have fun."

I knew I was back in peacock-mode, wanting to perform in front of her, hoping to impress her, but I couldn't help myself. Impressing Gabi had suddenly become of number one importance in my life. I messed around with my kit, keeping an eye on the front of the garage, waiting for her to show. I worried she'd change her mind, but then she appeared, wearing a summer dress with the type of short skirt that showed off her beautiful legs, and I jumped up and ran over to her.

"Hey, you made it," I said, dropping a kiss to her lips.

"Sure. I said I'd come." She peeped over my shoulder to where the guys were tuning their guitars. A couple of other people hung out on beanbags in the corner, laughing with their heads together, but they were Ryan's friends and I didn't know them.

"Hey, Gabi," Ryan called over to her.

Gabi gave a reserved smile and lifted her chin in a greeting, but didn't say anything.

"You ready to get started, Cole?" he asked me.

"Sure."

We started to play, a couple of covers first, and then one of our own songs. I noticed Ryan's friends had gravitated toward Gabi, and I was pleased to see her exchanging words with them. She still didn't look completely comfortable, but she didn't appear quite as uneasy as she had when she'd walked in.

Eventually, we took a break, and some of the guys headed out back for a smoke. Ryan passed a bottle of something around—a brown paper bag disguised its contents—and when it reached Gabi, she looked between the older guys and took it. I opened my mouth to say something and then shut it again. I'd had a few drinks plenty of times, and I knew she'd kill me if I said something about her not being old enough in front of everyone. Plus, I'd be a total hypocrite if I did. Anyway, Gabi was as sensible as they came. I figured she knew her limits.

Gabi took a swing from the bottle, and grimaced as she swallowed. I didn't know if it was beer or wine, or something stronger, but she didn't cough or splutter. Instead, she handed it to the girl next to her, and carried on chatting. Perhaps her having a drink or two wasn't a bad thing. It might make her enjoy herself more, and I wanted her to enjoy herself. I wanted her to be a part of the thing I loved doing, and if it took a couple of swings of booze to do it, then it was no big deal. Gabi wasn't a child, and she was more than capable of deciding whether or not to have a drink.

Despite this, I kept an eye on her while the band started up again.

The bottle was still being passed around, and she took a drink every time it reached her. Her laugh grew louder, and she kept touching the arm of whoever she was talking to. Admittedly, I had promised her a party, and it was Saturday the next day, so at least she didn't need to worry about going to school, but I still didn't want her getting completely trashed.

We played a few more songs, and then took a break for the guys to go out and smoke some weed. I knew this normally meant the end of practice, as they'd end up getting too wasted to bother playing again, so I took the opportunity to whisk Gabi out of the way.

"Where are we going?" she asked, as I pulled her out of the front of the garage, and away from Ryan and the guys.

"I'm going to take you home," I said.

Her lower lip pouted. "Aww, and I was having fun!"

"I know, but it's getting late."

I thought she might give me a fight about it, but instead she wrapped her hand around my waist and tucked in under my arm. I liked how we fitted together like this—two pieces of one whole.

"Bye!" she yelled to the people we were leaving behind, though no one paid us any attention. "They were really nice," she said, and then giggled. I couldn't help smiling with her. Drunk Gabi was actually kind of cute.

I kept my arm around her as we walked toward her house, her giggling and falling against me so I had to half hold her up.

"Do you want to know a secret?" she said as we walked.

I glanced down at her, wondering what she was going to say. "Sure."

"You can't tell anyone. You super, extra promise?"

"I promise."

"No, you *super, extra* promise."

I laughed and repeated her words.

"I love you," she said, jabbing me in the chest with her finger. "I really, truly, properly am in love with you. I mean, it's like you've taken over my mind or something," I noticed she was slurring, "because I seriously cannot stop thinking about you for even one second of the day."

I held back my grin—I didn't want her to think I was laughing at her confession, though the thought of it did make me smile. "I love you, too, Gabi."

"Nope. You're only saying that 'cause I said it first."

"Well, I would have preferred you to say it when you were able to stand up straight, but that doesn't mean I don't believe you."

"'Cause you just know, don't you?" she said. "We don't even have to say it. You can just tell. Like when you look at me, it's like the most intense thing in the world, and I know you're thinking exactly the same as what I'm thinking."

"And what's that?"

She smacked me on the chest this time. "That I love you, dummy."

The bubble of happiness swelling inside of me needed to get out and I swung her into a hug, kissing her neck and swinging her off her feet.

I set her down again, and she pressed her fingers to her mouth. "That kind of made me sick."

"Oh, shit, sorry."

But she managed to hold it together, and even her nausea didn't dampen my joy. I didn't think anyone had ever said that to me before. No, I *knew* no one had ever said those words to me. Having someone tell you they loved you wasn't something you ever forgot.

We reached her house, and I was relieved to see her driveway empty. Thank God, her dad wasn't home. I wasn't keen on the idea of having to explain to him why his daughter wasn't able to stand up straight.

We made it to the front door, and Gabi fumbled for her keys. It had just started to get dark, the street lights flickering on one by one. We were almost through the door when car headlights swung up the drive.

Shit.

"Uh-oh," said Gabi at my side, though I could hear the drunken giggle in her tone. "My dad's home."

The headlights blinded us for a second, making us both squint until the engine fell quiet and the beams flicked off. I debated whether or not I would get away with shoving Gabi through the front door and making a run for it, but I didn't think that would go down well with either her or her father.

The car door opened and slammed shut, and then he was walking up the driveway toward us.

"Gabi, you're home," he said.

She lifted a hand and waved. "Hi, Dad."

"Hi, Mr. Weston," I said, wishing desperately that I didn't have to be forced into having a conversation with the guy. I'd never been good with girlfriends' parents—not that I'd met many. Hell, I hadn't been good with parents of my own, so I had no reason to expect anyone else's to like me. I was also painfully aware of the fact Gabi had been drinking. Even though she seemed to have sobered up a little during the walk home, he was bound to spot it.

He did, sniffing as he got closer, his forehead creasing into a frown. "Gabi? Do I smell alcohol?"

She giggled. "Are you like a bloodhound now, sniffing out the booze?"

"Gabi," he said, a warning tone in his voice.

"I should probably get going," I said, giving Gabi's hand a squeeze and stepping away.

"No, you don't," Mr. Weston said. "Stay right where you are."

Double shit.

"I'm serious, Gabi, if you've been drinking, you need to tell me."

"Why?" she replied. "You never tell me when *you've* been drinking."

I glanced at her in surprise. I'd never taken her for someone who would talk back to her father, especially considering she'd just been busted for under-aged drinking. Perhaps it was the booze talking.

He exhaled a frustrated sigh. "You have, haven't you?"

"I was having fun for once," she shot back. "Maybe I learned from my dad, huh. It's not like you ever set a good example."

Happy, giggly Gabi had suddenly morphed into angry, bitter Gabi. I'd never seen this side of her, and the anger appeared to be directed at her father. His cheeks were flushed bright red, his mouth a hard line.

He turned to me. "I think you should go home now."

I was worried to leave her here. Things weren't right between her and her dad, but I wasn't sure what it was about.

"Are you okay, Gabs?" I asked her softly.

"Don't speak to her," he snapped. "I asked you to leave, young man. You're standing on my property, and you've just gotten my under-aged daughter drunk. I suggest you make yourself scarce before I decide to take things further."

"Gabi?" I said again, not knowing what to do. I didn't want to leave her like this, but I had a feeling her dad would physically force me to leave if he wanted to. I didn't want us to end up tussling on the front lawn.

"It's fine, Cole. I'm going to bed."

She had tears in her eyes, and I wanted to pull her into a hug or kiss her goodbye, but I didn't dare, not with her father watching.

What the hell was going on with them? I remember the night when I'd picked her up walking the streets in the rain. I knew her home life wasn't perfect—whose was?—but for the first time I wondered if there was more going on than she'd told me about.

"Get in the house, young lady," he ordered.

"Fine, I'm going," she snapped back. Then she looked over to me. "I meant what I said, Cole."

I gave her a smile. "Me, too."

And then I turned and walked away, hoping beyond hope her dad didn't lay a finger on her.

If he did, I wasn't sure I'd be responsible for my actions.

TWENTYFOUR

GABI—ELEVEN YEARS EARLIER

I woke the next morning with a headache and a niggling certainty something had happened last night. Flipping back in my memories, I remembered going to Cole's band practice, drinking something, and then staggering home. I cringed slightly at my drunken declaration of love, but then also remembered his reply back to me. Despite my hangover, I hugged myself with happiness. When he'd approached me all those weeks ago, when I'd been reading in the park, I never would have imagined Cole and I would have ended up in this position.

So things didn't go badly with Cole last night, even if I may have embarrassed myself slightly, so why did I have this sickening sensation in my stomach—I didn't think it was just down to the effects of last night's alcohol.

A knock came at my door, and my dad walked in holding a glass of water. The sight of him caused a light bulb to ping on in my head, and I barely restrained myself from groaning. Dad had caught me coming home with Cole last night, and had made Cole leave. I was more concerned about what Cole thought of me now, than the fight with my dad.

"Gabriella," he said, as he sat on the edge of my bed. "You and I need to have a talk."

I groaned and rolled over. "Just leave it, Dad. All kids my age have the occasional drink. It's not a big deal. And if it makes you feel any better, I feel like crap this morning, so I won't be drinking for at least another three years, okay?"

"I'm glad to hear it, but that isn't what I wanted to talk to you about."

I sat up and looked at him. "It isn't?"

"No. I've been asking around about that boy you've been hanging out with."

"His name is Cole."

"I want you to stay away from him, Gabriella. I deal with kids like him every day, and they're bad news."

Anger burst through me. "Yeah, you'd know all about bad news, wouldn't you, Dad? Because you're such a fine, upstanding citizen yourself."

"This isn't about me. I'm only doing what's best for you, and I don't want you seeing him again."

"You don't own me! I'll be eighteen in a few months, and then I can do anything I like."

"But you're not eighteen yet, young lady, and while you're under my roof, you go by my rules."

I wanted to say that I'd been following his rules on life just last night, but I managed to keep my mouth shut. I didn't want to fight with him, but there was no way I was going to let him stop me seeing Cole. Even a single day without Cole felt like torture. I couldn't bring myself to imagine longer.

"Listen to me, Dad," I said, trying to stay calm. "If you want to push me away, you're going about it in the exact right way. I'm going to be eighteen in a few weeks, and Cole will be eighteen this month. Don't make me choose between the two of you, because right now I'd choose him."

"He'll hurt you, Gabi. Boys like him always hurt girls like you."

"So be there for me for the fall-out if you want to be a good dad."

He stared at me as though finally seeing me in a new light, and I thought I might have convinced him, but then he shook his head. "What about that band he plays with. They're on our radar, Gabi. They've already been noticed and they're bad news. If I can't get you to agree to stay away from Cole, will you at least stay away from the band?"

I'd enjoyed myself last night, something I'd been surprised about, but not having to spend time with them again didn't sound like a bad thing in my book. Something about them just didn't sit right with me. In particular, Ryan set my teeth on edge. I didn't know exactly what it was about him, but I thought my dad might be right about the band.

"Okay," I agreed. "I'll stay away from band practice."

"And it might be an idea for you to suggest to Cole that he should do the same thing."

I nodded, knowing I'd never suggest such a thing to him. I didn't want him to think I was the type of girl who tried to change a guy once she'd gotten her claws into him.

The truth was, I'd be happy if Cole gave up the band. I didn't like the way they treated him. Sure, they were a couple of years older, but I almost felt like they were laughing at him behind his back. I didn't want to say anything to Cole—not only did I feel like it wasn't my place, but I also didn't want to hurt his feelings. Plus, he really loved playing with the band, even if they weren't particularly good—and I didn't want him to feel awkward about going just because I'd opened my big mouth.

The other thing that bothered me was how they treated me when I was there. I was basically ignored, with the exception of creepy Ryan and the way his eyes traveled up and down my body. I could just tell he was thinking about what I looked like without any clothes on. Perhaps I should say something to Cole, but I didn't want to put him in that position. These guys weren't just his friends, they were his band members, and if he fell out with them, he would no longer have a spot in the band.

My dad reached out for a hug, his arms enveloping me, and I squeezed him back. As he pulled away from me, he noticed something. He picked up Cole's hoodie from my pillow, a number of lines appearing between his brows. He held it up, allowing the material to open out, showing from the size that the sweater was obviously not belonging to a teenage girl.

"I assume this is his?"

Blood heated my face, and I snatched the sweatshirt back. "Yes, Cole loaned it to me."

"Do I need to be worried about how close the two of you are getting—physically, I mean?"

"Nothing's happened between us, Dad," I muttered, mortified. Dad and I didn't have these kinds of conversations. We talked about books, and the sports teams he followed, and what needed to be picked up from the grocery store. We certainly didn't talk about the opposite sex.

He clutched his hands in his lap and glanced down at them. "So, Gabi, I know I've probably left this a little late, but if you are starting to get interested in boys, there's a conversation we should be having."

Dear Lord, please let the ground open up and swallow me ...

"Dad, seriously, you don't need to be doing this."

"I know I haven't been much of a replacement for your mother ..."

"You've been great, Dad," I said, not wanting to fill in the hole of 'apart from the drinking.'

"Anyway," he continued, "There are things you need to know about as you're growing into a young woman."

"Dad!" I practically yelled. "Stop, now, please. You don't need to be having this conversation with me. I learned it all for myself several years ago."

For a moment, his mortification appeared to equal my own, and it dawned on me that he thought I'd learned the practical way.

I raised both hands. "No, Dad, not like that. I mean, it's the modern day. Girls talk." I widened my eyes, hoping to get the point across without having to say any more.

"Oh, right." It was his turn to flush red, and he got back to his feet. "As long as you're … safe … you know."

"I know, but honestly, that hasn't happened." I stopped myself adding, 'yet.'

He flicked imaginary dust off the front of his pants and headed to the door. "Well, I'm glad we had this chat."

"Yeah, me too, Dad," I replied, doing my best not to roll my eyes. He really was completely clueless at times.

He shut the door behind him and I dropped back onto my pillow, my hands covering my face. That was the most embarrassing conversation, *ever*. At least my dad hadn't banned me from seeing Cole, though I did feel like every time he saw us, he would be wondering if we'd slept together yet. Ugh.

I picked up Cole's hoodie and placed it over my face, inhaling the scent of him. What would be the future for Cole and me? Did we even have one? I'd be leaving town to go to college in the not so far future. What would happen to us then?

As well as my potential separation from Cole when I went off to college, I was also worried about how my dad would cope. Even though he kept telling me how he was the grown man, and I was the child, that didn't stop me worrying about him. He was excellent at hiding his drinking around the house, doing his best to keep up appearances on my behalf, but what would happen when I wasn't around anymore? Would he still make an effort to appear normal on the days when he wasn't at work, or would he just give up even trying? I'd told myself that it was ages away, and I didn't need to be concerned about it yet, but the weeks became months, and all of a sudden it felt like leaving was all too soon.

Was leaving for college even what I wanted anymore?

TWENTYFIVE

GABI–ELEVEN YEARS EARLIER

Over the next few weeks, Cole and I became inseparable. We were now officially a couple in the eyes of pretty much everyone, and we'd regularly be seen walking down the school hall, with his arm over my shoulders, and mine around his waist. We'd part for our various classes and then meet back up for breaks or lunch. I couldn't explain it, but being with Cole had somehow elevated my position at school. More people acknowledged my existence now, though I wasn't sure I wanted them to. When I was with him, I felt like I was walking taller, or perhaps it was just that I was walking a foot in the air.

Taylor still wasn't talking to me, and Jasmine appeared to have taken her side about the whole thing, which seemed crazy to me, though Jas still spoke to me when Taylor wasn't around. People on the outside probably thought I was wrong for picking a guy over a friend, but as far as I could tell, I didn't think Taylor was being much of a friend in the first place for getting upset over a misunderstanding. Now I'd gotten to know Cole better, I could see that someone like Taylor would never be for him. He couldn't stand any kind of fakeness—girls who wore too much makeup, or who liked to bitch behind each other's backs. Cole felt bad he'd come between me and Taylor, but I told him things would work themselves out eventually.

My dad had managed to keep things civil between him and Cole. He'd spotted Cole picking me up and dropping me off a couple of times, but so far their interaction had consisted of Cole waving and shouting, 'Hello, Mr. Weston,' and my dad waving back, a tight smile on his lips. I was relieved my dad hadn't attempted to have some kind of 'if you hurt my daughter, I'll kill you' conversation with Cole, though it wouldn't have surprised me if it was somewhere in our near future.

Cole was turning eighteen in a few days, and I still didn't have a gift for him. There was one thing I could think of, but the idea made my stomach roil with both nerves and excitement. Due to my dad's erratic working hours, we got to spend plenty of time alone in the house, and the kissing—which we would happily do for hours on end—had progressed to second base, and quickly on to third. I didn't kid myself for a second that Cole was as innocent as me. I knew of ex-girlfriends, and they weren't exactly of the reserved kind, which filled me with an intense jealousy for his past. He was all I wanted, and I didn't want other girls to have had a part of him that I hadn't, to have done things with him that I hadn't. But that wasn't my only reason.

I wanted him, too.

On the day of Cole's birthday, I had the house to myself. I hadn't told my dad about the importance of the date, and so he'd gone out for the day. If I'd mentioned it was Cole's eighteenth, I was sure he'd have made an excuse to stay home.

Excited and nervous, I'd spent the morning baking Cole a cake, and then I dressed in the sexiest underwear I owned—a black lacy bra which pushed up my breasts, and a tiny thong, that was definitely built for speed rather than comfort. Feeling a bit silly, I wrapped a length of red ribbon around my tummy and tied it into a bow, and then slipped my silky robe over the top. I hoped he wasn't going to laugh at me.

The doorbell rang and I yelled down the stairs, "It's open."

Sudden fear it wasn't him and I was about to be spotted by a delivery driver filled me, but then I heard Cole's voice, "Gabi?"

"Up here," I called back. I heard his feet on the stairs. "I'm in my room."

The bedroom door pushed open and I braced myself. As soon as he appeared in the doorway, I allowed the robe to slip from my shoulders and drift to the floor. Cole's eyes opened in surprise.

"Happy birthday!" I said, trying to appear seductive, rather than stupid and completely out of my comfort zone.

His mouth dropped open and then a smile spread across his face. "Holy shit, Gabi. Is this what I think it is?"

"If you're thinking that my birthday present to you is me, then yes, it's exactly what you think it is."

He bit his lower lip and took a slow step forward.

"Gabi," he said, his blue eyes suddenly appearing a shade darker, "if you're hoping I'm going to ask you if you're sure about this, and then we end up just cuddling on the couch, I've got to tell you you're going about this the wrong damn way."

I repressed a smile and shook my head. "I promise that's not what I'm doing. I'm your present." I gave a shimmy, making the ribbon rustle. "Happy birthday."

He growled. "And you know I'm going to unwrap you like a candy bar?"

I giggled. "That was exactly what I was hoping you'd do."

He took another step closer, so we were only a foot apart now. He reached out and snagged the end of the ribbon bow I'd tied around my stomach and slowly pulled it apart. His breathing had grown deeper and my own breath was shallow in my chest, my heartbeat racing.

He took the other end of the ribbon and tugged it hard between his hands, as though testing its strength. He gave me a wicked look. "I might need that later." Then he frowned slightly. "But I didn't bring anything, you know, protection-wise."

"It's okay. I'm fully prepared." Truth was, I'd asked Jasmine to hook me up. I hadn't been able to bring myself to go into a drugstore and buy condoms.

He dropped the ribbon to the floor and then wrapped his hand around my narrow waist and pulled me hard against him. I could feel he was already excited, a hardness pressing into my stomach. He kissed me, and I melted into the kiss. His hands trailed up my back to the catch of my bra. I didn't know how much experience he'd had undoing them, but this one didn't seem to cause him any problems. Within seconds, it was hanging free and he pushed the straps from my shoulders.

His kisses left my lips, trailed down my jaw and down the side of my neck. "Hell, Gabi, you're so damn sexy."

I'd never felt sexy before I'd met Cole, but now I felt sexy every second I was with him. I wanted to share this with him. I was ready to have this most intimate thing happen between us, to connect our bodies as I felt our hearts were already joined. We weren't kids anymore, and this felt like a completely natural progression.

He paused kissing me to allow me to pull his shirt over his head. He was slim, but wiry with muscle, his chest only with a fine spattering of blond hair. I ran my hands over his skin, aware that now when we kissed, our naked torsos would be pressed together. But he moved me backward, the backs of my thighs bumping with the bed, and then he lowered me down, my back against the mattress. He stood at the end and undid his jeans, toeing off his sneakers and socks, his eyes never leaving me for a second.

He kneeled at the end of the bed and reached for my very skimpy underwear. Hooking the sides with his fingers, he rolled the black lace down my thighs. I was conscious of what he'd think of me naked—would he think I was too hairy, too skinny? Too fat, even. He'd touched me down there before, just as I'd touched him, but we'd never been completely naked before.

I shook the thoughts from my head. He loved me, and I was a girl, naked in bed, offering myself to him. I could probably have two heads and he wouldn't even notice.

Cole crawled back up my body and I got my first eyeful of him, erect and ready for me.

He covered my body with his own, his hand slipping between my thighs. I opened my legs for him, and his fingers pushed inside me, readying me for him, and making me moan.

"The condom," I said, suddenly, reaching up behind me where I'd hidden it beneath my pillow. I pulled out the square packet, feeling awkward once more. Would he expect me to put it on him, to do something sexy with my mouth? I'd heard people talking about that kind of thing, but didn't think I'd be able to do it myself. I'd probably end up ripping the latex with my teeth.

"Here," he said, taking the foil packet from me. "I'll do it."

I almost wilted with relief.

"Touch me while I open it," he said, his voice growly.

I did as he asked, happily wrapping my fingers around his erection. I loved the feel of him, so hard and silky soft all at the same time. I ran my fingers up and down his length, hoping I was holding him tight enough.

"Slowly," he warned. "I won't last long if you keep that up."

His words caused a ball of warmth to swell inside me, loving that what I did to him turned him on so much. He tore the packet open and pulled out the condom. I released my hold on him to allow him to roll the condom onto himself.

He kissed me again, holding himself above me on his elbows, his narrow hips between my thighs. "You sure you're ready?" he said against my mouth, his fingers knotting in my curls.

"I thought you weren't going to ask me that." I smiled against his lips, and kissed him again, lifting my hips to meet his. "Yes, I'm ready."

He kissed me, long and deep, and our hips met. His erection wasn't quite in the right place, pushing against the outside of me, but not entering, but then he reached between us and steadied himself where he needed to be. We both laughed a little, but then he pushed harder and breached me, and the laughter died on my lips.

He was inside me.

This is it, my mind shouted. *It's happening. Your first time.*

And then a sharp pain speared me, and I sucked air in over my teeth, causing Cole to pause. "You okay?" He looked down at me, studying my face with the blue eyes I loved so much, his blond locks falling in his face.

I nodded and dug my fingers into his hard shoulder. "Yes, keep going."

And he did.

It took us a moment to find our rhythm, but as soon as we did, I felt the excitement inside me starting to build. But it was over too soon. Within a couple of minutes, Cole jerked inside me and let out a groan.

He dropped his forehead to mine. "It was too quick, wasn't it?"

I held him close, pressing my lips to his shoulder. "It was perfect."

"I'll make it better next time, I promise" he said. "Just you wait."

I gave a wicked smile. "When's next time?"

He pretended to look at a non-existent watch on his wrist. "Oh, I don't know. In about thirty minutes."

I laughed. "Sounds good to me."

"I love you," he said, kissing me again. "This is the best birthday present ever."

"I love you, too," I replied. "Happy birthday."

And half an hour later, he kept his promise.

TWENTYSIX

COLE—PRESENT DAY

The bright glare of sunlight pressed against my closed eyelids, demanding they open.

I groaned and flung the back of my hand over my eyes. I wasn't sure my eyelids would part if I tried—it felt as though they'd been glued together. My mouth was bone-dry, a disgusting taste lining my throat, tongue, and teeth. My dehydration was so intense, I'd been dreaming about downing long glasses of water. My head throbbed, and I worried if I moved it would explode. I also had the horrible feeling something bad went down last night, but right at that moment I couldn't remember a thing. Was it the fight I'd had with Gabi? She'd told me to stay out of her life, so I'd gone and gotten drunk. That must be what was bothering me, though something else niggled at me.

The sunlight continued to assault me, and I knew I wouldn't be able to remain lying here. I needed water, and my bladder was full to the point of being painful.

I forced my eyes open and cautiously sat up. The room spun and my head pounded, but I didn't think I was going to throw up. I stood and stumbled over to the bathroom to relieve myself. Next port of call was the kitchen for water, and to find some painkillers.

With both in hand, I dropped myself down at the kitchen table and knocked back the tablets with the rest of the water.

I groaned, folded my arms on the table, and dropped my aching head onto their cushion. I needed to go and see Gabi. As soon as I started to feel better, I would march right over there and tell her she wasn't going to get rid of me so easily. Maybe she did still hate me for what I did ten years ago, but that didn't mean we couldn't get past it. I didn't think she'd pushed me away because she no longer had feelings for me. No one held onto that kind of anger for so long if they didn't care about someone. If I wasn't important to her, she'd have forgotten all about me by now, or at best she'd be apathetic. But no, she was heated, and passionate, and still as beautiful and vibrant as the first day I'd plucked up the courage and spoken to her.

I pulled myself together enough to brew some coffee and fry up some bacon for a sandwich. I needed salt and grease to line my stomach. I ate and then took a shower to rid myself of the alcohol fumes from the night before. A couple of cups of strong coffee helped me feel more human.

An hour later, I stepped out of my house, ready to drive over to Gabi's and tell her I wasn't going to give up. With a frown, I paused and looked around. Where the hell was my car?

Damn, I must have left it outside the bar. I figured it was a good thing I'd had the sense to walk considering I couldn't even remember getting home. It didn't matter. A walk back to the bar to pick up my car would help to clear my head and figure out exactly what I would say to Gabi.

This time, I wasn't going to take no for an answer.

TWENTYSEVEN

GABI—PRESENT DAY

I woke the next morning emotionally exhausted.

I'd cried myself to sleep, and then sprung awake after a couple of hours and cried again. I knew I shouldn't feel like this—after all, I was the one who told Cole to leave—but I couldn't help what my heart felt.

A knock came at my door, and my dad pushed it open, carrying a cup of hot coffee. "Hey, sweetheart. I thought you could use this."

I forced a smile. "Thanks, Dad."

With my puffy eyes, and swollen face, not to mention insane bed hair, I was a total mess, but my dad only looked at me with sympathy. I took a sip of the coffee and smiled. He'd remembered for once that I no longer took sugar.

"So," he said. "Who do I need to go and kill for making my baby-girl cry like this? I can't help but think this has less to do with your leg and more to do with the young man who was here the other night."

So he did remember Cole being here when he'd gotten stuck.

I nodded. "The problem is, Dad, the two things are joined together."

"How's that?"

I hated saying my worst fears and feelings out loud, but my dad had always been good at getting me to talk, even when sometimes it ended up with bad results.

"How can I ask him to take on this?" I gestured to my missing limb. "He doesn't need to have a woman like me in his life."

"No? Seems to me that young man could do with someone exactly like you in his life." He lifted up both hands in a stop sign. "I'm not going to say I approve, Gabi, but I figure I'm hardly able to take the moral high ground. I know things didn't go the way you wanted with the two of you ten years ago, but you've both paid for it, and here you are, drawn back together again. Sometimes the universe has a way of making things happen, even when it feels like the worst thing in the world at the time."

I stared into my coffee. "I'm afraid of getting hurt again."

"Oh, sweetheart. We're all afraid of getting hurt. Are you really going to allow fear to be the thing that controls your life?"

Tears filled my eyes again and I pressed my lips together to hold back a sob. I wanted to thank my father for his advice, and tell him I loved him, despite everything, but a painful lump blocked my throat, and all I could do was blink and nod.

He patted my knee. "Listen, I have to pop out for a while, but I'll run you a hot bath. You can manage okay?"

"Yes, Dad, I can manage." I was practically an expert at sitting on the edge of the tub and removing my prosthesis, and then slipping over the side and into the water. Getting out again was more of an effort, but my upper body was stronger now than it had ever been, and I was able to haul myself back out again without too much of a struggle. "Where are you going?" I added.

He smiled. "Just seeing a man about a dog," and then he reached out and ruffled my hair as though I was ten again.

The moment where I'd felt like I had my old father back again vanished and my stomach sank with disappointment. He was going out to get a drink.

He left the room, and within a couple of minutes, I heard the thunder of water hitting the bathtub. I sighed and maneuvered myself to the side of the bed to put on my prosthesis, knowing I'd only have to take it off again when I crossed the hall to the bathroom. At some point I'd find the money to have the bathroom converted into a wet room, so I wouldn't have the hassle of baths, but until then I would have to make do.

I reached for my prosthetic leg and remembered I no longer had to go through the nightmare of putting the old leg on with the rubber sleeve. No, I had the new pin-lock leg, which was quick and easy to attach and detach again.

I smiled for the first time that morning.

I was out of the bath, dressed, and attempting to drag a comb through my corkscrew curls when the doorbell rang.

I made it downstairs and opened the door to find Cole standing on my porch. He appeared even rougher around the edges than normal, dark shadows beneath his eyes, his cheekbones hollowed. He looked rough, but more than that, something about him appeared vulnerable, and I didn't think I'd ever seen Cole Devonport vulnerable before.

"Gabi," he said, one hand out held. "Hear me out, please."

My father's words echoed in my head. He'd told me I shouldn't be ruled by fear. He was right. I wasn't a coward; I never had been.

I stepped back and nodded. "I guess you'd better come in, then."

He stepped into the entrance hall with me and glanced around. "Is your dad at home?"

"No, he's gone out, and I doubt he'll be back any time soon. So what did you come here to say?" Just being in Cole's presence sent my heart racing, and made me aware of my body in a way no one else did. My skin tingled when I was around him, and I felt like we were two magnets drawn together.

"I came to say that I'm not giving up."

"On what?"

"On us. Kissing you yesterday felt so right, and I won't just walk away. I love you, Gabi. I've loved you since I was seventeen years old. There's never been anyone else for me, and there never will be. You may hate me, and still resent me for when we were teenagers, but as far as I can tell, that simply means you still care. And that's worth fighting for."

I stared at him. I wanted to give in and fall into his arms, but despite not wanting to be afraid, I was. I was terrified, and the sad thing was most of my anxiety came from my fear about how he would react when he saw my stump for the first time. Assuming our relationship went the same way most adult couples' did, he would see me naked again, and my body wasn't the same one he knew so well when we were younger.

"What happened between us when we were teenagers isn't the only thing holding me back," I admitted. "I'm worried about how you're going to react when you see what's left of my leg."

He reached out and took my hand. "I don't care about your leg, Gabi. I'm not going to pretend that I didn't love your body—and I still love your body now—but it's *you* I'm in love with. You're the person I want to be with, not your leg."

I wanted to believe him, my heart longed for it, but the thought of showing him the result of the bomb explosion sent my stomach tumbling with nerves. I would be opening myself up to him completely, and being open meant exposing myself to being hurt again.

I wanted him to understand exactly how I felt.

"You broke me back then, Cole," I started, "shattered me into a million tiny pieces, and for a while I didn't think I would be able to come out of it, didn't think I'd be able to see a future. But you know what? I fixed myself. I didn't need any man rushing to my side to be a god-damned hero. I went out and became the hero myself. And if this had been a movie or something, I'd have gotten my happy ever after, just being strong for me, but instead God, or fate, or whatever other fucker likes to screw us over, decided I hadn't dealt with enough in my life yet, so then this happened," I gestured to my prosthetic leg, "and here I am having to fix myself all over again."

"But you don't have to do it alone this time. I'm here, and I'm not going anywhere."

I shook my head and pulled my hand from his. "And what happens if I let myself lean on you, and then one day you decide you're not going to be there anymore?" He opened his mouth to speak but I lifted my hand to stop him. "I'll tell you what happens—I fall down again, and one day I'm not going to be strong enough to pick myself back up."

"I'm not going anywhere, Gabi. Let me prove that to you."

I searched his blue eyes. "How? How can you prove it to me?"

He didn't say anything else. Instead, he stepped in toward me, closing the gap between us, and then his hands cupped my cheeks, his fingers slipping through my hair, and he kissed me. His lips were soft but firm, gentle but insistent. I melted into him, forgetting all of my worries, focused only on the sensation of his mouth capturing mine. It *did* feel right. In fact, kissing Cole felt perfect, just as it always had when we were teens. We'd been able to kiss for hours back then, and I felt like I could stand here and kiss him for hours again now.

His hands moved from my hair, slipping down my back to clutch my bottom and drag me against him so our bodies met. I could feel the beginnings of his erection pressing into my stomach, and the nerves I'd been experiencing joined with the first flutterings of excitement and arousal. I hadn't allowed sex to be part of my life for some time, had wondered at times if it would ever happen for me again, or if I would die a dried up old maid, but it seemed my body had other ideas.

His kiss transported me back to being seventeen again, and I forgot all of the pain and trauma of the last ten years. All that was important was how I felt in his arms—young, desired, and whole again. I didn't ever want to feel any different.

His kiss grew urgent, his hands skimming the curves of my body. My breath grew shallow, and he laced his fingers in the back of my hair, tugging back to expose my throat. His lips left my mouth and feathered across my jaw and down the outside of my neck. I shivered in his arms, a sudden slave to desire. I wanted Cole, and I knew he wanted me, too, despite everything.

"Upstairs," I managed to gasp, aware my dad might come home.

He caught me up around the back of my thighs and lifted me so I straddled his hips. He was strong, his muscles bunching beneath his shirt, and lifting me in such a way he made me feel light and feminine and sexy. He carried me up the stairs with little effort and kicked open my bedroom door. Cole transported me to the bed and laid me down, before climbing on top of me, his knees either side of my hips so his big body hovered over mine.

He stared down at me. "God, you're so beautiful."

I smiled, and his lips made contact with mine again, kissing away my expression. My hands reached for the bottom of his t-shirt, suddenly desperate to feel his skin against mine, to feast my eyes upon the man Cole had grown up to become. He helped me, breaking the kiss to sit up slightly and tug the t-shirt over his head.

Cole sat above me. I reached up and traced my fingers across his chest, the lines and swirls of tattoos, my palms skimming the hard bulk of his biceps, shoulders, pectorals, and abs. I wanted to learn what each and every tattoo on his body meant to him, his reasons behind them all.

He was the same boy I'd known all those years ago, and yet he wasn't. He still had the small mole he was born with on his collarbone, still had the scar on his hip where he'd fallen off his skateboard when he was twelve. His hands were still the same, his fingers long and strong, the nails square. His eyes and features hadn't changed. But that was where the similarities ended. The dark blond hair which had once been barely a spattering across his chest was now thicker, and ran in a line down to his navel, and then farther down again, disappearing beneath the waistband of his jeans. But mostly it was the muscles and tattoos that marked the difference. How he'd bulked out to a man.

"Cole," I breathed, as he leaned down to kiss me again, and then he began to pull my t-shirt up my body and over my head. I had scars from the bombing, twisted, raised lines across my stomach and hips, and after he ran his fingers over those lines, he dipped his head and kissed them. Then his fingers were at the button of my pants, yanking them undone, and I knew the time had come when I would have to show him.

This wasn't going to be a surprise to him. It wasn't as though he didn't know what he was getting himself into. But even so, I couldn't help the churning in my stomach, worrying what his reaction was going to be.

I had to do this.

"I need to show you."

He understood exactly what I meant, and gave me a final kiss before moving himself to one side of the bed, allowing me some space. With my stomach in my throat, I rolled up the leg of my jeans, exposing the prosthesis. I undid the pin holding the prosthetic leg to my limb, and removed the sleeve and the extra socks I had over the stump to make the prosthetic more comfortable. Then I completed the job he'd started of removing my jeans. Sitting only in my underwear, I was exposed, and it felt like the first time he'd seen me naked. Of course, it wasn't. Cole had seen me naked more times than I could count, but I'd been a slip of a girl then, and, like him, I'd filled out. Oh, and now I was missing a leg.

"It's okay, Gabi," he said with an encouraging smile. "It's not as big a deal as you're telling yourself. Not for me, anyway."

I wanted to believe him. I *had* to believe him. I sat, rigid in bed, not wanting to look at him. Sudden tears filled my eyes, and instantly he pulled me into his arms again, kissing my tears away.

"Don't be sad. Don't be ashamed," he said between kisses.

"I'm sorry."

"You're still you, Gabi. Still as beautiful as the day I met you."

He kissed me again, lowering me back on the bed, so we lay side by side.

His hands ran over my body, caressing my breasts and dragging a moan from my throat, my nipples crinkling into tight buds at his touch. His hands slipped lower, skirting over the front of my lacy underwear, and then onto my thighs. I realized where he was heading, and reached down to place a hand over his.

"Cole ..."

"I want to get to know you, every part of you, and this is a part of you now."

I released his hand and he moved lower, getting to know the new landscape of my body.

He lowered his head and kissed my stump, and I held back a sob.

"You know," he said, one corner of his lips tweaking, "I think I love this part of you even more than the rest."

I blinked. "Why? It's ugly."

"No. You have this because you lived. You sacrificed your leg, but that meant you were able to come to home, to me. If this hadn't happened, maybe we'd never have found our way back together again."

Could I let myself believe that? Everything happened for a reason. But no, the soldier I'd been with that day hadn't died for a reason. Life was cruel and heartless, but sometimes we needed to focus on the good parts, however hard they were to find among the rubble.

Cole's attention left my legs and moved back up my body. He looked at me with a hunger in his eyes. "Now, where were we?"

Feeling braver, I took his hand and placed it over the front of my panties. "I think about here."

He grinned, the desire in his eyes deepening. "Sounds good to me."

We wriggled down the bed together, to lie side my side. I reached for the front of his jeans, and was pleased to discover the sight of my limb had done nothing to make him lose his erection. The length and shape of his cock pressed tight against the denim, and I stroked him firmly. His hand slipped inside my underwear, fingertips raking through the patch of tight curls to find the fleshy bud, making me gasp. Then his fingers parted my lips, found me already wet for him. He pushed one finger inside me, and then a second, and finally a third so I felt like I was impaled on his hand. My back arched and I pressed down on him, feeling so impossibly full. With frantic need, I tugged at the button of his fly and then unzipped him. His erection met my hand, so long and hard, his skin silky soft and hot beneath my palm. The scent of male musk filled my nostrils, so achingly familiar, and once again my mind blurred, taking me back to when we'd been young and discovering each other for the first time.

Cole shucked the jeans from his hips, toeing off his boots and socks, and kicking the whole bundle off the bed. He was commando, and gloriously naked. I wanted to feast on him, to lick and taste and nibble every inch of his skin.

His erection, so long and hard, drew me. I wriggled down the bed, dislodging his hand from my underwear. I took him in my mouth, inhaling the scent of him. I slid my lips up and down his length, reached out to take his balls in my hand and gently squeezed. The smooth bell of his cock head hit the back of my throat and I swirled my tongue around him as I bobbed back and forth. His breathing grew ragged, his hand knotted in my hair.

"Gabi ..." he gasped. "Not yet. I want to be inside you."

I craved to taste his cum again, wanted more than just the salty pre-cum which coated my throat now. I was greedy for him. But I also wanted to give him what he desired.

I realized I hadn't been prepared. "I ... I don't have anything ..."

"Ah, shit."

Then I remember my wash bag. I was sure I still had a couple of old condoms in there. I just hoped they were still in date. I instructed Cole, and he jumped off the bed, completely naked, to grab the wash bag. I admired his ass as he walked, the strong, lean lines of his thighs. He truly was a beautiful sight, and my heart skipped.

He was mine.

He found the bag and checked inside and then pulled out a couple of condoms.

"Check the date," I hissed, realizing the fact they were ancient showed how bad my love life had been over the past few years. Cole checked and grinned. "We're good."

Standing at the end of the bed, he took his cock in his hand and masturbated himself slowly. It was an erotic sight, this big, tattooed man with his erection pumping in his fist. He tore open the condom packet with his teeth, and, with my eyes glued to him, he rolled it down the length of his dick.

Oh. My. God.

Hurriedly, I rid myself of my panties, rolling them down my thighs and flicking them to the floor.

Cole crawled back over me, pulling the cups of my bra from my breasts and drawing my nipple into his mouth. I wrapped my thighs around his hips, lifting my bottom, wanting him to impale me. I clutched at his back, trying to pull him down, but he was teasing me.

"Not so fast, Gabs."

He took hold of my arms and pressed them over my head, pinning my hands onto the pillow. Holding both my wrists in one of his hands, he reached between our bodies with his other hand and positioned himself at my entrance. A lift of my hips this time brought us together, and Cole thrust downward, penetrating me with one smooth, firm stroke.

I cried out, my back arching. I wanted to touch him, to claw my nails down his back, but he held me writhing and gasping beneath him as he thrust into me again and again.

Our movements grew faster, almost angry. I cried out his name as I exploded around him, my eyes squeezed shut, every muscle tensing as pleasure rippled through my body in waves, again and again.

Seconds later, Cole thrust hard and held himself deep, and then pulled out and thrust again. He lowered his face to my throat, his body shuddering, and finally released my hands so I could wrap my arms around him and hold him tight.

"You have no idea how much I missed that," he said and kissed me again.

I nuzzled my nose and mouth against his hair and skin. It felt so good to be able to immerse myself in the scent and taste of him again. I remembered how I'd always slept with his sweatshirt.

I do know, I thought, *I know exactly how much.*

TWENTYEIGHT

COLE—ELEVEN YEARS EARLIER

I knew something was wrong as soon as I approached the garage where we met for band practice. No sound was coming from inside the walls, and normally, if the guys weren't jamming already, there would at least be music blaring from the stereo.

I hadn't wanted to go to band practice without Gabi, but she had an algebra test the next day to study for, so was spending time holed up in her room. I'd offered to hang out in her bedroom and quiz her, but she'd told me I should go and spend some time with the guys. I knew I shouldn't be disappointed, but I felt like I was addicted to her in a way, wanting only to spend time in her presence. If she wasn't with me, it felt like a piece of me was missing, yearning to get back to her. My body needed to be in some kind of contact with hers at all times, and I'd have kissed her all day if she'd let me. But I loved practice as well, and I couldn't let the guys down. The band had meant everything to me before Gabi had entered my life, and I was aware that I was letting it take second place.

Besides, I knew what Ryan would say if I said I didn't want to go because Gabi wouldn't be there. The usual kind of taunts would emerge—pussy-whipped, under the thumb, blah, blah, blah. Mike and Adam would join in and I'd be leaving with my tail between my legs. I didn't want them to think that of me. I had a reputation I needed to uphold, and acting like a pussy was never going to keep me safe. If you showed any weakness in my world, it was guaranteed you'd end up with your ass handed to you.

I swung the garage door open to find Ryan, Mike, and Adam all standing in a circle, their heads together as they discussed something that appeared important. They stopped talking as I walked in and looked my way.

"What's up?" I asked, frowning.

"Hey, Cole," said Ryan. "We were just talking about you."

Uh-oh.

I tried to appear nonplussed. "You were?"

"Yeah, no biggy. We were just wondering if we could make use of your truck again."

"My foster family's truck," I corrected.

He waved a hand, as though to dismiss my concerns. "Whatever. We need to move something, and right now you're the only one who has access to a vehicle."

I looked between them. "None of you do?"

Ryan shook his head. "Nah, my car's still in the shop, and Mike's just lost his license for a DUI." Mike gave an apologetic shrug. "And Adam is a pussy who never learned to drive."

"Hey, dude!" protested Adam, punching Ryan on the arm.

Ryan just laughed.

"So anyway, you're the only one who has access to wheels and we need your help. There will be some cash in it for you."

That piqued my interest. "How much are we talking?"

"Five hundred bucks."

My eyebrows shot up. "Five hundred? How far are we moving the equipment?"

"That's the thing, it's not equipment exactly."

"It's not?" A sense of unease settled in my gut.

"No. We've got some guys who are after a decent amount of weed. We can get our hands on it, but now we don't have any transport, we've got no way of getting it to them. Then your name sprang to mind, so we figured we'd ask you first."

My lips twisted. "I don't know, Ryan. That's not really my thing."

"It's no big deal. Just a bit of weed. You drive for an hour, meet my guy, hand it over, and you get five hundred dollars in return."

Most people smoked grass these days, and even though I didn't myself that often, I didn't have any issues with anyone who did. Weed was practically legal anyway. I had to admit, the thought of five hundred dollars was tempting. I was only too aware of the fact I would be making my own way in the world in the scarily near future. Five hundred dollars would be enough to get me started. I'd be able to rent a room in town, and feed myself while I found other work. A couple of hours driving for that amount of money sounded like a good deal.

But I wasn't a total idiot. To get that money, I was essentially drug running, even if it was only a bit of weed.

"I don't know, Ryan. When do you need it moved by, and can I think about it?"

"We need it done in the next couple of days, so there's not much thinking time."

"I'd have to make sure I can borrow the truck, so I can't give you a definite yes or no right now."

"You can ask your fake dad tonight, though, can't you?" he pressed.

"Yeah, I guess ... "

Ryan huffed air out through his nose. "If you don't want the job, just say so, Cole. There are plenty of other people I know who would gladly do it, and I thought you would be in need of the money, especially now you've got that little lady around to impress."

My shoulders stiffened at the mention of Gabi. "What do you mean?"

"Well, not being funny or anything, Cole, but she's a little hottie. At some point, she's going to realize she can do better than a kid like you. I know her type. They tend to date older guys—guys who have their own places, their own rides, and money to treat her right." He laughed and grabbed his crotch. "Plus us older guys can show a girl what it's like to fuck a man."

The other two laughed and punched each other.

I wanted to lay out all three of them, starting with Ryan, for talking about Gabi like that, but I knew I'd come out worse off. Plus, they had a point. I always wondered what Gabi saw in a loser-guy like me, who had no prospects, and whose own family hadn't even wanted around. We always went to her house, as I didn't want to invite her around to mine, and her dad didn't exactly think much of me. With that money, I could start looking around at getting my own place.

"I'll need to check I can borrow the truck," I said, holding back my fury at Ryan's comments about Gabi. "I'll let you know if I can move the gear tomorrow."

"Nice one," Ryan said, punching me in the arm. "I knew we could count on you."

I was able to borrow the truck without any problem, and so I told Ryan I would do the job for him. The whole time, I felt sick with nerves, but Ryan told me it would be easy. Just hand the bag over to the guy I was meeting on the other end, take the money from him, and get the hell back to Dodge.

Norburn, the town I headed to, was located a little over an hour away. By the time I got there, the guy was already waiting—a greasy looking guy who reminded me of Ryan. Not much was said. He took the bag, checking the contents—not that he could see much as it was all wrapped in brown tape; I'd already checked—and then handed me an envelope of cash.

I drove back to Willowbrook Falls, handed the money over to Ryan, who then gave me my cut.

It was quick and easy money, but it had left me edgy and nervous. For a couple of days afterward, I jumped at my own shadow and started snapping at Gabi. Though she asked me what was wrong, I could never tell her. Instead, I hid the money behind one of the wall panels in my bedroom and told myself I'd done it for the right reason. I had a matter of weeks, and I would be out of this house with nowhere to live. I'd had no choice but to do what Ryan had wanted.

Hadn't I?

TWENTYNINE

COLE—PRESENT DAY

As much as I didn't want to leave Gabi for a second, I had a shift at work which I couldn't afford to miss. My hangover was long gone, cured in Gabi's arms. A smile felt like it was permanently fixed to my face, and I held her tight, never wanting to let go.

We'd dozed together, talked, and kissed, and then made love again, slow and sensual. When I finally told her I needed to go to work, she groaned and buried her face against my neck.

"No, don't go."

I laughed and kissed her. "Believe me, I'd much rather be here with you than scrubbing out pots at Frankie's grill. But I could do without getting fired right now."

"Well, since you put it like that, I'd better let you go. Will you come back after your shift?"

"It'll be late—early hours of the morning."

She shrugged. "I'll leave a key out for you. I'll hide it under the mat, and you can let yourself in."

"Are you sure? Won't your dad mind?"

"We're not seventeen anymore, Cole," she said, smiling at me. Her crazy hair was tousled around her face, and her lips were slightly swollen from all the kissing we'd been doing. I felt myself growing hard for her, but I couldn't fuck her again. I literally didn't have time.

"Okay, I'll come back when I've finished my shift." It wasn't exactly a difficult choice. Come home to Gabi in bed, or go back to my rundown rental to spend the night on my own. "But I should probably warn you that I'll stink of grease and trash by the time I get back."

She laughed. "I love grease and trash."

"You're weird, you know that, right?"

She hit me with a pillow. "Yeah, and you wouldn't have me any other way."

I loved how we'd fallen into the comfortable banter we always used to share. It was so easy, being with her again. I felt as though the last ten years had never existed. I could finally put all that time I'd spent in jail behind me and think about the future.

I leaned in and kissed her again. "I love you, Gabi," I told her.

She smiled "I love you, too, Cole."

My heart sang with happiness.

Not wanting to leave, I forced myself to dress, and drove home quickly to shower and change. I made my shift by a matter of minutes, receiving a glare from the manager as I slipped in and got to work. Nothing was going to spoil my mood that evening. I caught myself singing while I washed dishes.

Deano overheard and nudged Ben. "I'm going to bet Cole got laid last night."

I just grinned. Though I would have loved to let them know it had actually been a couple of times this afternoon, I wasn't going to screw and tell. As Gabi had pointed out, we weren't teenagers anymore.

The hours dragged by, and I did my best to keep my mind off Gabi and focus on my job. It wasn't easy, though, when all I wanted to do was remember every time my mouth touched her skin, and the feel of her fingers wrapped around me. On several occasions I found myself needing to spend longer standing at the sink while I forced myself to think of something else. I didn't want to embarrass both myself and my colleagues.

Finally, the last of the customers finished their meals, and I was able to slip away, back to Gabi's. Sure enough, she'd left her key under the mat, and I let myself in, listening out for her father, and wondering what he'd say if he saw me. I didn't hear or see any sign of him, something I was thankful for. I'd never felt more like an eighteen-year-old again as I did sneaking up the stairs and tiptoeing into Gabi's room. She lay in a bundle beneath her covers, her breathing soft and regular.

I shrugged off my clothes and climbed into bed beside her. She smiled in her sleep and rolled toward me. I slid my hands down the long line of her back to discover she was completely naked, and immediately my cock sprang to attention. I'd nipped into the men's bathroom during my break and bought some new condoms to replace the old ones Gabi had made me dig out. I didn't want to think about her reason for having condoms. I'd had enforced celibacy when I'd been behind bars, but I couldn't have expected her to stay away from men. I couldn't help the little surge of jealousy that rose within me at the idea of another man's hands being on her, but I pushed it away. I would fuck the memory of any other man away from her.

Her skin smelled clean and of coconut body-wash, as though she'd spent the evening relaxing in a hot bubble-bath. She was warm beneath the covers, and I wanted to drown in her body heat. Ducking beneath the duvet, I kissed down her stomach, and then spread her legs, the covers over my head. I heard her murmur, "Oh, Cole," as she realized what I was doing. I buried my nose in the small patch of curls at the apex of her thighs and then placed my mouth over her pussy. With my tongue, I drew a line down the crease of her slit, licking her open. Gabi moaned and wriggled in the bed, parting her thighs further and opening the sweet petals of her pussy to me. She tasted sweeter than any sort of candy that could be bought, and I drove my tongue deep inside her, feeling her inner muscles try to clamp around me and pull me deeper. Her breathing became ragged, her moans louder as she squirmed beneath my administrations. Sensing she wanted more, I replaced my tongue with my fingers, and concentrated my mouth on her clit, first licking her with long, strong strokes, and then flicking the little bundle of nerves faster.

"Oh, God, Cole," she gasped.

I loved hearing my name from her lips once more.

She tugged on my shoulders. "I want you. Now!"

I wasn't going to disobey her demand. I kissed my way up her stomach, lingered for a moment on her breasts, licking and sucking each nipple in turn, and then kissed her mouth. She'd be able to taste herself on my tongue, and the thought made me harder than I'd ever thought possible.

Quickly, I sheathed myself in one of the new condoms I'd brought, and then pressed open her thighs and sank my cock into her tight, wet heat. I didn't think anything else in the world would ever feel better than being inside Gabi. She was my everything—the girl I had loved since I was seventeen years old, and the girl I planned on loving until the day I left this world. Being with her like this wasn't just about seeking pleasure, it was about joining myself to her, about giving her a part of my soul and praying she would cherish that part of me as much as I worshipped her.

We moved as one, slowly at first, but gradually building until we clung to one another, sweating and panting, both climbing toward that final release. When we found it, I kissed her hard, swallowing her cries, inhaling a part of her as I gave her a part of me.

We fell asleep with whispered declarations of love on both our lips, holding each other so tightly it was as though we both feared someone would steal the other person away.

Over the next week, we fell into an easy routine, with me only using my rented house to shower and change when I needed. Whenever I finished work late, I used the key Gabi had hidden to let myself into the house. Her father had gotten used to seeing me at the breakfast table, and when Gabi had asked him if he minded, he simply said that if having me around made her happy, then he was happy, too. Like Gabi, I turned a blind eye to his drinking. He was a grown man, and unless Gabi said she wanted something to change, it wasn't my place to force things. We all had our demons. Some just had a tighter hold on us than others.

I left work after my evening shift, planning to head back to Gabi's as usual, to find someone waiting for me outside.

He stood, leaning against the outside wall of the diner, his arms folded across his chest. "Hey, Cole. Good to see you again."

I scowled. "What are you doing here, Ryan?"

He pushed himself away from the wall to stand up straight. "Catching up with an old friend."

"Bullshit."

I hadn't seen him since that evening at the diner, and so I'd assumed he'd just been passing through and I'd been in the wrong place at the wrong time. Now, however, it was clear he had come here to see me.

Ryan shrugged. "Okay, maybe you've got me on that one. I actually need your help with something."

"I'm not going to help you with a single thing."

He ignored me. "I need another man on a job. I've been let down at the last minute, and it'll all fall apart if we don't have someone else."

"I'm not your guy, Ryan. Now get lost." I turned away from him, intending on crossing the parking lot to head to my car, but Ryan continued to speak, calling over to me.

"I noticed you and sweet Gabi have been spending a lot of time together again."

I froze, and slowly turned to him, fury rising up inside me. "You stay the hell away from her."

He gave a nonchalant shrug. "Sure, if you come and help on this job. There will be a decent paycheck in it for you."

"I don't want any money from you—in case you've forgotten, that didn't turn out so well for me in the end—and if you go anywhere near Gabi, I'll fucking kill you."

Ryan's stance changed, his shoulders rounding, his upper lip lifting in a sneer. "You owe me, Cole. Don't screw with me."

My eyebrows shot up my forehead in disbelief. "*I* owe *you*?

"You messed up that run ten years ago, and now it's payback time. If you don't do what I ask, I'll make sure your pretty girlfriend suffers the repercussions."

Red descended on my vision, my blood pounding in my temples.

Without thinking of the consequences, I stormed up to him and swung my fist. My knuckles connected with his jaw and sent him stumbling. I didn't stop there. I strode over to him, and dealt a kick to his side, so he rolled to the ground.

"I'm not some teenage kid you can push around anymore, Ryan. I dealt with a hell of a lot meaner sons-of-bitches than you when I was inside. You don't scare me, you don't intimidate me, and if you so much as breathe in Gabi's direction, I will cut your fucking balls off and make you swallow them. Do you understand?"

His face was white, nostrils flaring. "You're making a big fucking mistake, Cole. I was doing you a favor, offering you a way to make some decent money instead of working in that dump, and this is how you repay me."

"Mistake? You're the one who made a mistake coming anywhere near me. Because of you I spent ten years behind bars. I should have tracked you down and fucking killed you by now."

"Don't act like such a fucking victim. You knew exactly what you were doing."

"I had no idea! I'd just turned eighteen, remember? I wasn't exactly a drug lord."

He crawled back on his hands and choked laughter. "No, you were a stupid kid who thought too much of himself."

I couldn't help myself. I pulled back my boot and kicked him again. He gave an *ouff* of breath exploding from his lungs, and he coughed and curled in on himself.

"Oh, you've made a big fucking mistake, Cole" he gasped. "You have no idea who I am."

"I know exactly who you are. You're the guy who should have been behind bars for the last ten years."

Resisting the urge to spit on him, I turned and walked away.

THIRTY

COLE—ELEVEN YEARS EARLIER

"Hey, Cole," Ryan shouted to me from across the street. "Got a sec?"

I'd been avoiding both the guys and band practice. It wasn't just about the run I'd done for them down to Norburn a couple of week ago. The things Ryan had said about Gabi had been running around in my head, fueling my anger. Gabi had been asking why I hadn't been going to practice recently, and I'd made the excuse that I wanted to spend more time with her. Truth was, I didn't want to spend time with Ryan. I worried I'd lose my temper if he so much as mentioned her name again, and after the fights I'd gotten into with my foster brother, I couldn't afford to get into any more trouble with my foster parents. I had another few weeks, and then we would graduate and life would start anew. I had a decent sum of money hidden in my room, and I was looking forward to being independent. I didn't need problems just because Ryan didn't know how to keep his mouth shut.

I shoved my hands in my jeans pockets and kept my head down, my hair falling over my face.

"Hey, Cole," he shouted again. "Don't pretend like you can't hear me."

I huffed out a sigh and stopped walking. "What is it, Ryan?"

"I'm not going to shout across the street. Just come over here for a minute."

I was tempted to make him come to me, but I didn't want to get into a yelling match in the middle of town. The sooner I found out what he wanted and then told him to get lost, the sooner I would be away from him.

Checking the street both ways, I ran across the road.

"What do you want?" I asked.

He moved closer and lowered his voice. "Me and the guys have got another run for you to do."

My stomach sank. "Nah, I don't think so."

"It's the same money. Same setup. What have you got to lose?"

I cocked my eyebrow. "My freedom."

He laughed. "You're such a girl. Don't be so dramatic. It's just a bit of weed. Nothing to get your panties in a twist about."

"So you take it, then."

"I can't. My car couldn't be fixed, and I don't have any money to get a new one yet. Another run or two, and I should be sorted, though."

I shook my head. "Sorry, Ryan. You're going to have to find someone else for this one."

His eyes narrowed, his head tilting to one side as though listening hard for something. "I don't think you've quite understood what I'm saying. We need someone to do another run, and that person is going to be you."

I folded my arms across my chest. "And I don't think you understood what I said. I'm not doing it."

"You don't want to go saying things like that, Cole. I'd take it kind of personally, and when I take things personally, I like to hurt things that are personal to you."

I stiffened. "What exactly are you saying?"

He sucked and licked his lower lip. "That girlfriend of yours is mighty sweet. Get a couple of drinks in her, and she's practically humping the leg of the nearest guy."

"Gabi's not like that!"

"No? I've seen her all flirty when she's around us older guys. Don't pretend you haven't, too."

I suddenly regretted guilting Gabi into coming to my band practices. It had gotten her in trouble with her dad, and now Ryan had set his sights on her. She hadn't wanted to come in the first place, but I'd wanted to show off my gorgeous girlfriend. What an idiot I was.

"I get the impression your girl has a bit of a reputation to uphold as well. I don't know what she was thinking hanging out with the likes of you, but I can tell she definitely cares what people think of her." He nodded slowly, as though considering his words. "I imagine if word started getting around that she let me and the other guys gangbang her, how we'd all taken our turn and loved every second, it wouldn't exactly be good news for her reputation."

I balled my fists, a muscle in my jaw twitching. "You wouldn't fucking dare!"

"Just watch me, kid. And I'll tell you something else, if you don't play ball, or you cause some kind of trouble for me and the guys, I'll make sure that little scene happens for real."

The idea of all my band members raping Gabi was like a punch in the gut.

"You fucking bastard!" I swung my fist, but he side-stepped it, sending me reeling out into the street.

"Don't cause a scene, Cole. You need to learn to keep your head down."

It took every ounce of self-control I had not to throw myself, roaring, at him. Only the idea that he could tear Gabi down with just a few words stopped me from doing so. If rumors like that started going around about her, she would be utterly heartbroken. Devastated. Rumors had the power to destroy a person—especially someone as sweet and innocent as Gabi. I couldn't let it happen and I would do everything within my power to make sure Ryan kept his mouth shut.

I'd always known I would be bad for her, that I should have kept my distance, but yet I hadn't been able to help myself. I'd been drawn to her, and fallen head over heels so hard in love with her I hadn't been able to control it. She deserved better. She had an amazing future ahead of her, and being with me only put that in jeopardy.

"I guess I don't have any choice, do I?" I managed to growl.

Ryan smiled. "Now we're starting to see eye-to-eye."

"When is the run?"

"A couple of nights from now."

"Fine, I'll do it."

I knew this wouldn't stop. Even if I did this run, Ryan would still be here, threatening Gabi and making me do another and another to keep her safe. If I wasn't around, Ryan would haven't any reason to threaten her.

My staying in Willowbrook Falls wasn't good for Gabi's safety.

THIRTYONE

GABI—ELEVEN YEARS EARLIER

I started the walk home from school alone.

Cole had chores he needed to do for his foster-dad right after school, but he said it wouldn't take long and he'd meet me at my place. I worried about him. He seemed distant lately, but I didn't know why. The idea that he might be starting to go off me had been working its way into my soul, and I couldn't seem to stop thinking about it.

Lost in thought, I didn't look up in time to avoid someone stepping out in front of me. I gave a strange squeak of shock, and the next thing I knew, strong hands grabbed my shoulders, yanking me to one side. The hands shoved me down a side alley, away from the main road. My head spun, adrenaline spurting through my veins. A man was standing directly in front of me, and though I tried to dart away, he pushed me back again.

"Now, now, little girl. You stay right where you are."

I know that voice, I thought with alarm. I suddenly realized who had attacked me.

"Ryan, what the hell?"

He gave me a sly smile. "Hello, Gabi. You and I need to have a chat."

"No, we don't. My dad is expecting me home."

I tried to move again, but Ryan pushed me up against the wall and then put his hands against the brick on either side of my head, boxing me in. I felt dwarfed by him, and wished I was taller, so I could at least appear intimidating. I'd never hated my small, curvy frame any more than I did right at that moment.

I froze, pinning myself against the brick wall behind me, as though hoping I could push myself through it and disappear. My heart beat so hard it felt as though it filled my whole body, blood pounding in my ears, the pulse thrumming in my fingertips. I glanced around frantically, my eyes darting from side to side, praying for someone to come along and ask Ryan what he was doing, but the street remained deserted.

He leaned in closer, his head tilted to one side so he brushed his nose up my neck and jaw, to exhale in my ear. I held my breath, just wishing he would go away. Tears filled my eyes, but I didn't want him to see them, knowing they would only give him another reason to taunt me.

"Mmm, sweet," he rasped against my skin. "I can understand what our little Cole sees in you."

"Please, I need to go," I managed to say. "My dad is waiting for me."

But he ignored me. "I can see what Cole sees in you, but what do you see in him? You know you could have one of us older guys, if you wanted?"

"Really, I'm fine as I am. Thank you."

Thank you! Where the hell did 'thank you' come from? I should be telling him to get fucked, not thanking him. And yet, I guessed part of me hoped if I just played nicely, he'd let me go without anything bad happening.

I tried to duck under his arm, but he stepped in quickly, reducing the space between my body and his, so one more inch of movement and he'd be pressed right up against me.

"He's just a boy, you know. Me and the rest of the guys, we're real men. I assume Cole has fucked you already?"

My cheeks burned and I quickly glanced away.

He laughed. "That's right. You're not a sweet little virgin anymore, are you? None of the girls your age are these days. You're all just a bunch of sluts, spreading your legs for the first guy who comes along. If you'd waited awhile, you could have had me do the dirty with you instead. I'd have loved to have popped your cherry."

The tears I'd been fighting won the battle and spilled down my cheeks. I didn't know what Ryan was going to do. Surely he wouldn't try and assault me out here, in the middle of the street. Statistics about how you were more likely to be assaulted by someone you knew rather than a stranger ran through my head. What else was it they said? You should always put up a fight. A woman who screams and makes a nuisance of herself is more likely to be released than someone who does nothing. Cowards like Ryan only ever went for an easy target.

I wasn't going to be an easy target.

I sucked in a breath and lifted my booted foot as high as I could manage. With all of my strength, I stamped down, making contact with the bridge of his foot. At the same time, I shrieked, "Fire! Help! There's a fire!"

Ryan automatically ducked down to grab hold of his injured foot, looking at me with utter fury in his eyes. "What the fuck, you crazy bitch!"

But he'd moved away, and that was all that mattered. I ran, my arms pumping wildly, my only thought to put distance between me and Ryan. I didn't think he would chase after me—he would know he'd be seen eventually and I was pretty sure he'd decide I wasn't worth the trouble it would cause. Either that or he figured he would catch up with me later. I wondered if he knew who my dad was. Surely he wouldn't try to pull this kind of shit if he did. Or perhaps he'd thought he was being seductive and sexy, and I'd taken it all the wrong way.

I wheeled around the corner, barely staying on my feet, feeling as though they were flying out behind me. My tears blurred my vision, and as I collided with a strong, solid body, I let out a shriek of shock.

"Gabi! Hey, Gabi! What's wrong?"

I realized Cole had hold of me and I crumpled in his arms, crying in fear.

"I was just heading over to your house to meet you," he said. "What's happened?"

With heartbreaking sorrow, I realized I couldn't tell him. If I did, I'd ruin the one thing he had going for him, the one thing in his life he loved. He'd never forgive Ryan for upsetting me in such a way. In fact, he'd probably head right over there and punch the guy in the face. I didn't think for one moment that Ryan didn't deserve to be punched, but I didn't want Cole to be the one to do it. He was in enough trouble for getting into fights with his foster brother.

I untangled myself from his arms. "Nothing, Cole. Just leave me alone, okay."

Putting my head down, I kept going for my house.

"Hey, Gabi, wait up!"

His feet pounded the sidewalk behind me, and his hand wrapped around my arm as he pulled me back.

"I said leave me alone!" I shrieked at him.

It was too much. I knew it even as the words left my mouth, but it was too late to take them back. He dropped his hold on my arm and his mouth fell open, his blue eyes full of confusion and pain. He didn't know why I'd reacted to him in such a way, and I couldn't tell him.

"I'm sorry, Cole," I said, shaking my head and turning to run-walk toward my house. I just wanted to get into my bedroom and shut the door and not open it for a week.

Though I knew I couldn't have Cole follow me, for fear of breaking down on him again and telling him exactly what had happened, I wanted nothing more than to be pulled into his arms so I could sob against his chest. I was still shaking from my encounter with Ryan, and I wondered how I would ever be able to face the guy again. From now on, if Cole ever invited me to band practice, I would need to have some seriously good excuses on hand.

I reached my house and fumbled with my keys, managing to unlock the door, despite my hands shaking. Dad was at work, and even though I was used to taking care of myself, right at that moment I wished he was home more than anything.

But I shook the thought from my head. It was better I was on my own. Just like Cole, my dad would know something was wrong right away, and then he'd be full of questions, and would get the truth out of me eventually. One thing my dad was good at was asking questions.

Despite it barely being evening yet, I took myself to bed, and climbed, fully clothed, beneath the covers. I ran the events leading up to what had happened over in my head. Had I done or said something to make Ryan think I was interested in him? I'd always done my best to be friendly toward him and the other guys, because I'd wanted them to like me. I'd thought Cole would like me even more if his friends had approved of me, and, because they were older, I knew they'd have more influence over him. How stupid of me. Had I taken things too far? Had what happened been my fault? Cole would be devastated if he thought I'd been flirting with Ryan.

Heavy despair clutched my heart and dragged it into the pit of my stomach. What if Ryan said something to Cole? What if Ryan told him I'd been flirting with him? I wouldn't put it past him to do something so low.

Fresh tears sprang from my eyes and I buried my head beneath the cover, not knowing which way to turn, and I cried myself to sleep.

THIRTYTWO

GABI—PRESENT DAY

For the first time since Iraq, my life was starting to make sense again. For a while, I'd believed happiness was out of my reach, but instead it filled me once more—giddy, ridiculous happiness. Cole and I spent every moment we could together, as though making up for the ten years we had lost. My confidence about my leg was growing, and though I still felt self-conscious, Cole's constant desire for me made me start to no longer care what other people thought. The only person who was important to me was him, and if other people didn't like my leg, they could look the other way.

My dad even appeared to be drinking less. I thought he felt bad about not being around the night of the fireworks. Cole had been unable to contact him all of that night, even though Cole had sat up with me, and called my father's house every half hour. My dad confessed he'd been passed out on the couch from ten-thirty, and had barely even noticed the fireworks, never mind heard the phone ringing. He seemed to be getting better, though I didn't know how long it would last. He'd gone through phases of getting a better control on his drinking before, only to relapse again at a later date, so I was taking each good day as it came.

With my better state of mind, I'd also taken to walking as much as I could. I knew I wouldn't be running again until I was ready to be fitted for a blade, but I figured I could still work on my fitness. Plus, now Cole and I were spending so much time in bed, I'd started to care about my figure again. Just because I was missing a limb didn't mean the rest of my body couldn't be smoking hot. Not that Cole seemed to mind what my body looked like—he loved me just the way I was—but I wanted to feel like I was looking the best for him, and all those months of being immobile hadn't been kind to my waistline.

I began walking each morning, or afternoon, when Cole was at work. I started with twenty minutes, and gradually built up to thirty, then forty-five, and then an hour. It wasn't easy, but I felt good doing it. I'd also discovered a fantastic little coffee shop about halfway into my route, and so treated myself to a latte midway. Okay, I knew that part wasn't so good for my waistline, but I figured I'd been getting a lot of exercise in bed lately, too.

That day, I ordered my coffee and then lurked at the end of the counter, waiting for my takeout to be made. My name was called, and I took my drink and headed back outside, planning to finish my route. I stepped out of the doorway, onto the street, and someone blocked my way.

He had less hair than when I'd known him ten years ago, and had put on a little weight, but otherwise I'd have recognized him anywhere. It was the attitude surrounding him—the cocky, smug, superior air that followed him like a cloud of fog. He also had a graze beside his left eye and his lip looked swollen. I didn't know what he'd been up to recently, but it appeared someone else had taken a disliking to him.

Over the years, I'd played this moment in my head. I'd imagined exactly what I would say to him, about how he must have felt like such a big man, threatening a teenage girl. I'd imagined that when I ran into him again, we'd both be adults, able to have a heated, but mature conversation, and he'd see how I was now a grown woman—an Army Captain, no less—who wouldn't be intimidated by some little weasel of a man. I'd put my point across concisely, with just enough edge and bite to make him feel pathetic, and then I'd turn on my heel and march away, leaving him shrinking into the sidewalk.

The reality of that imagined conversation was very different. Just from his smile, and the way his eyes ran up and down my body, I could tell thirty-year-old Ryan was no different from twenty-year-old Ryan. Nothing I said to him would make an ounce of difference. Whatever he'd been doing over the last ten years, I didn't think it had affected his personality a single iota.

"Well, well, well. What do we have here? It's the little prick tease Cole Devonport used to hang out with." I could hear the sneer in his tone.

I tried to shrug him off. "I don't have time for this."

Glancing away from him slightly, perhaps hoping that if I didn't engage him, he'd leave me alone, I moved to walk past him. He stepped into my way, blocking the sidewalk and forcing me to stop. I'd managed men like him plenty of times in the Army. Cocky young guys who didn't think a woman belonged there, who would tell me I was only going to get myself and other people killed. I'd proven them wrong back then— perhaps I'd been a little cocky myself. I'd shown myself to be an equal by being fast, and strong, and smart. But that was before the incident where I'd lost my leg and a good man had died. Going through that had shaken my confidence to the core. I'd rebuilt myself after Cole had broken my heart in so many different ways, but I was still in pieces from the bombing. I'd quite literally left a piece of myself in Iraq.

Plus, there was that niggling worry in the back of my mind which said those men had been right. I *had* gotten a man killed by not acting quickly enough, and I had almost gotten myself killed, too. How could I believe anything else about myself when my worst fears had come true?

I forced myself to lift my eyes to his. "Get out of my way, Ryan."

"No chance. We're having a little catch up."

"I don't want to talk to you. Not now, not ever."

I willed for someone else to walk down the street, or for a car to pull up beside us and ask what was going on, but everything remained quiet. Perhaps I should turn around and go back into the coffee shop, but I didn't want him to think I was afraid of him. I was in this on my own.

"Now, that's no way to treat an old friend."

"Old friend? You were never a friend. Not to me, not to Cole either. If he hadn't known you and your buddies, he might have gone on to live a whole different life."

"Bullshit. He was old enough to make his own choices. We gave him an opportunity, that's all, and he took it." He studied my face for a second and one side of his upper lip lifted. "Don't tell me you're still hot for Cole? Does he know that?"

I hated my face for coloring at his suggestion. "That's none of your business. But I cared about him back then, and you screwed his life up. What are you even doing back in Willowbrook, Ryan? Surely you had bigger and better things to do with your life than hang around here?"

"I heard Cole was out, and thought I'd see what the big guy was up to these days."

Sudden anger spurted inside me. "You stay away from Cole!"

He laughed. "Aww, are you worried I'm going to lead your boyfriend astray?" His expression hardened. "Oh, but wait, he's not even your boyfriend anymore, is he? He dumped you pretty hard, from what I heard. He's also no longer a boy. He's a man, and a fucking criminal at that, so I'm pretty sure he can make up his own mind about who he does and doesn't want to hang out with. He seemed pretty pleased to see me the other night at the diner, shook my hand and everything. Perhaps he's getting sick of washing up other people's pots for a living, and is interested in something a little more profitable."

"Just stay away from both me and Cole," I said, trying to sound braver than I felt.

His nostrils flared. "Or what?"

I opened my mouth to speak, but a different voice came from behind me. "You okay, Miss?"

I turned to see an older man who'd also been in the coffee shop, standing behind me.

"Yes, she's fine," Ryan snapped.

"Actually, I was just leaving." I turned to the man who'd come to my rescue. "Thank you."

"No problem, Miss. You take care of yourself."

I walked away, feeling Ryan watch me go.

THIRTY THREE

GABI—ELEVEN YEARS EARLIER

I spotted Cole walking away from me down the hallway, so distinctive with his jaw-length blond hair and swagger. I hurried to catch up with him. We'd not seen each other yesterday—something that was almost unheard of—and he hadn't returned my calls. I was worried Ryan had said something to him. I'd barely slept, worrying about what Ryan had said to me, and wondering if I should have told Cole the truth. I knew Cole would be furious, though, and I couldn't risk him getting into a fight with Ryan. Ryan was older, and Cole would lose. Plus, it would mean he'd get in more trouble with his foster family, and I dreaded something happening which would get Cole sent away.

"Cole?" I shouted as I got closer. "Wait up!"

He glanced over his shoulder at me and slowed, but didn't stop. "Gabi, I'm sorry, but I've got somewhere I need to be."

I frowned. What was going on? In the space of a few days we'd gone from being joined at the hip to barely seeing each other. I missed him horribly, but he didn't seem to be missing me at all. Quite the opposite.

"You do? Where?"

"Just somewhere. I'm almost eighteen, Gabi, I don't need someone keeping track of me every second of the day. You're kind of smothering me."

I stepped back like he had struck me.

"What?"

His expression had turned hard, his eyes expressionless. I'd never seen this part of him before, and it frightened me. "You heard what I said. I need a bit of space. All of this …" he waved his hand in the air between us, "just has to cool down a little. I'm starting to feel like an old married man."

Someone, who must have overheard our conversation, sniggered beside me. I didn't even care if other people were listening in. My world was crashing down around my ears, and right now I was in complete denial rather than accepting it.

"What are you talking about, Cole? Is this some kind of joke or dare, 'cause it's really not funny."

"I told you, Gabi. I just want to cool things. I don't see why that's such a hard thing to understand. I thought you were smart."

Tears filled my eyes, blurring the hallway around us, and the sight of his strange, stone-like face. "Well, you weren't saying that two days ago in my bed! You told me you loved me, and we'd be together forever."

He gave a cold laugh that pierced my heart. "Guys always say things like that." He gave an almost apologetic shrug. "How else are we going to get what we want?"

Why was he doing this? I knew it wasn't the truth. Perhaps guys did tell girls they loved them to get them into bed, but that wasn't the case with me and Cole. He loved me, I knew he did. I'd known it from the first moment he cupped my cheek with his palm and stared into my eyes. Love wasn't just a word; it was a feeling, a connection. We had that, and something had happened to make him want to pretend it had never existed. Had Ryan told Cole I'd come on to him? Was this Cole's idea of saving face? Had Ryan put these words into Cole's mouth?

Rage bubbled up inside me. "What the hell do you think you're doing? I know this isn't you talking."

He lifted a hand. "Sorry, Gabi, but yeah, it is. I'll catch you later, okay?" And, with that, he turned from me and carried on sauntering off down the hall as though he hadn't just blown my whole world apart with a couple of cold-hearted lines.

As I stood, staring after him, I became aware of all the other kids around me, watching me and commenting behind their hands. Cole and I were known to be high school sweethearts, and that he'd just dumped me in the middle of the hall was going to be whizzing around the gossip mills within seconds.

Unable to stand their scrutiny any longer, I ran for the bathrooms. I banged in, and hurried for a stall, slamming and locking the door behind me. The pain in my chest was so bad, crawling up my throat so I felt like my airways were closing over. I gasped between silent tears, certain I would die from heartbreak. I couldn't believe Cole had just said those things to me.

I heard the bathroom door open again, and then came a female voice. "Gabi? You in here?"

Jasmine.

With my hand shaking, I managed to undo the lock on the stall.

Taylor was with her.

Jasmine took one look at me and her face crumpled. She pulled me into her arms, and I sobbed on her shoulder. "Oh, Gabi, honey. I'm so sorry. I heard what happened. What a total jerk."

"That ... that's the thing, though," I managed to say between hiccupped sobs. "He's not a jerk. I don't know what's come over him. It was like that wasn't Cole speaking back there."

"Sweetie, it was Cole. Unless he's been taken over by aliens, which I think is highly unlikely, it was definitely Cole."

I knew she was trying to coax a smile out of me, but it refused to come.

"Gabi," said Taylor, though I wasn't sure I wanted to hear what she had to say. "Cole is trouble. He's a heartbreaker. We've told you that from the start."

I wanted to retort back that she would have been quite happy to jump into his pants herself if I'd stepped back, but I didn't want to fight with her as well right now. I needed support, not another argument. I got that she didn't like Cole, but at the same time I knew the main reason was because he liked me, not her. Or at least he had.

I sniffed. "Yeah, maybe you're right." I agreed with her to keep the peace, but I didn't believe what I was saying for a second. Something had happened. I was sure of it. Perhaps I was just in denial, but I couldn't bring myself to believe Cole had only used me for sex.

We stood together, creating a little circle while my friends rubbed my back in comfort. "Do you want to go to class?" Jasmine asked me, her tone doubtful.

I shook my head. There was no way I was going to hang around school now. Everyone would be talking, and besides, I looked a mess. I'd never been a pretty crier, and right now my whole face felt swollen, my eyes red, and my nose so bunged up I couldn't even breathe out of it.

"I'm going to skip class. I'll head home."

"Are you going to be all right on your own?" Taylor asked.

"Yeah, I'll be fine. I'm going to go to bed with a pint of ice-cream and listen to sad music for the rest of the afternoon."

Jasmine gave a tight smile. "That's my girl."

The truth was, I didn't intend on hiding under my covers. I wanted to see Cole again and find out what was really happening. I loved him with every single cell in my body, and I knew he felt the same way about me.

I needed to see him so he would tell me the truth.

Perhaps it was a bit stalkerish, but I decided to hang out on the street corner a block from Cole's foster parents' house. I knew he would need to come home at some point, and I was willing to wait it out. We needed to be able to talk in private if I was going to get the truth out of him.

I was so caught up in my own thoughts, I barely noticed the time go by. I tried to hold back the tears, but every now and then a sob burst through my defenses and I'd discovered my cheeks wet and salty. I didn't give a single thought to anyone else. The only person I cared about was Cole.

Finally, I spotted him walking down the street, his hands stuffed in his pockets, his head down so his blond locks fell over his face. I stood, rooted to the spot, hoping he would notice me and come running, saying how sorry he was and covering my face in kisses. Perhaps I was pathetic for being there, and still desperately wanting him despite what he'd said, but he meant everything to me and the thought of a future with him not in it felt like I might as well just tear my heart out and lie down on the sidewalk to die.

But Cole didn't notice me, and, if I wasn't careful, he'd disappear inside the house. Then I'd have to go and knock on the door, and my presence would be noticed by the rest of his foster family. I didn't want to have to speak to anyone else.

"Cole?" I called out, stepping out into the street so he would see me.

He stopped dead and his head snapped around to face me. His expression was strained, his face tight, and crazily he appeared thinner than he had earlier in the day, his skin paler. The cocky, blasé attitude had vanished, and instead he just appeared stressed and worried. Something was wrong. I knew it was. I'd known it from the moment he'd opened his mouth that afternoon.

"What's happened?" I asked him, my gaze searching his face.

"Please, just go home, Gabi. You can't be around me anymore."

"Why not? Please, tell me the truth, Cole."

He shook his head, not even looking directly at me. "Just go home."

"No." I was resolute. "I'll sit on your damn doorstep until you tell me what's happening. I don't believe you want us to break up for one second."

"We don't always get what we want in life."

I stared at him. "That's not good enough."

"Listen to me, Gabi. Being with me will get you hurt. Do you understand? Whether I want to or not, I will end up hurting you, and I can't let that happen. From now on, we're over. Just go and get on with your life, and leave me alone."

I was baffled, hurt, frustrated, and angry.

"Let's go and get a coffee and talk about this," I said, grasping onto straws.

"I can't. I have stuff to do."

"Tomorrow, then, after school?" I offered, thinking the next twenty-four hours would be hell, but that I was willing to wait it out if it meant I got to spend time with Cole again.

But he shook his head. "I have somewhere I need to be tomorrow."

What on earth could be more important than talking about our relationship?

"Where do you need to be?"

His gaze shifted from side to side, his sneaker scuffing the sidewalk. "I've got to move some gear for the band."

My stomach lurched. "Is that what this is about? Is Ryan giving you a hard time about me?"

Alarm brightened his eyes and the certainty Ryan had said something about me grew deeper. "No," he said. "I just have to move some stuff, that's all."

"Fine. I'll come with you."

He flung his arms up in the air, startling me so I reared back. "For fuck's sake, Gabi. Why don't you listen? I've told you I don't love you. I've told you I don't want you around anymore. Why won't you listen to me?"

"No." I said, stubborn, tears rolling down my face. "No, no, no."

He grabbed me by the upper arms, not pushing me, but giving me a shake. He'd never touched me in anything other than affection before, and his reaction shocked me.

"I don't want you involved, Gabi," he hissed at me, his face in mine. "Ryan's got me doing stuff for him, and I don't do as he asks, he's going to ruin you. So please, I need you out of this situation. You are the only thing he has over me. I couldn't give a shit about anything else."

I stared at him in horror. "So let him! I don't care."

"Well, *I* care, which is why I need you to get away from me."

"What's he got you doing for him? Is it illegal?"

His lack of an answer confirmed what I needed to know.

"Jesus, Cole. Please, whatever it is he's making you do, just tell him no. I don't care what he does to me. Just get the hell away from him."

He shook his head. "No, Gabi. You're the one who needs to get the hell away from me. I won't say it again. Leave me alone."

And with that, he turned and stormed back to his house, leaving me standing alone in the road, tears streaming down my face.

GABI—PRESENT DAY

A couple of days after bumping into Ryan again, I was surprised to get a call from Jasmine. I'd not heard from either of my old friends since they'd come to the house, and Jas asked if I'd like to meet them for lunch in a little bistro in town. My first instinct was to say no, but Cole was working, and I didn't have anywhere else to be. I needed to get out with other people more. This bubble Cole and I had created was bliss, but it wasn't realistic. We couldn't live like this forever.

I was feeling guilty about not telling Cole I'd bumped into Ryan again, but I didn't want Cole trying to make contact with his old band-mate. The last thing I wanted was the two of them becoming friends again. Cole was far better off without the likes of Ryan in his life.

Now I was on my way downtown, to meet my two ex-best friends.

I arrived at the bistro feeling nervous. It was silly to be anxious around women I'd known for fifteen years, but they still didn't know about Cole, and I hadn't yet decided if I would tell them. I guessed I worried they would tell me I was making a huge mistake. I wouldn't blame them if they did. They'd witnessed the fallout when we'd been teenagers—though Taylor couldn't say much about that—but I knew their disapproval may also be because Cole was essentially an ex-con. They'd give voice to all the worries that had been flitting around my head, and I really didn't want to hear them. The best thing to do was simply keep my mouth shut, but he filled my thoughts constantly, his name ready to slip off my tongue at any moment.

Jasmine and Taylor were already sitting at a table near the back of the restaurant. The girl working as hostess showed me over, and both women stood to kiss my cheek as I arrived at the table.

"Wow, you're looking amazing," said Jasmine. "Seriously. Your skin is glowing."

I blushed. "Thanks."

Taylor nodded. "You look like you've lost a ton of weight as well. What's your secret?"

Mind-blowing sex every night, sometimes twice a night, I wanted to say, but couldn't.

"Oh, I've been walking a lot," I said instead. "I'm up to about four miles a day."

Jasmine smiled at me encouragingly. "That's great. It's really working for you."

I ducked my head into the menu so they wouldn't read the secret on my face. "Have you guys ordered yet?"

Taylor shook her head. "We were waiting for you, but I recommend the chicken Caesar salad. It's delicious."

"Sounds good."

The waitress came over and took our orders. We went for a bottle of sauvignon blanc to accompany our meals. I was starting to relax.

"So what have you two been up to since I last saw you?" I asked, wanting to divert attention away from myself.

Jasmine shrugged. "Absolutely nothing. Work, sleep, repeat. My life is boring as hell."

Taylor hunched up her shoulders and leaned over the table. "Well, I've got some gossip," she said, all conspiratorial. "You'll never guess who I spent the evening with the other night."

"Who?" Jasmine asked, slipping into her co-conspirator role easily.

"Only a certain Cole Devonport."

If she'd punched me in the stomach, I wouldn't have felt more winded. My breath tightened in my chest, and a sickening dread clutched my heart.

Jasmine glanced at me, suddenly gone from playful to awkward. "Taylor ..." she said, her tone warning.

Taylor, clearly as self-centered now as she'd always been, fluttered her eyelashes and gave a shrug. "Oh, sorry, Gabi. You don't mind, do you? I mean, it's been over ten years now since you two were a thing."

The world spun around me, and I opened my mouth to speak, but no words would come out. Seemingly oblivious to my discomfort, she continued with her story. "So, it was the other week when I went out with Poppy to meet that guy she'd been talking to online. She didn't want to go alone, understandably, but he didn't show up and she hooked up with someone else anyway ..."

Taylor babbled away, while I tried not to throw up.

"Anyway," she continued, "Cole was at the bar and recognized me right away and offered to buy me a drink. Let's just say, one drink led to another, and the next thing I know, we're making out like a couple of kids in the front of my car." She looked to me and winked, "I've got say, Gabi, I can see what got you all hot and bothered about him all those years ago. He's not exactly small below the waistline." She giggled.

I couldn't hear any more. I stood up, awkwardly, my chair falling back. "I'm sorry, I have to go."

The room was closing in, blood rushing through my ears.

I heard Jasmine say, "Jesus, Taylor," as I staggered from the restaurant, and Taylor's not so innocent reply of, "What did I do?"

I left the restaurant, but Jasmine chased after me. "Hey, Gabi, wait a minute."

"I'm sorry," I said over my shoulder as I hurried toward the car. "I forgot I had to be somewhere."

"Don't be silly. I've known you for how many years? It's obvious Taylor upset you, *again*." She pulled me to a halt and studied my face as I tried to hold back tears. "It was a long time ago, though. I didn't think you'd still have feelings for him."

I shook my head, unable to speak, and understanding dawned on her pretty face. "Oh!" Her eyes widened. "You and Cole hooked back up again?"

How could I tell her it was so much more than that? What we had wasn't just a hook up. I'd thought it was the real thing—a true love that would keep us together until we were old and grey. Clearly, Cole didn't feel the same way. In my mind, I tried to piece together the dates. Had it been before we'd first had sex again, or after? I hated the idea that he'd touched her first, but also hated the idea of him cheating on me after as well. It was as though she'd come in and tainted everything that had happened over the past few weeks. If only it had been anyone but *her*.

"I have to go," I said, turning and hurrying away again. I didn't want her to see me crying.

I wanted to see Cole, but at the same time I couldn't stand to look at him. Had he been there for me, holding me when I'd been struggling with everything, while all the time knowing he'd been with her? The images of them together filled my head, the thought of his tongue in her mouth, and him pushing inside her. Had his fingers been inside her, too? The same fingers that had stroked my hair and face, and told me he'd take care of me and that I'd never be alone again.

I felt sick.

I just wanted to get away from there. I wanted to run home, shut my door, and never open it again.

GABI—ELEVEN YEARS EARLIER

I burst through my front door, tears streaming down my face. I couldn't believe what was going on with Cole. He'd never laid a finger on me before, and tonight he'd frightened me. I didn't like seeing that side of him—it made me wonder how much further he would go. Plus, it made me feel like I didn't really know him at all—something that broke my heart as much as the awful things he'd said to me. If I didn't really know him, then the past couple of months were nothing but a lie.

I ran up the stairs to my bedroom, my feet pounding on the treads. My dad was home, but I couldn't face him right now. I just wanted to be on my own. In fact, I didn't think I'd ever want to face anyone ever again, especially after my humiliation at school. But I was worried about Cole as much as devastated by how he'd treated me. I'd never liked Ryan, and after he'd come on to me, it didn't surprise me in the slightest that Ryan had used me to threaten Cole. I also didn't doubt Ryan's threats were true. I bet that bastard would do anything to get back at me for stomping on his foot and running away that day.

I threw myself on my bed, tears pouring down my face. Despite wanting to be left alone, I heard my dad's feet coming up the stairs after me. He must be worried about me, too, and honestly, right at that moment I just wanted to be a little girl in my dad's arms again, and not have to worry about all the bullshit that came with being older.

A knock came at the door, and then it opened a crack. "Gabi, honey? What's happened?"

I turned from him and buried my face in the pillow. "Nothing. I just want to be left alone."

His footsteps crossed the room, and the bed dipped with his weight as he sat on the edge. "I'm not going to leave you on your own when you're so upset about something. Now you might as well tell me what's happening, because you know I'm going to get it out of you at some point."

"Please, Dad, I don't want to talk about it."

"Gabi, if Cole has done something to upset you, I want to know. I'm not going to go all crazy, but I want to be able to support you. I love you more than anyone else in this world, and I want you to be able to confide in me."

The truth was, I wanted my dad, too. I was hurt and confused, and worried to death about what Cole was getting himself into.

My dad had a way of getting the truth out of people—I guessed that was why he did the job he did.

I wiped my face and sat up. I stared down at my hands in my lap. "Cole said he doesn't want to see me anymore."

"Oh, sweetheart, I'm so sorry. Do you want me to go and break his kneecaps?"

I gave a forced bark of laughter. "No, Dad, of course not."

"I thought the two of you were really close."

"That's the thing, we are. I'm worried about him, Dad. He's gotten himself caught up in something with the guys he plays in the band with, and he thinks by breaking up with me, he's protecting me, somehow."

He frowned. "What sort of thing?"

I shook my head. "I don't know. He's been borrowing his foster parents' truck and heading off to places, though. I don't know if it's connected, but he's been acting strangely ever since it started. I'm so worried about him." Tears were close again. Cole had made me believe whatever he was doing was illegal, but I didn't plan on telling my dad that. I knew how he felt about Cole being caught up with the band. I just wanted some advice from him about where to go from here.

"I have to admit that I'm pleased to see you out of it, Gabi. You know how I felt about those boys."

"Dad, please. I don't need a lecture. I just need to know what I'm supposed to do about Cole."

"I don't want you doing anything. It's not your place. He's still under his foster family's roof for the moment, so they should be the ones to handle whatever trouble he's gotten himself into, not you." He thought for a moment and then said, "Would it help if I had a word with him?"

"No! Please don't, Dad. That won't help at all."

"Maybe I should have a word with his foster parents instead. If I was able to convince them to keep him home, or not let him borrow the truck, would that help?"

I allowed my heart to lift with faint hope. "I don't know how much, but maybe a little."

"When does he need to borrow it?"

"Tomorrow night, I think."

My dad nodded. "Okay, I'll see what I can do."

I didn't want to get Cole in trouble, but I had to do something. He was under his foster parents' care for the moment, and perhaps it would be a good thing for Emily and Stephen Cowen to speak to him. Even though Cole had butted heads with them on occasion, he did respect that they'd done their best for him. I didn't think I had any other choice. He wasn't going to listen to me, and he'd hate it if my dad tried to talk to him—in fact, if he knew I'd spoken to my dad about this at all, he'd go crazy.

I just hoped they would be able to talk some sense into him.

I went to school the next day, trying to ignore all the whispered comments and nudges that followed me as I passed through the halls. I'd hoped Cole's treatment of me in the hall the previous day might have been forgotten, but it clearly hadn't.

Jasmine caught up with me. "Hey, how are you doing?"

"I've been better. Have you seen Cole today?"

She shook her head, but glanced away.

I frowned. Why did I get the feeling she wasn't telling me something?

We went to class, and I sat through my lectures, not listening to a single word said. My mind stayed on Cole the whole time, wondering if my dad had been to see his foster parents yet, and if Cole would hate me for saying something. I hoped he'd understand I was desperate. Plus, it didn't matter if he hated me as long as he agreed to stay away from Ryan and his gang.

Jasmine and I decided to have lunch outside. I was happy to find a tree, where I could sit in the shade and hide behind the trunk. People were still looking at me, though I did my best to keep my head down and ignore any comments, though I couldn't miss a couple.

"—going to be a cat-fight when she finds out."

More giggles.

"—cut off his balls ..."

I turned to Jas. "What are they talking about?"

"No idea. I'm sure it's nothing about you and Cole."

But as soon as she said it, I knew she was lying. "Jasmine, just tell me."

She shrugged. "It's nothing, I'm sure. People are just gossiping …"

"About what?"

Her eyes widened, staring in the direction of the building which housed the gym. I followed her line of sight and my heartrate skyrocketed. I'd have recognized Cole anywhere, even from behind as he was standing now, one hand pressed against the wall, his head ducked slightly as he talked to someone. The position made my stomach drop and I suddenly felt sick. He had someone pinned up against the wall, and it wasn't in a violent, aggressive way. Quite the opposite. I could tell from the way his body was positioned that he had no intention of fighting the person he was speaking to.

Jasmine's hand on my arm drew my attention momentarily. "Come on, Gabi. Let's go back inside."

I tugged my arm away. "No, I need to see this for myself."

I suddenly understood what all the gossiping in the halls was about. It wasn't just that Cole had dumped me in the middle of school yesterday, it was that he was now hooking up with someone else.

With my heart pounding, I stomped across the grass toward him.

He must have sensed me coming, because he glanced over his shoulder and spotted me. I thought seeing me might have made him jump away from whatever tramp he had cozied up to, but he did quite the opposite. Instead, he wrapped his arms around her waist, ducked his head, and kissed her.

I froze.

This wasn't a 'peck on the lips' kind of kiss. It was a full, 'bodies pressed together, tongue in mouth, dry-humping' kind of kiss. The same kiss we'd shared on so many occasions.

Well, never again.

And then, just when I thought it couldn't get any worse, I realized who the bitch was he was kissing.

Taylor.

With blood pounding in my ears, the world distant and faint around me, I turned and ran. I only wanted to get away from there. I was done. With my friends. With school.

With Cole.

THIRTYSIX

COLE—ELEVEN YEARS EARLIER

This would be the second and last time I would ever do anything for Ryan. To say I resented the guy would be the understatement of the century. He'd taken everything from me by making me push Gabi away. She hated me now, and I didn't blame her. Everyone had warned her I was trouble when we'd first gotten together, and it had turned out they were right.

I'd had to make sure Ryan would hear that we'd broken up, and by her seeing me making out with Taylor, I'd known the news would spread and Gabi would hate me. Ryan couldn't use her if she no longer wanted anything to do with me, and he didn't know where I was.

As soon as I'd made this drop and got my money, I was getting the hell out of town. I didn't know where I was going yet—my plans went no further than packing my stuff, taking the money I'd made, and the little extra I had saved up from doing chores over the years, turning up at the bus station, and taking whichever bus was heading out of town next. Everyone would find life better if I wasn't around.

I collected the parcel from Ryan. I wanted to kill him, but he had Adam and Mike standing around him like his fucking bodyguards, and short of buying a gun and shooting the son-of-a-bitch, nothing was going to get rid of him. I figured I was in enough trouble already without heading down that route.

No, my best option was taking the money I made and leaving as soon as possible. I tried not to think about Gabi, the crack in my heart steadily widening as each hour passed, knowing I would be leaving her for good. She'd never want me back now anyway, not after seeing me kiss Taylor like that. I didn't think it would make any difference if I told her I'd hated doing it and had been thinking of her every moment of the kiss.

She'd tell me I was sick in the head, and she was probably right.

I drove for a little over an hour. I reached Norburn and pulled into the spot where I was due to meet Ryan's contact. I was nervous, but not as much as the last time. At least now I knew what to do and how to act. We weren't friends meeting to hang out. This was business only, and would be quick.

No one was waiting for me when I arrived, so I stayed in the truck, the bag containing the couple of kilos of weed sitting on the passenger seat beside me. I was glad when I'd be rid of it, and heading back to town. I would hand over Ryan's money and be out of there.

Headlights lit the parking lot behind me, and I turned to see another vehicle pulling in.

Inhaling a steady breath, I opened the driver's door, grabbed the bag, and climbed from the truck.

"Hey, you Ryan's friend?" the guy called out.

"That's right."

"You got something for me?"

I lifted up the bag, so he could see it in the car's headlights. He waved

227

an envelope, which I assumed contained a wedge of bills, at me in return.

I handed the bag over at the same time he passed me the envelope.

Sudden sirens blared through the night, making me jump, my heart lurching. My first thought was a storm warning, but then the roar of engines filled the air and a number of vehicles tore into the parking lot, the headlights blinding me. People jumped from the cars, doors slamming like gunshots. I was surrounded in a rush of movement, and noise, and men shouting. Confused, I lifted my arm to cover my eyes, squinting at the new arrivals. Police. I was surrounded by the cops. What the hell was going on?

"Get down on the ground!"

"Hands in the air!"

The whole of my insides plummeted as I realized the men were shouting at me.

Fuck, fuck, fuck.

I had no choice but to do what they asked, letting the envelope I had been clutching drop to the ground. It broke open, and instead of the twenties I had been expecting, hundred dollar bills spilled out onto the asphalt. My mouth dropped. There must have been thousands of dollars scattered across the ground.

The guy I'd met up with copied my movements, dropping the bag to the ground and lowering himself down.

"No one move," one of the cops told us, and I saw weapons pointed in both our directions.

"Let's see what we've got here," said the officer who appeared to be in charge.

He went to the bag I'd brought to the scene and opened it, pulling out the couple of fist sized, tape-wrapped, bundles of marijuana. Taking out a penknife, he cut open the first of the bundles, but instead of dried leaves falling, he pulled out a white powder.

Nausea washed over me and the world spun in a circle.

"What you got, sir?" another cop asked.

"Looks like cocaine, and a lot of it." He turned to his colleague. "These boys are going to be going down for a very long time."

THIRTYSEVEN

GABI—PRESENT DAY

Shaken to the core, my heart shattered into a million pieces by Taylor's revelation about the night she'd spent with Cole, I stumbled into my house. I only wanted to be alone for a few hours, but when I walked into my living room, I discovered someone sitting on my couch.

I froze. "Ryan?"

He got to his feet and smiled. "Hello, Gabi."

I looked around, frantic, for my dad, but as far as I could tell, he was nowhere to be seen. "How did you get in here?"

He held up something small and metallic between his fingers. "You left me a key, didn't you?"

Damn it. The key I had been leaving out for Cole. The thought of him stabbed a knife into my heart, but I had other problems right now.

I reached out to snatch the key from Ryan's fingertips, but he jerked back and laughed.

"That wasn't meant for you, asshole," I spat. "Now get the hell out of my house."

His eyes narrowed, a muscle in his forehead twitching. "Now, that's no way to welcome an old friend." His tone, initially jovial, gradually grew colder. "Where are your manners, Gabriella?"

My stomach lurched. *Shit.* It suddenly occurred to me that I'd walked into a dangerous situation. Without moving my head, I tried to glance toward the living room door, trying to judge if I could make it out of the door and slam it behind me before Ryan moved. I wanted to try, but I knew my leg would make me a lot slower than a fully-functional, grown man.

He must have seen the look on my face. "Uh-uh, Gabi. Don't even think about trying to make a run for it."

"What do you want, Ryan?" I tried to keep my voice level, though my heartrate thrummed.

"I need you to convince Cole to do something for me."

"Not a chance. He's not going to listen to me, anyway."

He shrugged. "I don't know about that. You must know he only ran those packages for me because of you all those years ago."

"I know you threatened me. But Cole was only a kid back then. He's a grown man now, and he's not going to let you push him around."

"Oh, I don't know about that. I think Cole is pretty protective of you. If I let him know I'll blow your fucking brains out if he doesn't do as I tell him, I think he might wise up to the situation."

My eyes widened. "What?"

He reached into the back of his jeans, and pulled out a gun. "You heard me, bitch."

I felt sick, a sudden rush of heat blasting through my body, followed by ice-cold water though my veins. I couldn't believe this was happening. I wanted to believe he wouldn't shoot me, but I had no idea what kind of man Ryan had grown into, or what he'd been doing these past ten years. I could only guess from the fact he was here in my house now, holding a weapon and threatening me, that none of it had been good.

But when the initial shock ebbed away, I realized it wasn't fear I was left with but anger. I was suddenly furious he was doing this, coming into my home and threatening me. I'd been threatened by men with guns on numerous occasions in the Army, though of course then I'd been armed myself, and the playing field had been even.

"What's your obsession with Cole?" I said, anger burning hot inside me. "He could have handed your name over to the cops when he was arrested, but he didn't. He kept his mouth shut. You should be thanking him, not trying to churn up shit with him all over again."

"The thing is, Gabi, that's what makes Cole a trustworthy guy. Trustworthy guys are people I like to do business with."

I tried not to think about Cole and Taylor. Just how trustworthy was Cole?

"Well, he's not going to want to do business with you," I said. "In case you didn't notice, the last time didn't turn out so well for him."

He waved the gun as a gesture, and I reared back, inhaling a breath. "I'm trying to help Cole," he said. "I want to give him the opportunity to make a better life for himself."

I snorted, unable to help myself. "Like the last ten years have been better?"

His face hardened, his eyes narrowing. "I tried to help that kid. He was a nobody who was going to be homeless within a few months. He had no job prospects and nowhere to live. It's easy for you to judge with your family, and middle class home, but what do you think guys like him always end up doing? It wasn't my fault something went wrong. In fact, Gabi, I can't help wondering a few things."

Prickles of unease pinched my skin. "What?"

"What's your father doing these days?"

I stiffened. "What do you mean?"

"Over the years, I couldn't help wondering just who was the

untrustworthy one? I guess I joined the dots. It seems like more than a coincidence that Cole told you I'd threatened you—or perhaps you told him about that stunt you pulled when you got all feisty about me being a little friendly—and then he gets arrested when he was doing one of our runs. We lost a lot of money that night, Gabi. It wasn't just that Cole was arrested. We were down several hundred thousand dollars. Can you even imagine how much money that is?"

He moved in closer, the weapon held between us, the muzzle pointed at my stomach. "So, Gabi, what did you tell your daddy-dearest about Cole and the rest of us? Was it malicious or just sheer stupidity? I mean, it's not as though you didn't know he was a cop."

I held my breath. He was right. My dad had been a cop back in those days, before his drinking had taken hold. He'd been discharged from the force, but he'd still been on active duty the day I'd told him about Cole getting into something he couldn't handle. He'd told me he would speak to Cole's foster family, and stop Cole from borrowing the truck to do the run, but instead he'd used the information to get Cole busted and sent down. It was part of the reason I'd left town, together with the fact Cole had cheated on me and broken my heart. After I graduated, I'd reinvented myself completely. I'd thrown away the bookish girl who'd been happy to stay in her room and keep herself to herself. Where many would crumble, I decided to go the other way. I realized to get through life I needed to be strong, physically and mentally. I started running and lifting weights, pouring my heartbreak into exercise. I knew I couldn't go back to a school setting, not after everything that had happened, and so when I'd seen an advertisement for recruitment for the Army, I'd locked onto it. It was perfect. I knew now I could be stronger than I'd ever thought possible, and the job would take me a long way from Willowbrook Falls, and from my dad. My resentment toward him had reached the point where I couldn't even look at him, never mind live in the same house.

As I'd grown older, some of that resentment had faded. Perhaps it had been time, or distance, or simply that by growing up I'd realized not all of it was his fault, but my own guilt had set in about abandoning him. He'd betrayed my trust, but he'd also believed he'd been protecting me.

"So the thing is, Gabi," Ryan continued, "both you and Cole owe me a hell of a lot of money. I know you don't have that kind of cash, so I think Cole needs to work off his debt, and I have a couple of perfect jobs for him to do."

I shook my head. "The police will be watching him. He's an ex-con. Surely there's someone better to do your damn drug runs for you. He's just going to end up back behind bars, and you're going to end up broke again."

"Yeah, and what about you, Gabi? What's your punishment for blabbing to your father? Does Cole even know you were the one responsible for getting him locked up for ten years?"

Tears filled my eyes, and I blinked them back angrily. Of course he didn't know. Perhaps he suspected, but he'd never said anything to me. He blamed himself for everything that had happened, and I'd been too much of a coward, and too broken-hearted, to go and see him in jail. I hadn't been able to stand the thought of the pain I would have seen in his eyes when I'd told him what I'd done. Cole had told me in confidence about what Ryan had planned, and I'd gone and told my cop-father. I had never broached the conversation with my dad about what he'd instigated, but I knew he must have either followed Cole himself, or gotten someone else to keep an eye on Cole.

He'd been arrested because of me.

I'd ruined his life.

"Please, Ryan," I begged, "Cole doesn't need to know about that."

"You mean you haven't told him. Tsk-tsk. What sort of relationship could you possibly have if it wasn't one built on trust?"

"We don't have a relationship. Cole has been seeing Taylor—the same girl from when we were at school. Maybe it should be her house you're lurking in."

I instantly regretted what I'd said. However much I hated Taylor, she had a son, and I wouldn't want any harm to come to either of them.

"No relationship? What kind of person leaves a key under a mat for someone who they're not in a relationship with?"

I should have just given Cole the key. I deeply regretted not doing so now. It had just felt like such a big step, giving him a key to my place, and I hadn't wanted to say or do anything to ruin the happy little bubble we'd been in.

I guess I shouldn't have worried. It had burst eventually anyway.

THIRTYEIGHT

COLE—PRESENT DAY

I was supposed to meet Gabi after my lunch shift finished. She'd said she was having lunch with a couple of old friends, and so I'd planned on turning up a little early and surprising her. We'd been keeping our relationship fairly quiet, with only a couple of public appearances, but I wanted that to change. I wanted to shout about her at the top of my lungs, and I had a feeling she felt the same way. I didn't want to pressure her into telling people about us—perhaps a part of her was worried others would judge because of me recently getting out of prison—but I felt like we just needed to rip the Band-Aid off and let everyone know.

I turned up at the restaurant and peered through the large glass front before I headed inside. I couldn't see Gabi anywhere, but I did recognize Jasmine sitting across from another woman at a table near the back. Perhaps Gabi was in the bathroom.

Entering the restaurant, I felt everyone turn and look at me. I'd done my best to smarten up after my shift, but I couldn't hide the way I looked. I knew I had a hard edge about me now. Growing up in the system and then spending most of my adult life behind bars, it was hardly surprising.

Jasmine's gaze flicked to me as I crossed the restaurant, and then the woman she was sitting opposite turned in her seat to see what Jasmine was looking at. Instantly, my heart sank. Taylor. The last person I wanted to see. I only barely remembered seeing her the other night, but knew I'd been drunk when I had. I remembered talking about Gabi, and her leg, something I felt like I'd betrayed Gabi over just by speaking to Taylor. I really didn't want to see her, and hoped she hadn't said anything to Gabi. I should have told Gabi myself that I'd seen her at the bar, but things had taken off between us when I'd gone to her house the next morning, and after that it hadn't even occurred to me again.

Until now.

Taylor gave a wide smile and got to her feet. "Oh, my God, Cole. What a coincidence."

I frowned. "Is it?"

She rose from her chair and stood on tiptoes to kiss me on the cheek. I jerked back, alarmed by the sudden invasion of space. But the waft of her perfume conjured a memory in my head—her kissing me, her hands all over me.

Oh, shit.

"I thought you were going to call me after the other night," she said, her hand lingering on my chest. I took a step back, dislodging the contact.

"Why would I do that?"

Her fine blonde eyebrows lifted. "Umm, because that's what a decent guy does after he gets all hot and heavy with a girl, Cole."

I scowled. "Since when did you mistake me for a decent guy?" Jasmine was looking awkwardly between us. "Where's Gabi?" I demanded. "I thought she was meeting you guys here."

Jasmine got to her feet as well, so we were all standing around the table, drawing curious glances from the other patrons and the couple of waitresses working. "She left, Cole. Sorry. I think Taylor said something that might have upset her."

"What?" I snarled at Taylor. "What the hell did you say?"

She flicked up her hand in defense. "Hey, I didn't know the two of you were an item again. I mean, really, Cole, you shouldn't go hitting on other women if you're supposed to be dating someone else."

A second memory of that night suddenly swept over me ...

I'd been sitting in Taylor's car, dreaming about Gabi, and that we were making out. I'd felt like her hand was on me, pressing down against my cock and making me hard. I'd wanted her so badly, just to claim her for my own again, to fuck away all of the hurt and pain from the last ten years. I'd wanted to hear her moan and gasp my name.

The pressure against my cock had grown firmer and the rhythmical stroking had made me buck my hips in a drunken response. And then a mouth had been on mine, kissing me, fingers around the back of my neck, thighs straddling my hips.

I remembered confusion washing over me. I hadn't understood where I was, or what was going on. A tongue had pushed between my lips, and I'd realized the person kissing me hadn't tasted like Gabi.

I'd opened my eyes at that point and found myself surrounded in a halo of golden hair. Blue eyes had smile down at me seductively and narrow hips had ground into mine.

Taylor!

"Jesus fucking Christ, Taylor," I'd exclaimed, suddenly sober. "What the hell are you doing?"

She'd pouted, "We're making out, Cole. What do you think we're doing?"

I'd pushed her off me then, throwing her back into the driver's seat. I would never normally have gotten rough with a woman, but the idea of her hands on me while I was semiconscious had made me sick.

I'd shoved open the car door and staggered up to my front door, Taylor's voice chasing after me. "Cole, wait…"

The memory retreated and I was left staring at the woman in question.

"Jesus fucking Christ, Taylor! What the hell is wrong with you? I never hit on you. We were talking about Gabi, and I was so drunk you drove me home. I was passed out in the car, and I woke up to find you all over me."

I could still feel the pressure of her fingers rubbing my erect cock, the taste of her mouth against mine. Even though I'd been dreaming about Gabi while it had been happening, I felt sick and guilty that my body had responded to Taylor's touch. My mind replayed the events of that evening. Had I led her on? Given her the wrong impression that I was interested in her? I couldn't see how—we'd talked about Gabi all evening—but perhaps just by sitting and drinking with her she'd thought I wanted more.

I wasn't completely blameless. Hadn't I used her, too, all those years ago? Perhaps it was no surprise she thought I still liked her. I'd been locked away not long after. Had she thought I'd been harboring feelings for her this whole time?

Taylor flipped her hair behind her shoulder. "It wasn't like that. You were giving me the eye all evening. You kept staring at my tits, and I knew you really wanted it. I was only playing. As soon as I started touching you, you got hard for me." She reached for me and I smacked her hand away.

"You know what, Taylor, if that was the other way around, and you'd gotten drunk and woken up to find me all over you, I'd be arrested for sexual assault."

She laughed. "Since when did you become such a drama queen? Most men would love to have been in your position."

"No. Consent is consent, and you didn't have mine. My guess is you didn't tell Gabi that, though, did you?"

Her cheeks flamed red under her tan.

"Jesus, Taylor," said Jasmine in disgust. "You really are something else."

"Where's Gabi?" I demanded.

"She left," said Jasmine. "I don't know where she went. I'm so sorry, Cole."

"You don't have anything to be sorry for. It's the other one who needs to be sorry. I swear, the only thing saving you right now is that you have a kid, and I wouldn't want to see another boy grow up without a mother."

Taylor hung her head.

I didn't have any more time for her. I needed to find Gabi. I couldn't even imagine how devastated and angry she must be right now. Did she think I'd willingly slept with Taylor? Just the thought of the sort of pain she would be in right now stole my breath.

Turning from the two women, and ignoring all the curious stares which followed me out of the restaurant, I stormed from the building and out into the parking lot.

I pulled my cell phone from my pocket and dialed her number. It rang several times, and for a moment I thought she wasn't going to answer—not that I blamed her, the caller I.D. would be showing my name—but then someone picked up.

"Cole!"

But it wasn't Gabi's sweet voice answering the phone, but a man's, and my stomach dropped as recognition sank in.

"Ryan? What the hell are you doing with Gabi's phone?"

He laughed and every muscle in my body tensed. "I'm at her house. We're having a little get together, aren't we, Gabi?"

I heard her voice in the background; she sounded frightened.

"Gabi!" I shouted, as though I hoped she might hear me.

"The thing is, Cole," he continued, "the two of you owe me for your little escapade ten years ago. You cost me a lot of money, and now I want payback."

The line went dead.

"Fuck! Fuck, fuck, fuck!" I wanted to throw the phone and punch walls, but there was no time for any of that shit. Ryan had told me where they were, which meant he wanted me to be there, too.

I jumped in my car, leaving Taylor and Jasmine staring out of the restaurant window after me, and drove as fast as I could to Gabi's house.

GABI—PRESENT DAY

Cole was on his way—something I couldn't decide if I should be happy or worried about. It wasn't that I wanted to be left alone with Ryan, far from it, but I didn't want Cole to get into an altercation with the other man. Plus, part of me still couldn't stand the thought of seeing Cole. The memory of what Taylor had told me was so raw, I felt like someone had scraped out the inside of my heart and replaced it with shards of glass. I wouldn't be able to look at him without wanting to simultaneously collapse into a weeping heap, while launching myself at him and battering him on the chest, demanding to know why he'd done it.

I also knew that when Cole arrived, Ryan would take great delight in telling Cole the truth about what I'd done when we were teenagers.

In the end, it hadn't mattered that Cole had slept with Taylor again. When he found out I was the person responsible for getting him arrested, he would never want to see me again.

"So, Gabriella," said Ryan. "How about you and I get to know each other a little better while we wait for lover-boy?"

"Stay the hell away from me!" I threw back.

Where was my dad? I was worried he'd come home and get himself shot. I couldn't just stand here and allow Cole, or my dad, to walk into this situation. I needed to do something.

But what? He was holding a gun, and I had nothing. More than anything, I hated feeling helpless, and right now that was the overwhelming emotion swamping me. Cole was going to arrive, and Ryan would make him do something that would most likely get him put back behind bars.

I was at the mercy of a man with a ten-year grudge, and there was nothing I could do about it.

"Please, Ryan," I said, holding up both hands and taking a step backward, reducing the distance between myself and the door. "This is crazy. You're not going to shoot me. Why don't you just let me go, get the hell out of here before Cole arrives, and we'll forget this whole thing ever happened."

"Sorry, Gabi. Not happening."

"Please," I said again, glancing around for something I might be able to use as a weapon should I get my hands on it. My dad's taste in décor was simplistic—a couple of picture frames on the walls, a rug on the floor, and that was about it. There was nothing I could snatch off a shelf and use as a weapon. I suddenly wished I'd tried to add more of a woman's touch to the house during my time here, but I'd had other things on my mind.

I edged another step back.

"Gabi," he said, a warning tone to his voice. "Just where do you think you're going?"

"Nowhere," I said, standing still. "It just makes me nervous when someone waves a gun in my face."

He jerked his head toward the couch. "Take a seat, Gabi."

"I'm fine standing."

He raised the gun higher, so it pointed at my head instead of my stomach. "I said, take a seat."

Reluctantly, I was forced to walk farther into the room, and I lowered my backside to the couch.

Ryan came and sat next to me, uncomfortably close. I had learned how to disarm a man during my time in the Army, but I'd had two legs then and had been at the peak of my physical fitness. I worried that if I made the wrong move, I'd only end up getting myself shot.

"So," he said, "while we're waiting, I thought we could catch up. I hear you had an unfortunate accident recently."

I stiffened, my mouth running dry.

"You know, I've never fucked a girl with one leg before. Is it freaky? Does Cole like it? Is it one of his kinks?"

I couldn't even look at him, but stared at my hands in my lap. "Fuck you."

"Now, now. I'm the one with the gun, here. I suggest you speak nicely to me."

I wanted to cry, but didn't want to give him the satisfaction.

He laughed. "I don't need the gun, do I? I can just take off your leg, and then you'll have no way of running off." He laughed a big, belly laugh, wiping tears of mirth from his eyes, finding himself hysterical at something that wasn't even remotely funny.

Ryan was dangerous and unstable, and I had no idea how this was all going to end.

The roar of a car engine came from outside, the squeal of brakes in the driveway as it came to a standstill. *Oh, God. Cole.*

The front door slammed open.

I opened my mouth to yell a warning. "He's got a—"

Something slammed against my temple, knocking me sideways. The other side of my face hit soft cushions as I fell to one side, bright lights dancing around my vision.

Another male voice. "Gabi! What the hell is this?"

I came around enough to realize it wasn't Cole who had arrived, but my father.

"Dad," I sobbed. "Go, run!"

But it was too late for that. "What the hell did you do to my daughter?" He snarled at Ryan. My heart pounded, and I stared at my dad, trying to spot any signs that he might have been drinking. That would be the worst thing, if he was drunk and stumbling and capable of making terrible decisions, but it appeared that his good run of late had paid off, and he was either sober or doing an excellent job of *acting* sober.

Ryan had jumped to his feet when my dad burst in. But now there were two of us and only one of him, and only one weapon, he couldn't keep it trained on both of us at once.

"I'm going to guess this is the cop who cost me all that money ten years ago," Ryan said. "Looks like fate, or destiny, or whatever, is on my side today. Maybe you're all supposed to end up dead."

"And then you'll go down for a very long time," said my dad.

"Mr. Weston, isn't it? Bill? Or Bob?"

"Bill," my dad confirmed. "Now, I suggest you put that weapon down, young man, before someone gets hurt."

Ryan laughed. "Someone getting hurt is the whole point of the gun. You cost me a lot of cash ten years ago, and now you have to pay."

My dad glanced over at me. "What's he talking about, Gabi?"

"Ryan organized the drug run you busted Cole on ten years ago."

He frowned. "I didn't bust Cole."

"Well, no, not you personally, but you told the rest of the police department about Cole being mixed up in something with the band, and how he was using his foster parents' truck to move stuff around."

My dad shook his head. "I never told anyone else, Gabi. I didn't even manage to get hold of Cole's foster parents. I'd ... I'd been drinking too much, and forgot, and then by the time I remembered again, Cole had already been arrested. But I had nothing to do with it."

I stared at him in shock. Was he just saying this to try and protect both of us from Ryan, or was he telling the truth. "Really?"

He focused his gaze on mine. "I swear to you, Gabi. I wasn't the one who reported Cole. The police department had been keeping an eye on the band for a while before Cole was arrested. It was part of the reason I made you promise to stay away from them. Someone on the county taskforce screwed up, and arrested Cole rather than waiting for the money to make its way back to the real perpetrator. By the time they tried to make something stick to this scumbag, he'd cleaned up all the evidence."

I couldn't believe it. I'd been blaming him, and myself, all of these years, but my father had never betrayed my trust. It was just a coincidence.

"Perhaps I should have done more," he continued, "but despite everything, I'd believed Cole was a good kid. I was as shocked as everyone when he was arrested. I wasn't even on duty that night, Gabi."

Tears blurred my vision. "I'm so sorry I didn't trust you."

He shook his head. "It's okay, sweetheart. You were barely more than a kid yourself."

I'd abandoned him for so long, feeling resentful and angry at him. If I'd just sat down and talked to him, I could have saved us all those years of pain.

But Cole still would have been behind bars, and he still would have cheated on me with Taylor in front of the whole school, just like he'd betrayed me again now.

Ryan interrupted. "This is all very heartwarming, but it doesn't change the fact you didn't know how to keep your mouth shut, Gabriella."

"It wasn't her fault your drugs run went bad," my dad snapped. "You'd have been busted sooner or later. In fact, you should be thanking Cole for going down on your behalf. If he hadn't gotten arrested that night, it would have been your ass the cops would have gone after."

I resisted the urge to add, 'that's what I said.'

A second engine roared to a halt outside, and I glanced behind me, my mouth running dry.

Cole had arrived.

COLE—PRESENT DAY

Anger drove me now.

I was furious. Furious at Taylor for coming on to me when I'd been unconscious, and then telling Gabi we'd spent the night together. Furious at Ryan for going to Gabi's house and upsetting her. And furious at myself for being such a total fuck-up and not giving Gabi the sort of happiness she deserved.

I would fix that. I was determined to. My current plan was to kick the shit out of Ryan, and then drop to my knees and tell Gabi the truth of what had happened with Taylor. She had to understand, and forgive whatever needed to be forgiven. Gabi and I were meant to be together. The thought of a future without her felt utterly futile.

Her dad's car was in the driveway, but that didn't mean he was in. He tended to walk more these days because of the drinking; I guessed he didn't want to end up with another DUI and possibly a prison sentence. He could be out walking somewhere.

Perhaps I should have thought about my action more carefully, but I only wanted to wrench Ryan away from Gabi, and put things right.

I jumped out of the car and ran to the front door. It stood ajar, and so without bothering to knock, I shoved it open.

"Ryan!" I yelled.

Gabi's voice. "Cole?"

I turned in the direction of her voice and stormed into the living room. Gabi was sitting on the couch, her face pale and worried. Her father stood inside the room, his expression like nothing I'd witnessed on him before. He'd always appeared to be a fairly relaxed man—something I guessed was partially down to the booze—but right now I could see the cop in him. His gaze didn't even budge as I burst into the room. Something about that expression jarred me even more than knowing Ryan was in the room.

I followed Bill Weston's line of sight, and my eyes made contact with the black muzzle of a Glock 19.

Time froze.

It hadn't even occurred to me Ryan would go down this route. I still thought of him as the twenty-year-old dope-smoker, but it appeared he'd upped his criminal status since then. Was this the result of me punching him the other day? Did he plan on taking his revenge?

My focus needed to be on Gabi. If I was shot while making sure she was safe, that was a price I was willing to pay.

"Are you okay, Gabi?" I asked her.

She nodded, but she wouldn't even look at me, staring down at her hands instead, and I knew her pain didn't come from anything Ryan had done. I was the one who had hurt her, even if it was unintentional. I hated myself for that.

I turned my attention to Ryan. "Your beef is with me, Ryan. Let Gabi and her dad go, and you can do whatever you want with me."

Frustratingly, he smiled. "I'm glad we're on the same page, Cole. I tried to talk to you man to man, but you flipped out on me and gave me this." He gestured to the graze beside his eye, and the green and yellow bruises I'd blessed him with. "If you'd just agreed to work with me then, we wouldn't be here now, so really you can blame yourself for our current situation."

"No, if you'd just left us alone, none of us would be here."

"But as I explained to Gabi here, you owe me. The three of you managed to screw up a big job, and I lost a lot of money, so now it's payback."

Gabi spoke up. "My dad already explained how that was never our fault. You would have been busted at some point anyway."

I frowned, confusion rippling through me. Why would any of it have been their fault?

Ryan must have noticed my bewilderment. "Oh, you don't know yet, do you? Your girlfriend here told her cop dad about the drug deal you were doing. He's denying he said anything that got you arrested, but honestly, if I had a gun pointed at my head, I'd probably be denying it, too."

Bill spoke up. "I'm telling the truth."

Ryan jerked the gun and shouted. "I wasn't asking you!"

"It doesn't matter what happened ten years ago," I said, trying to keep my voice level. "We're here now. I did my time for that drug run going wrong, but I guess ten years of my life wasn't enough for you, Ryan?"

"Your ten years made no difference to the cash in my pocket, so no, I want back the money you cost me, and if you don't agree to do what I want, I'll put a hole in Gabi's head." He gave a wild-eyed grin, and it suddenly occurred to me that perhaps Ryan wasn't altogether with it. "In fact," he continued, "I might just fuck her first, so I can feel what it's like to screw a cripple. I'll do it right in front of her darling daddy, here, and then I'll shoot the pair of them."

It took every ounce of strength I had not to let out a roar and tear him apart with my bare fingers. Only the threat of Gabi being shot held me back. I also worried if I did something crazy and Ryan shot me, there would be no reason for him to keep Gabi alive.

I held up both hands. "There's no need to say any of that. I'll do what you want. Just tell me."

A smug grin appeared on his face. "Good. I need you to go and meet a guy and collect a package from him. Come straight back here when you do. If you're gone any longer than three hours, she dies."

I had a bad feeling about this. "What if I get a flat tire or something?"

"Don't get a flat," he snapped back.

"Why can't you just do this yourself?"

"Apart from you owing me, I've also got people watching me, and like I told you before, someone let me down. In case you hadn't noticed, I don't like it when people let me down."

I bunched my fists. "What makes you think I won't go straight to the cops when I leave here?"

"Because I'll be watching out that window until your return, and if I even get a hint that the cops have been involved, I'll put a bullet in your girlfriend's head."

"I'm not his girlfriend."

Gabi's words shocked me as much as Ryan's threat.

"Really?" said Ryan, unimpressed, his eyebrows lifting, his head tilting to one side.

She finally lifted her eyes to me, and the expression in them broke my heart. "Ask him. Ask him how he slept with Taylor behind my back only a matter of weeks ago."

I hesitated. I didn't want her to believe I'd cheated on her, but if this was the thing that would save her life, then I'd take her hating me over her being dead.

"Tell him, Cole," she said, though I could hear the desperation in her voice which begged me to set her right, to tell her it was all a big mistake. I couldn't do that.

"That's right," I told Ryan, hating every single syllable coming from my lips. "I've been seeing Taylor as well. I've spent the last ten years behind bars, and if you think I'm not going to use my freedom to make up for all the pussy I've missed, then you're very much mistaken."

Frustratingly, he laughed. "I'm not buying it. I've seen how you're looking at her."

To my left, Gabi's dad had taken a tiny step toward the dresser which was up against the far side of the living room wall. I didn't think Ryan had noticed, he was too caught up in the discussion between Gabi and me. Bill Weston appeared hard and focused, and his silence hadn't gone unnoticed by me.

I needed to keep Ryan's attention away from the other man.

"I look at all women that way. Like I said, it was a long time behind bars."

Ryan sneered. "Looks like little Cole finally grew into a man."

"There's nothing manly about lying and cheating," said Gabi. "Or threatening a woman, for that matter. The pair of you make me sick."

"Gabi," I said, wanting to tell her that was wrong, that I hadn't wanted anything to do with Taylor, but I noticed her dad had taken another step toward the cabinet. I didn't know what he had planned, but I didn't want Ryan noticing what he was doing.

"Just stop talking, Cole," she said, "I've heard enough lies come from your mouth."

My heart broke. If we survived this, would she ever trust me again?

The click of a lock suddenly sounded, too loud in the room, followed by the scrape of a drawer yanked open. Ryan's head twisted toward the noise, his eyes widening as Bill Weston spun back around from the cabinet he'd been edging toward, a gun of his own in his hands.

Immediately, Ryan swung his own weapon toward Gabi's dad. My only thoughts were to keep Gabi safe, and so I threw myself toward her, covering her body with my own to protect her from flying bullets. She struggled, her hands pushing against my chest, her skin burning against mine, her muscles taut and compact beneath me.

A bang shattered through the room, quickly followed by another, both impossibly loud, making my ears ring. Gabi screamed beneath me, and I realized if Gabi's dad had been shot, and Ryan was still alive, Gabi and I would be next.

Still covering her body with my own, I twisted to look toward Ryan.

"Dad!" Gabi screamed.

Ryan's shot had hit its mark. Bill Weston was still upright, his hand clutched to his shoulder, the other hand loosely holding the gun. Ryan's attention was focused on the ex-cop, not us.

If we weren't all going to end up dead, I needed to do something.

Not allowing myself to think further, I pushed away from Gabi and launched at Ryan. I heard her shriek 'Cole!' as my body slammed into his. The gun went off again, so incredibly loud, and I felt the bullet graze my face, like a hornet sting.

I didn't have time to analyze any potential injuries. Ryan and I both hit the floor, and beside us I sensed, rather than saw, Bill Weston drop to his knees. I lifted my fist and smashed it back down, connecting with Ryan's nose, and slamming his face sideways. He gave a roar of anger and pain. Where was the gun? I glanced around, frantic, to see the weapon still in Ryan's hand. He seemed to remember its presence at the same time my gaze alighted on it, and Ryan lifted the hand holding the handgun.

Only reacting, I slammed my hand onto his wrist, pinning his arm to the floor. But Ryan was no lightweight wimp, and with a grunt of fury, he pushed back on me.

I gave a roar of my own, knowing if I lost this fight, it would mean a bullet in my head, and most likely Gabi would be next. I couldn't lose.

Ryan pushed up as I pressed down. We were equal in strength, both our arms trembling with the force of our struggle. My teeth clenched, my upper lip curled in a snarl of ferocity. Ryan's hand edged off the floor, his fingers tightening around the weapon. I needed to do something else—hit him again, perhaps—but if I diverted my concentration for a moment, I knew Ryan would win. I sensed movement to the side, the briefest thought that Gabi must be checking on her father went through my head, but then a shoe, not containing soft tissue and bone, but hard metal, smashed down on Ryan's hand.

Ryan let out a howl of pain, his fingers releasing the butt of the handgun. It clattered to the floor and skittered away, out of his reach.

Gabi bent and picked up the gun up.

Her voice was cold and calm. "Get up, Cole." She didn't sound like herself. This was the soldier I was seeing now.

"Gabi," I said, worried if I got off Ryan, he would try to attack again.

"Do as I say," she replied.

She had the gun, and right now she wasn't a woman I'd dare to disobey. Slowly, I climbed off Ryan.

She lifted her foot and kicked him. "Roll onto your stomach, hands behind your head."

"You broke my fucking fingers," Ryan wailed. His face was pale, his eyeballs rolling in their sockets.

"I'll break your fucking head if you don't do as I tell you," she snapped back. "Move. Now." She shoved him with her foot again, and

Ryan rolled over, linking his fingers behind his head.

With Gabi covering Ryan, I turned my attention to her father. Blood was dripping in my eyes, blurring my vision, but I wiped it away with the back of my hand. My injury hurt, but he looked a lot worse.

I crouched beside Bill. His breathing was shallow, his face pale, but he had his eyes open. Blood spread across his shirt from where he'd been shot, but the fact he was still alive meant it had missed his heart. Blood loss was the thing most likely to kill him now.

"Take the other gun," Bill told me, his voice weak, nodding toward the weapon he'd taken from the dresser. As an ex-cop, I should have known he'd have kept a gun somewhere in the house. "Help her."

I understood what he meant. I picked up the weapon and covered Gabi, just as insurance so Ryan wouldn't try anything stupid.

From outside came the wail of a police siren, which was quickly joined by another.

Someone must have heard the gunshot and called the cops.

FORTYONE

The police burst through the door, armed and demanding for Cole and me to put down our weapons.

We both did as we were told, slowly lowering the guns to the ground. As I placed the gun carefully on the floor and sank to my knees, my hands behind my head, I glanced over at my dad. Thank God he was still conscious. I wanted to tell the police we were the good guys, but I knew how this looked—both of us armed while two men were bleeding on the floor.

Handcuffs clicked around our wrists, but neither of us put up any kind of struggle. Not taking any chances, the police also cuffed Ryan's hands, and I took satisfaction in his yelp of pain as his smashed hand was forced into the metal bracelets. It was over for Ryan now. I just hoped this wasn't going to get Cole in trouble as well.

"These people assaulted me," yelled Ryan from the floor.

"Shut up, asshole," said the arresting officer.

"Please," I begged the first cop who had entered. "My dad's been shot. He needs help."

The police officer's eyes widened as he glanced over in my dad's direction. "Oh, shit. It's Bill Weston."

He hurried to my dad's side.

My father was still able to speak. "It's okay, Nate. This wasn't done by my daughter and her boyfriend. The guy on the floor came in here with a gun and threatened us all. He's the one who shot me."

I nodded. "It's true."

Cole nodded, too, his lips pressed together, his square jaw tight.

"Okay, I trust you," said the cop, Nate. He turned to the other officers. "Take the cuffs off those two. That's Bill's daughter."

The cuffs were undone, and I breathed a sigh of relief as I pulled my arms free.

On shaking legs, and struggling a little because of my prosthesis, I got to my feet. I turned to Cole, who had also stood, and he reached out and pulled me into his arms. My feelings about him were so mixed up, but right now I didn't have the energy to fight him.

Paramedics entered the house, stabilizing my dad. "We need to get him to the hospital," one of the EMTs said, as she placed an oxygen mask over my father's face.

"I need to go with him," I told Cole.

"You go. I'll follow in my car."

"We're going to need a statement from each of you," the police officer, Nate, said.

Cole nodded. "Of course. But first we need to make sure Gabi's dad is going to be all right."

I rode in the ambulance while the paramedics worked on my dad.

He was taken straight to surgery, leaving me worried and frightened in the corridor outside. Cole showed up and once more I fell into his arms. Even when I was hurt and betrayed, and angry with him, it seemed that was the only place I ever wanted to be.

Blood dribbled down one side of his face from where a bullet had grazed him. A nurse came to try to patch him up, but he shooed her away.

"You should have let her fix you up," I said.

"I'm not going anywhere until we know your dad is all right."

"Do you think he will be?" I asked, my voice breaking.

"He'll be fine," Cole said, soothing me. "Your dad is almost as hard to kill as you are."

I choked back a mixture of a sob and laughter.

"Gabi, we have to talk about everything that was said back at the house, and what Taylor told you."

"Please, Cole, not now." I couldn't hear any more. My heart was already broken.

"No, you have to hear this. I only said what I did to Ryan because I was trying to stop him hurting you. I thought if he felt you weren't important to me, he might let you go."

I shook my head. "But why did you do ... what you did... what you did with Taylor?" To my horror, I had started to cry. That hurt worse than anything else.

"I didn't do anything with her. She just happened to be at the same bar I was in. I'd already had a few drinks, and she wanted to talk about you, which I was more than happy to do. You're all I've ever wanted to talk about. Then I was too drunk to drive, so she offered to drive me home. I fell asleep—or passed out, I'm not sure—in the car, and when I woke up she was all over me. I'm telling the truth, Gabi."

I wanted to believe him so badly.

He must have sensed my hesitation. "I swear to you, Gabi. Nothing happened between me and Taylor. Nothing has ever happened. I kissed her once, ten years ago, because I thought I was protecting you from Ryan by driving you away from me. Nothing else ever happened between us, and I hated myself for doing it. I love you now as much as I loved you back then, and I'd never do anything to jeopardize that."

"You did do something, though," I said, quietly. "You did something so stupid, you were taken away from me for ten years."

"I was an idiot, but again, I thought I was protecting you. I planned on taking the money and getting out of town, so Ryan would never have had a reason to threaten you again."

"But you were still arrested," I said, needing him to know the truth of what I'd been thinking all these years, "and I'd believed it was my fault."

He frowned, his face still handsome, despite the blood. "Was that what Ryan was talking about when he said you'd been responsible for getting me arrested?"

I bit my lower lip and nodded. "Part of the reason I left town and joined the Army was because I believed it was my fault you spent the last ten years behind bars. After you told me about getting involved with Ryan, and that you were doing trips for him and implied it was illegal, I went home and told my dad. I thought he'd taken that information and had you followed and arrested." I covered my face with my hands and shook my head. "I'm so sorry, Cole."

He pulled my hands away from my face so he could look into my eyes. "It wasn't your fault, Gabi. None of it was. You were seventeen years old, and your dad was a police officer. I was getting myself into trouble, and you were worried about me. You did the right thing. I was the one who was stupid enough to go along with Ryan's plans, rather than ask for help myself."

"I know, but I could have done things differently. When I heard you'd be going down for so long, I felt horrible. It was part of why I ran off and joined the Army. I couldn't stand to be around my dad, because I blamed him in part, too, but also because I couldn't live the next ten years in the same town, knowing you were locked up not far away."

"I knew you'd told your dad, Gabi. Perhaps a part of me wanted you to. At least it brought the sorry mess to a close. Of course, I didn't know it was coke I was carrying, I did truly think it was only weed."

"I'm so sorry," I said again.

"Hey, stop saying that. Maybe this whole thing was fate. Maybe if you hadn't told your dad, I would have ended up heading down the same route in life and gotten myself killed by some drug dealer, or ended up hooked on drugs myself. Who the hell knows? The point is we're here, now, together and safe. Ryan won't ever touch us again, and Taylor knows not to come anywhere in our vicinity, but even if she does, she can't hurt us. I'm yours, Gabi, for as long as you'll have me. I always have been."

I nodded through my tears. "I'm yours, too."

Cole pulled me into his arms and kissed me.

THREE MONTHS LATER

GABI

We stood outside of the single story house, looking up at the green wooden cladding and white painted window shutters, a set of keys in Cole's hand. The moving truck containing all of our worldly belongings sat in the street behind us, a couple of guys waiting in the cab for the word to start unpacking our gear. We didn't have a whole heap of stuff, but we'd been accumulating bits and pieces over the past few months.

This house was to be our home, mine and Cole's. Our first real place together. We hoped this would be the start of our new future, one that would hold many years of happiness, with hopefully marriage and children at some point. We hadn't started trying yet, but we talked about it when we lay together in bed at night—how many we would have and what we'd call them. That I would be raising children when I had a disability didn't worry me at all. They wouldn't miss out on a single thing.

I'd finally gotten my blade, and was running again, even spending time on the track, which was something I'd never even bothered to do when I'd been at high school. My body was strong and athletic, and I was no longer embarrassed or ashamed by my stump. I'd survived an incident in Iraq where a good man had died, but that wasn't my fault, and it wasn't my fault I had lived. Guilt had played a big part in my decisions over the whole of my adult life, but I wouldn't allow it to control me anymore. I'd started to let that guilt go, and be proud of who I was and how far I had come.

My dad was doing much better. He'd spent a couple of weeks in the hospital, but was now fully recovered from his gunshot wound. He'd even stopped drinking, though alcohol would always be a tempting demon for him. He'd had a couple of relapses, but had gotten back into the program right away. This was a long road for him, and I didn't expect miracles, but he was trying and that was the important thing.

Cole was still working at the restaurant, but he was also doing a lot of volunteer work with children from difficult backgrounds. He hoped that it would give him an inroad into what he really wanted to be doing—social work. He'd once told me that the only thing he knew was how to be a kid stuck in the system. I guessed he wanted to put that knowledge to good use.

His fingers wrapping around mine caused me to look up at him. My heart clenched with love. He still had a scar above his eyebrow where Ryan's bullet had grazed him, but it was fading as every week went by. Ryan had been sentenced on multiple charges—including drug dealing after a large quantity of heroin and amphetamines had been discovered in his apartment in a town fifty miles away—and he wouldn't be bothering us for a very long time. Soon enough, our memory of Ryan would be as faded as the scar he'd given Cole.

Taylor had also stayed out of our way, though Jasmine had been in touch. It was good to know I still had a friend.

"So what do you think of your new home?" Cole asked.

"*Our* new home," I corrected him, "and I love it already. But then I'd love anywhere if it meant we got to live together."

The house had been modified perfectly for me, a wet room, widened doorways and all on one level, just in case I ever needed to be in my wheelchair again for a period of time. My payout from the loss of my leg had come just at the right time, and allowed me to buy this place for us.

Taking me by surprise, Cole bent down and scooped me up. I loved being held against his chest, in his strong arms, but I smacked him on the shoulder. "Hey, put me down."

He laughed. "Isn't it supposed to be romantic for me to carry you across the threshold?"

"Cole, I love you, and as romantic a gesture as this is, I think I'd rather walk."

"Sure," he said, understanding, and gently set me down.

It was important for me to be able to walk, strong and tall, into our home. This was a new beginning for me, and I intended on starting as I meant to continue.

I smiled up at him and he grinned back down, before ducking his head and kissing me, firm and gentle on the mouth. "I love you too, Gabi."

I'd been wrong when I'd said there were no second chances. Perhaps we were different now, but that didn't mean we couldn't try again. It would take some adjustment, plenty of understanding, and patience, and love—love most of all—but we were doing it. We were getting a fresh start—a second chance at a first love—and I couldn't be happier.

With a smile on my face, and Cole's hand in mine, I took my first step into our new life.

Together.

THE END

LIKE WHAT YOU'VE READ?

So you never miss out, make sure you sign up to Marissa Farrar's new release list to stay updated about new releases, exclusives, and special offers! http://forms.aweber.com/form/61/19822861.htm.

ACKNOWLEDGMENTS

I often feel extremely lucky to have such an amazing network of generous, supportive people around me, and I don't think I've ever felt this more so than during the writing of this book.

The old adage is 'write what you know,' but you can't always do this as an author. I knew I wanted to write Gabi's story, but of course I had no experience of being an amputee myself. One of my friends was kind enough to put me in touch with one of her friends, who had recently had the same amputation as Gabi, and he was extremely generous with sharing his experiences.

So thank you a million times over, Geoff Ennals. This book wouldn't be what it is without you. Thank you for sharing your experiences of being heckled in the disabled spots in car parks and for your terrible joke about losing eight pounds in one go! And even more thanks for allowing me to be your 'sister-in-law', which helped me to write about Gabi's prosthesis in much better detail. Perhaps I may have got a few things wrong, so please forgive me if I did! I hope you enjoyed the book.

The second person I need to thank is fellow author Thomas S Flowers, for allowing me to see into his head, via his own novel, about what life is really like in Iraq. I would never have been able to get such an accurate feel for the yellow dust and smells if it wasn't for that book. Fellow readers, if you would like to read another story about a veteran who also loses a limb, please check out Thomas's book, Dwelling. Be warned – it's a scary one!

As always, I have to thank my long-time editor, Lori Whitwam. You made some excellent suggestions about certain things in this book, and I really think it helped the story overall. Apologies for getting more 'British' for this one!

Thanks to my proofreaders, Glynis Elliott, Karey McComish, and Linda Helme, for spotting all those annoying little typos that like to sneak through. I hope you all enjoyed the book, and that it didn't feel too much like work.

And a final huge thank you to you, the reader. I wouldn't be able to keep writing without you.

Marissa.

ABOUT MARISSA

Marissa Farrar is a multi-published romance, fantasy, and horror author. She was born in Devon, England, has travelled all over the world, and has lived in both Australia and Spain. She now resides in the countryside with her husband, three young children, a crazy Spanish dog, and two rescue cats. Despite returning to England, she daydreams of one day being able to split her time between her home country and the balmy, white sandy beaches of Spain.

Even though she's been writing stories since she was small and held dreams of being a writer, her initial life plan went a different way.

In her youth, inspired by James Herriot, she decided to become a vet, and would regularly bring home new pets to her weary parents. Upon discovering her exams were never going to get her into a veterinary degree, she ended up studying Zoology. Once she completed her degree and realised she'd spent the majority trying to find time to write, she decided to follow her dream of being an author. Seven years later, she was published and two years after that she was able to say goodbye to the day job.

However, she's continued to collect animals!

Marissa is the author of over twenty novels, including the dark vampire 'Serenity' series. Her short stories have been accepted for a number of anthologies including, *Their Dark Masters,* Red Skies Press, *Masters of Horror: Damned If You Don't,* Triskaideka Books; and *2013: The Aftermath,* Pill Hill Press.

If you want to know more about Marissa, then please visit her website at www.marissa-farrar.blogspot.com. You can also find her at her facebook page, www.facebook.com/marissa.farrar.author or follow her on twitter @marissafarrar.

She loves to hear from readers and can be emailed at marissafarrar@hotmail.co.uk.

Made in United States
Orlando, FL
02 August 2022

20480301R00167